PRAISE FOR
PREDESTINED

PREDESTINED

RACHEL BYRNE

Predestined
Published by Humboldt Press
Denver, CO

Copyright ©2024 by Rachel Byrne All rights reserved.

Names: Byrne, Rachel, author.
Title: Predestined / Rachel Byrne.
Description: Denver, CO : Humboldt Press, [2024] | Audience: young adult.
Identifiers: ISBN: 979-8-218-36948-4 (paperback)
Subjects: LCSH: Teenage girls--Fiction. | High school students--Fiction. | Elite (Social sciences)--Fiction. | Private schools--Fiction. | High school graduates--Fiction. | Predestination--Fiction. | Secrecy--Fiction. | Future, The--Fiction. | Young adult fiction. | LCGFT: Science fiction. | BISAC: YOUNG ADULT FICTION / Science Fiction / General.
Classification: LCC: PS3602.Y765 P74 2024 | DDC: 813/.6--dc23

Cover and interior design by Victoria Wolf, wolfdesignandmarketing.com, copyright owned by Rachel Byrne.

QUANTITY PURCHASES: Schools, companies, professional groups, clubs, and other organizations may qualify for special terms when ordering quantities of this title. For information, go to: rachelbyrneauthor.com

*To Mom and Dad for sparking and
nurturing my love of stories*

"He alone, who owns the youth, gains the future."
—*Adolf Hitler*

CHAPTER
ONE

I DIDN'T SENSE ANYTHING SINISTER about the brochure in our stack of mail. With the photo of a green meadow ringed with pine trees and the words *Foster Your Purpose at Haverford Pines*, it was not the dreaded ticket, so I left it with the bills, catalogs, and other junk.

During dinner, I pondered how quickly photo red-light tickets were mailed. Pushing bits of salmon and sweet potato hash around my plate, I failed to notice my mom's bright eyes and still mouth—not chattering about the houses she had shown, the country club bestie she had lunched with, or her latest Pilates class. She hadn't even filmed herself presenting her perfect paleo meal for her Instagram followers. My sister, Emma Claire, filled the silence with a story about her spelling test and how she had been the only one to spell arugula correctly.

As I forked overcooked hash into my mouth, my dad cleared his throat. "Lina, your mother and I would like to talk with you after dinner."

I swallowed hard, the mushy lump barely going down. A post-dinner talk was never good. It meant there had been a call from the school, or another parent. It meant I was in trouble. When I was younger, the calls were almost daily. I had climbed up on the play structure's roof, left the classroom and stolen donuts from the lounge, gotten into the tortoise enclosure at the zoo, etc., etc. On the bulletin board at preschool with the picture of a traffic light, the *Catalina* card always ended up in the red zone by lunchtime. I earned tokens for good behavior by sharing toys and listening to the teacher, but then lost them just as fast when Quinn stole Sophia's crayon, and I stomped on his foot to get it back.

After dinner, I flopped onto the couch in the family room. I had been determined to avoid trouble this year—I was a high school freshman so should be mature. My goal was to remain calm, make new friends, and avoid "outbursts". That plan had gone well in the fall but tanked by February thanks to Mason Kline. For absolutely no reason, aside from being a privileged asshole, he had kicked over an overflowing can outside the cafeteria, spilling trash all over the floor. When Mr. Hill—our sweet janitor who worked three jobs to support his family—asked him to pick it up, Mason snorted with laughter, nudged his friends, and walked away. I was fuming as I helped Mr. Hill put the trash in bags and, in biology, had stuck out a foot to trip Mason. I hadn't meant for him to fall on his finger, dislocating it and making him scream like he was dying. That's just the way it played out.

I picked at the edge of my thumbnail, trying not to let my anxiety show. If Dad knew about the ticket, he would not have waited until now to confront me. He would have blown into the house after work and started yelling. So, this talk must be about something else, probably my "sneakiness".

I glanced at my parents as they settled in the armchairs across from me. They were smiling. Oh no. Smiles meant I wasn't in trouble.

Worse. They wanted me to do something. Something I would detest. Smiles meant a tennis match with Dad's frat brother's pimply son, babysitting my sticky, drooling cousin, or sleeping on an air mattress in Emma Claire's room so a summer exchange student could steal my room for a month.

"I'm not doing it, DJ," I said, sitting up straighter and crisscrossing my legs.

My mom's smile flickered. She hated it when I called her by her initials. She glanced at my bare feet on the white Ethan Allen sofa. "Sweetie, it's a great opportunity," she chirped in her real estate voice—like she was trying to talk me into a four-bedroom, two-bath single-family home. "You don't even know what we're talking about yet."

Dad sat forward. "It's really exciting, Lina." He did look excited—his eyes were bright, and the corners of his mouth tipped up—a rare expression when it came to me.

I sighed and wriggled my thumbs in my lap, avoiding the urge to further pick at my nails. "What is it?"

Mom took a rectangular paper from the coffee table and held it out. I recognized the brochure with the photos of grass, trees, and brightly colored flowers.

"You want me to go on a yoga retreat?" She was always saying that her friends' daughters came to yoga class and hinted it was a way to get fit *and* have bonding time.

"Yoga?" My mom trilled, flashing Dad one of those *isn't she so funny* looks. "Sweetie, Haverford Pines Academy is one of the most prestigious programs in the country. Marcy Wright tried to get all four of her kids in and they wouldn't even return her calls." She raised an eyebrow. "And here, an invitation for you just pops up on our doorstep."

3

Nothing thrilled my mom more than being one of the elite. The more exclusive and snobbier, the better. It was why she had charmed her way into Green Hills Country Club and why Emma Claire had gone through an extensive audition process to train at the top dance studio.

I turned the brochure over—it did have my name and address written in fancy, scrolled letters. I unfolded it to see photos of trees, a lake, wood cabins, a football field, a swimming pool, and classrooms with computer stations. "You're sending me to boarding school," I said flatly. "In a forest."

"No sweetie, a summer academy. Just for six weeks. In the beautiful Rocky Mountains in Colorado."

"Discover your strengths and your destiny," I read from the first page. "Develop your full potential by determining what you are truly meant to do in life." I rolled my eyes. "Sounds like a scam."

Underneath in bullet points: *Comprehensive physical, cognitive, and personality testing; Focused, elite training with proven success; World-renowned staff.*

I tossed the brochure on the table, feeling a rumble of unease in my gut. "Is this one of those boot camp places?" I thought my parents had gotten past the incident with Mason, even though I hadn't explained the situation. I had been afraid that Mr. Hill might get into trouble, so my excuse—that I had been getting out of my seat and accidentally tripped Mason—had rung false and added another black mark against me in everybody's eyes.

Dad chuckled. "No, honey, just the opposite. Like your mother said, this is a prestigious program."

DJ clicked her pink manicured nails together. "They have an amazing track record. Graduates have gone on to become concert musicians and professional athletes. You know Senator Collensworth? Apparently, he was shy with no manners until he went to Haverford Pines. And that violinist we went to hear last month? A grad too." She and Dad exchanged a look. "This is the opportunity to find out where your strengths lie."

I tried to imagine myself as a tiny figure on stage holding a violin, a packed audience waiting for me to play. Not likely. I had tried piano and had quick fingers, but a horrible ear and zero desire to practice. Becoming a concert musician was about as likely as DJ dyeing her hair green and taking up fishing. Ditto for me being a politician or professional athlete.

"What about the counselor job? Remember, I'll be getting paid." I couldn't wait for summer break in two months when I would have my first job at the rec center—with unlimited access to the climbing wall! The manager, who had seen me practicing had offered me the front desk job. She had climbed Namaste and Cloud Tower and said she would coach me on my strength and technique."

My goal was to get to the top of *Denali*, the V6, in under three minutes.

DJ waved her hand. "Catalina, when I set my sights on making varsity, I gave up everything else that summer to train. Sometimes you need to sacrifice to achieve your goals."

I groaned inwardly. My mom compared everything to soccer. Yes, okay, she busted her butt to get on the varsity team at Choate, her fancy boarding school. Yes, her dedication had led to playing varsity at Wellesley. But my mom's running and drilling all summer in heat and humidity to make a soccer team was *not* comparable to every challenge in my life—getting an A on an algebra test, learning to water ski, or going to some lame place that promised the impossible.

"I'm too old for camp." I looked at my dad. "Earning a paycheck is important at my age, right?"

My dad, who loved to tell stories about his summers flipping burgers, was unfazed. "You can get an after-school job next fall. And it's a preparatory academy, not a camp."

Clearly, my parents had talked this through and prepared for my objections.

I lifted my chin. "What if I say no?"

Mom's smile tightened. "Who said it was a choice?"

Dad put a hand on my mom's knee. "This could make a difference in your future, Lina," he said gently. "It could give you some direction."

A familiar ache bloomed in my chest. It appeared when other kids talked about their plans to be marine biologists, lawyers, or doctors. Or when I thought about the fact that at my age, my mom had been playing competitive soccer by day and learning to charm her parents' friends at cocktail parties at night. And Dad had practically been born with a stethoscope in his hand—groomed for medical school from the moment Gramps and Gran got him into a "mini-Ivy" preschool. He had been excelling ever since, ending up at Choate, Princeton, then Harvard Medical School.

As if on cue, Emma Claire came into the family room, doing graceful turns around the furniture and swooping in to kiss Dad's cheek. Our fluffy bichon frisé, Daisy, trotted after her. I had wanted to name him Desi, after Desi Arnaz, the star of the 1950s sitcom *I Love Lucy*. But Mom and Dad had said nobody would know who Desi was and Emma Claire had liked Daisy. I still called my cute puffball Desi and he seemed to like it.

My ten-year-old sister, now she had *direction*. She was a devoted ballet dancer, practicing at least four days a week, competing on the weekends, and gushing about how much she loved it. At school, she did her work on time and was cheerful and polite. The teachers and other kids loved her.

I could feel my parents' expectations and disappointment weighing on me. Just like they had my whole life. The only thing I had excelled at so far was getting into the red zone. Just wait until they found out about my real red-light ticket. I'd be on the next flight to boot camp and forced to wait until I was twenty-one to even think about getting my driver's license.

My anger flashed, hard and strong. I threw the brochure onto the floor and jumped to my feet. "I don't want to go to some stupid academy in Colorado," I yelled, striding toward the stairs, giving all fifteen a good stomp, going into my room, and slamming the door. My heart was pounding and my face was red in the mirror above my dresser. I dug my hand into a jar of pennies on my bookshelf, pulled out the hidden pack of gum, and shoved two pieces in my mouth. My mom thought chewing gum was *crass*, but it helped me calm down.

Chomping hard, I felt a mixture of shame and relief. Shame that I had again overreacted and let my anger flash, after promising myself I would get it under control. Relief that at least anger was intense and energizing. It banished the crushing feelings of guilt and shame for not being what my parents wanted, and the fear that I would never become anyone important.

I focused on my posters, willing them to work their calming magic. The first was Lucy and Ethel, wearing oversized bakers' hats and frantically stuffing chocolates into their mouths during my favorite episode of *I Love Lucy*. My love of the show had sparked while watching with my gran, and I'd seen all 181 episodes at least twice. Lucy is a lot like me and constantly getting into trouble. Her husband, Ricky, accuses her of being sneaky—and she is—but her best friend Ethel is always right with her to defend her and share the blame.

If I had a friend like Ethel, I knew my life would be different.

The second poster was an Army Ranger, lying flat on his belly in a trench, his body slick with mud, his steel-blue eyes providing the only color. Clutching his gun, he is alert and ready, awaiting the right moment to strike. His purpose is clear—do anything necessary to defend his comrades and country. I had stolen the poster from the military table during Career Week. The Ranger's ability to radiate both intensity and calm reminded me that I could do the same—it would just take practice.

My breathing slowing, my face returning to its freckled paleness, I spit out the gum, worked my bra out from under my T-shirt and threw it and my shorts into the corner. DJ had given up buying me pajamas long ago—I heard her telling her friends she was 'choosing her battles.' Kneeling, I crawled under my bed and into a spot in the corner where I had molded blankets into a soft nest. By middle school, DJ had also surrendered the battle of making me sleep in my bed. I don't know why I felt safer and calmer underneath, I just *did*. I pulled my stuffed dog, Cairo, against my chest and willed my body to *hush*. I focused on my heartbeat, feeling it beginning to thump more slowly. My muscles began to relax.

As I drifted into sleep, a thought struck me. My mom had said that Marcy Wright had tried to get her kids into Haverford Pines, but they had to be invited. If that were true, then how had they found me? And what had made them send me an invitation?

CHAPTER
TWO

IN THE BACK OF THE RENTAL SUV, my stomach burned, and a sour taste flooded my mouth. One week into summer break and my family was dumping me at this strange academy. While I struggled to find my purpose, they would be in Aspen, Emma Claire enjoying a ballet workshop while my parents lounged at the pool.

I had planned to hold my ground and insist on the rec center job, but then Dad got the red-light ticket. As I heard him slam his way through the front door, I raced to intercept him before he could start yelling.

I had briefly debated telling the truth—my anger at the stricken look on Noah's face as pee ran down his legs and puddled on the floor. I imagined Dad puffing up with pride that I had stood up for a boy being bullied. That fantasy was discarded because I knew Dad wouldn't get it. He and Mom had never experienced classmates jeering at them and the way it made you curl up inside and want to die.

I then considered accepting the consequences he started listing— no screens, no permit or license until I was seventeen, no allowance, etc. I could handle those but DJ wouldn't stop until she knew why I had taken the car out in the first place. And that couldn't happen if I wanted to survive the rest of high school.

Instead of an explanation, I offered him a deal. If I agreed to go to Haverford Pines, he wouldn't punish me, tell DJ, or ask any questions. My brilliant doctor dad was a rule follower and believed in consequences. But he was also practical and knew weeks of DJ and me battling would be miserable. He grudgingly agreed on the condition that I not drive before starting Driver's Ed and promised to give Haverford Pines "the old college try."

Since stunning DJ by giving in, I had felt my parents' hopeful eyes on me. Could their daughter, who had been kicked out of tennis for slamming her racket on the court, or sat down in the middle of the soccer field because kicking a ball was stupid, be the next Serena Williams or Mia Hamm? Could their mediocre student be the next Bill Gates or Shonda Rhimes?

I dreaded how they would feel when they were yanked away from their poolside holiday to retrieve me. Disappointed? Humiliated? Angry? Yes to all. An emotion they would not experience—surprise. None of us would feel that. It was so clearly a mistake that the invitation had been sent to me. Obviously, there was another sixteen-year-old Jamison out there training for the youth Olympics who was meant to go instead.

"We're here," Emma Claire shrieked as we exited the highway and turned onto a two-lane road, thickets of dark green pines on both sides. At an iron gate with *Haverford Pines* scrolled at the top in dark metal, a man directed us to the visitors' lot. The road stretched a few hundred feet to a clearing where a circular drive fronted a towering building with brown-and-cream-flecked stones and interconnected blond wood beams. Oversized picture windows framed in steel led to a tall steepled roof.

Mom gasped and opened her window to start filming. "It's just gorgeous, isn't it Walker? It's like a chalet. Marnie said it was designed by the architect who did the Swiss Omnia."

To the right was a football field, a track, and another large stone building with a wooden peaked roof. Beyond the parking lot stretched the meadow—green and gorgeous with six log cabins perched on the far end. Thick pines, the border of the forest, ran along the long edge.

I climbed out, breathing in warm air with rich scents of pine and grass. So different from the salty breeze in California. Emma Claire scrambled to stand beside me, grabbing for my hand. "I wish I could stay here."

I squeezed her hand. "You're going to have so much fun dancing. And I hear that Aspen has the best ice cream in the country." I had no idea if that was true, but Emma Claire loved ice cream.

"Lee, look!" she yelled.

A majestic bird sailed over the meadow, its expansive wings casting triangular shadows across the grass. It had a regal cap of white feathers, a hooked beak, and sharp black eyes. A bald eagle.

"Wow," Emma and I said together, then laughed.

Dad got my duffel bag and we walked toward the building, my mom stopping every few feet to take a selfie. She insisted Emma Claire and I pose in front of a stone statue of a man wearing flowing robes, his hand resting on the head of a giant wolf. A stern-looking woman with a blonde pixie cut sat at a table, a row of teens lined up behind her, their hands behind their backs. They were dressed in purple T-shirts, white athletic shorts, and black tennis shoes.

The woman looked me up and down, and I was sure she was going to announce that I needed to leave. But she crossed my name off a list and informed DJ that no, there weren't celebrity graduates here to meet the families, the dining hall wasn't having a reception, and the rest of the grounds were off-limits.

My mom's expression morphed from disappointed to annoyed when the woman told her she couldn't record videos for her 986 followers who had "gone gaga" over my invitation. With an insider's view of HP, she hoped to propel herself into the thousands, or higher. She glanced over the woman's shoulder as if looking for a manager. Seeing only the teens, she flipped her hair and declared she was ready for Aspen.

I was surprised when she pulled me into a hug and held on for a long moment. The scent of her familiar perfume tickled my nose, and I had the sudden fear that I might get homesick. I had never spent more than a few nights away, and that was at my grandparents where Gramps took me hiking and Gran made us chocolate chip pancakes.

"Make us proud," she murmured, letting me go and swiping at her eyes. Dad kissed the top of my head while Emma Claire wrapped her arms around my waist.

You are too old to be homesick, I told myself as they headed back to the car.

"Take Catalina to Madison, room 206," the woman barked. A girl stepped forward and picked up one handle of my duffel while I took the other. The sleeve of her shirt had a wreath-shaped emblem on it. I wanted to ask her about that, and more about Haverford Pines. But I couldn't think of the right way to phrase my questions without sounding weird, so I stayed silent. At a cabin with *Madison* carved above the entrance, we went into a lounge, up ten stairs, and down a hallway with eight sets of facing doors to number 206.

"The welcome assembly is at six p.m. See you then." She gave a small smile and strode back down the hall.

I hefted my duffel, pushed into the room, and halted. Standing in front of a full-length mirror was the most beautiful girl I had ever seen. I know that sounds like an exaggeration, especially since I live in SoCal, but it's true. She was tall with creamy skin and caramel-colored hair that hung thick and straight down her back. Her facial features looked sculpted—smooth forehead, delicate straight nose, angular cheekbones dusted with pink, and bow-shaped lips. When she turned, her eyes were emerald green, framed by long lashes.

She smiled and identical dimples popped in each cheek. "Well, hi there," she said. Her voice had a soft southern lilt. "I'm Brittany Roselee Moore." She held out a hand with cotton-candy pink nails. "Call me Britt."

I dropped my duffel, suddenly aware of my brown hair in its limp ponytail, my athletic shorts, and Lakers T-shirt. "Lina Jamison," I said, shaking her hand which was soft and cool.

She smiled and gestured toward the bare side of the room. "Let me know if you need any help." Turning back to the mirror, she picked up a brush and began sweeping it across her cheeks. I felt the sudden urge to touch Britt's hair and see if it felt as silky as it looked.

Britt's side of the room was extremely pink. A shiny pink comforter covered her bed with matching bejeweled pillows. A bulletin board bordered with a pink ribbon hung over her desk, on which were pinned photos—models, actresses, boy bands. Her trunk, pink with white trim, was open, a pair of blingy flip-flops and lace underwear peeking out. The only non-pink item was a hanging green Texas banner with a giant star instead of the X.

I was suddenly glad that DJ had insisted on buying me new shorts and T-shirts. I would not be considered fashionable but at least my clothes were clean and stain-free.

My side had a wooden dresser, nightstand, and bed with a purple comforter. Unzipping my duffel, I took out my clothing and put it and the toiletries into the dresser drawers. I set Cairo on my pillow. He was named after the Belgian Malinois who had been a member of Seal Team Six—the squad that had killed Osama bin Laden, the terrorist who planned 911.

A knock and a girl with wavy dark hair, owlish eyes, and plump cheeks entered holding a plastic bin and shopping bag. Her T-shirt had a horseshoe emblem on the sleeve. "Hello, girls. I'm Samantha, and I'm your mater, your floor leader." She pulled a box of granola bars from the grocery bag. "Hungry?"

Brittany gave a polite "No, thank you," while my stomach let out a rumble. We laughed as I accepted a bar and ripped open the wrapper.

"We've got a bit of information to review." From the bin, Samantha pulled out a square speaker and a plastic shelf with a hook. "Since the cabins don't have Wi-Fi, we have this old-fashioned intercom system." She hung the hook on the footrail of Brittany's bed and set the speaker on the shelf. "If we need to reach you, we will talk through these speakers. And if you push the button on the top, you can talk back." She pushed it. "Hey there Jackson, you read me?"

"Loud and clear," a boy's voice responded.

"Excellent." Samantha hung the second speaker on my bedrail. "We do tones in the morning to wake you up and ten minutes before meals and lights out. In the evenings, we play music."

"How about our own music?" Britt regarded her speaker like it was going to sprout horns. "I like Taylor Swift and Luke Bryan."

Samantha gave a sympathetic smile. "Being chosen to train at HP is an honor and opportunity. Everything we do here is geared toward optimal performance. The music we play, the food we serve, and the training exercises are to promote neuronal functioning and growth."

"English please," Britt said.

I studied her pouty expression and wondered how much optimal neuronal functioning was needed to look gorgeous. "Luke Bryan doesn't help your brain," I offered through a mouthful of bar. "It's got to be like Mozart or some other famous dead guy."

"Exactly," Samantha nodded. "Now, let's go over some of the rules." She pulled two booklets out of the bin and handed them to us.

The cover had a pine tree with a stately wolf at its base and the words *Haverford Pines Handbook and Code of Conduct.* Ah, nothing like a book of rules that I was bound to break. *Be on time for class. Treat classmates with respect. Follow the teachers' instructions.* Sounded easy enough, but between getting distracted on my way to class, my occasional anger bursts, and overall hating stupid rules, it wasn't.

"Read this by tomorrow," Samantha said. "Pay special attention to page five. Important rules about how a trainee must comport themself."

I shoved the rest of the bar in my mouth and wiped my fingers on my shorts.

"No gum chewing," Brittany exclaimed. "No crop tops?"

"HP academy members are groomed to achieve ultimate success. Gum chewing can be construed as unprofessional, as can wearing revealing clothing." Samantha held up a hand before Brittany could protest again. "Of course, if it's related to your purpose, it's allowed."

This was my chance to ask about the purposes. What exactly were they, and how did HP know what mine was? Should I confess to Samantha that there had been a huge mistake? Or would it void my deal with Dad since I had yet to give it his "old college try"?

"No romantic relationships? No dating or physical contact?" Brittany slammed the booklet closed and crossed her arms. "There are athletes and models here. And we're supposed to focus only on training?" She waved her hand. "I know, I know. We're here to prepare to be at the top." She pointed at her bulletin board. "Just tell me, how many supermodels don't have hot celebrity boyfriends?"

"That comes later," Samantha said patiently. "Once your career is established."

"I'm not waiting that long," Brittany muttered.

Samantha looked at me, and for once I felt like the well-behaved one. It would be short-lived, but it felt good! I gave Samantha a look that said, *We can't all be perfect, can we?*

"Oh, and one more thing," Samantha said. "I need to see your phones."

Brittany and I glanced at each other, then pulled out our phones and handed them to her.

She dropped the phones in the bin. "Great, I've got two more rooms to get to. See you in a few."

"Wait," Brittany shrieked. "You're not keeping our phones."

"We need your entire focus to be on your testing and training." Samantha reached for the door handle. "Phones interfere with nurturing your purpose." She opened the door. "After a few days, you won't even miss them. I promise."

"But ... but ..." Brittany sputtered, as Samantha shut the door. She spun toward me. "I didn't realize I was going to prison. This is outrageous!"

I wasn't happy about my phone being taken away, but honestly, who was I going to text anyway? The theater gang I sometimes ate lunch with were at a performance workshop and sadly, I wasn't getting the chance to make new friends at the rec center.

She pressed her palms to her chest. "Daddy expects my call every night. He won't stand for this." Her breath started coming in small gasps.

Was she going to be one of those spoiled drama queens? I didn't think I could stand eight weeks of that. "Look at these rules," I said, hoping to distract her, like I did with Emma Claire when she got upset. I stabbed a finger at page five. "Wanna see how many of these we can break?"

Brittany's eyes widened. Her hands dropped and she reached for the booklet. "That could be fun."

I pasted on my sneakiest smile and held out my palm.

She slapped it and grinned. "Let's just try not to get ourselves kicked out on our asses, okay?"

I wondered if *ass* counted as profanity and hoped that rooming with Brittany might be okay.

CHAPTER
THREE

AS BRITT CONTINUED TO FUSS with her appearance, I opened the handbook to the map and went to the window. Assessing my surroundings, especially the ways in and out, always made me feel calmer. Madison faced the side of the big building, which—DJ would be thrilled—was actually called The Chalet. It had large windows, balconies, and a patio with a central fountain. On the other side of The Chalet were the sports complex and football field. A path between it and the cabins led to The Science Center, then a lake and zones labeled *Training*. Other buildings on the outskirts were Tutor Housing and Auxiliary Buildings. There was no scale indicator so I couldn't tell how big the grounds were, but, based on the length of the drive, I guessed it to be about two square miles. A fence surrounding the property had a lightning bolt symbol across it. Did that mean it was electrified?

A flash caught my eye. Light reflected off a pair of glasses in a second-floor Chalet window. A stout man stood looking toward the check-in table. He had thick gray hair and a deep scowl. His body was stiff and radiating negative energy.

As if sensing me watching, his head swiveled.

I jumped back, scolding myself for potentially being spotted. Normally I was more careful—some might say sneaky—than that.

Samantha's voice came through the speakers. "Madisonians, meet downstairs."

Britt applied a coat of lip gloss. "Let's rock this."

I pushed down a burst of nerves and followed her downstairs. A bunch of girls were introducing themselves and Britt jumped right in, saying hey and shaking hands. I hung back, hating how uncomfortable I felt. When I met new kids, I never knew what to say or how to behave. I wanted to make a good impression but that made it even harder.

As we walked, the other girls started comparing their purposes—one was a nationally ranked swimmer, another an actor in commercials, and another a computer science whiz who had created multiple apps. I gazed intently at the spindly aspen trees and hoped no one would ask me about my purpose. What would I say? I bake decent chocolate chip cookies and can shimmy up the rope in gym class faster than the boys?

The Chalet's flecked stones had decorative swirls etched into them and a paved courtyard stamped with images of elephants and lions. The fountain had a stone lion spouting water from its mouth. Towering doors opened into a long hall with a gleaming wood floor and framed photos on the walls. I examined a black-and-white photo of a woman with wide eyes, round curls, and a fur wrapped around her shoulders. The quote beneath it read, *"Without wonder and insight, acting is just a trade. With it, it becomes creation. Bette Davis."*

Above the auditorium were cursive HP letters and a carved elephant, along with another quote. *"If your actions inspire others to dream more, learn more, do more and become more, you are a leader. John Quincy Adams."*

The immense room had purple velvet-lined walls and sloped rows of plush chairs leading down to a stage. The Madison girls separated and I walked to the far side where I could watch the others enter. Like magic, cliques were already forming. Britt had merged with the other beautiful people destined to be actors and supermodels. A group of burly boys with tight T-shirts and cropped hair were athletes, the hunched skinny kids with oversized glasses were techies. Some, on the fringes like me, were harder to label. I wondered if anyone else had ended up here by accident.

As soon as we all sat, the lights went out. Gasps and giggles turned to oohs and aahs as a cloud of white glitter appeared above our heads, swirling and spinning. The particles grew larger and denser until they formed a sphere, which rotated and twisted, taking on the shape of a skull. As it floated toward the stage, features began to cover the bones and color seeped into the wavy salt-and-pepper hair.

The head, now the size of my mom's Mercedes, stopped in the center of the stage and rotated to face us. An older man with pale mottled skin, a jowly chin, thick brows, and fleshy lips. As his intense gaze swept over us, I felt a cold flash of recognition. This was the man I had seen in the window of The Chalet.

His lips spread into a smile, showing yellow, crooked teeth. "Welcome to all of you, the newest members of our HP family," his voice boomed and echoed. Samantha and her crew began clapping and the rest of us slowly joined in. Clearly, we were all thrown off by this creepy floating head—like something from the Haunted Mansion at Disneyland. And while the man was smiling, his eyes were cold and dark.

"Congratulations on your achievement. I remember well being in your shoes forty-five years ago when I was a Plebe. I wish I could be there in person to greet each of you but I am currently in Switzerland. Fortunately, we can take advantage of this holographic technology created by one of our illustrious graduates."

I stared harder, pretty sure that this was the man from the window. But why lie about being here? Many older people did look similar, so maybe I was wrong?

"My name is Edmund Blakewell, and I am the president of the Council, HP's governing body. One of the perks of my position is having the honor of welcoming the new trainees to our fine institution." Blakewell's head glided to the side of the stage and the apparition of a man in a black suit appeared in his place. "Above the door is a quote by the sixth president of the United States, John Quincy Adams. Our forefathers were pioneers in every sense of the word. They recognized Americans' unique abilities and the spirit and determination it took to forge this great country. Their desire to nurture boys with special talents, boys who would grow to become powerful leaders, was the inspiration for Haverford Pines."

Another man appeared with an intense expression and bushy eyebrows. "William Haverford was a wealthy merchant and a patriot during the Revolutionary War. He was the visionary who founded our magnificent program."

A cluster of cabins resembling an old-fashioned black-and-white photo replaced the two men. "Located near Philadelphia, our campus was originally named Haverford Hills." A chuckle. "Obviously, when we relocated to our current location in 1940, we had to change it."

I rubbed my eyes, feeling like I was in a psychedelic history class. More men appeared and disappeared. A few looked familiar. Was that Thomas Jefferson with his fuzzy red hair? Benjamin Franklin in round glasses?

A grainy apparition of a giant tent with boys lined up wearing what looked like long underwear. "This 1858 photo shows our annual selection process. Until recent technological advances, HP had to search far and wide to find its talent. We held events nationwide where we evaluated thousands of youths to select the cream of the crop." More apparitions—groups of teens competing in athletics or hunched over exams.

"That's a lot of white boys," a voice murmured. I swiveled to see a frowning girl behind me. Her thick, brown hair was pulled back in the ponytail she was twirling around her fingers. The girl's eyes fixed on me, and I felt a jolt, as if she were crawling inside my thoughts, trying to see if I was a friend or foe.

I must have passed the test because she continued, "Brownest thing in those photos is the dirt on their boots."

She was right—even in black and white, it was clear that every figure was a white boy.

A rotating globe appeared, points on its surface sparkling. "In 1945, with the creation of the United Nations," Blakewell's deep voice continued, "satellite centers opened around the world." Scattered cheers. "And in 1950, we welcomed girls, finally recognizing their contribution to the well-being and success of our planet."

An apparition of boys and girls posing at The Chalet brought a chorus of female cheers. "There you go," I whispered, pointing at the smattering of diverse faces. "You've got a few tokens there."

The girl sniffed. "I remain unimpressed."

Blakewell's eyes blazed. "You will continue HP's tradition of excellence by becoming the world's leaders, its greatest influencers. Many of you have begun to realize your purposes. We will strengthen your determination and hone your skills. Others have yet to realize your incredible strength. We will unearth that purpose and nourish it. Centuries of success show our ability to produce presidents, champions, and Nobel Prize winners." A figure of a beaming scientist holding up a medal.

I wondered how long it would take until they realized I was no Beethoven or Einstein. I had promised Dad I would try, whatever that meant, and I would. But if I still got kicked out early, I might get home in time to work at the rec center.

From the hall came a low hum. A group of teens filed into the auditorium, chanting in a foreign language. They carried lit candles and wore black jeans and dark purple cloaks. Lining the aisles, they continued chanting as a procession of adults followed, wearing purple robes. As they took seats in the front, I spotted the stern woman from the check-in desk, sitting next to a pale man with messy black hair.

We were silent, mesmerized by the chanting, the flickering light, and Blakewell's eerie grinning head. A boy emerged from the back and strode toward the stage, the tails of his cloak flowing behind him. He took the stairs two at a time, stopped next to Blakewell's head, put his palm across his chest, and bowed. The old man nodded, and his head vanished.

The boy turned to face us. The cloak fell to just below his waist, wrapped in folds around his left side, and was fastened at his right shoulder with a giant gold wolf pin. He raised his fist in the air and the room felt charged with energy. "Courage, loyalty, triumph," he said, his voice clear and strong.

The teens holding the candles raised their fists. "Courage, loyalty, triumph."

The boy made a slashing motion and, in unison, the others blew out their candles. The room was pitch black and silent as we all held our breaths.

The lights in the room came up and the boy picked up a microphone. "Welcome Plebes." He flashed a huge white smile and the tension in the room eased. He resembled the handsome Ricky Ricardo from *I Love Lucy*, with thick black hair swept off his forehead and an aura of comedic energy. The creepiness of Edmund Blakewell's head was replaced by excitement and anticipation. "I'm Matthew Drexler and am honored to be the president of the Youth Council and the youngest serving member of the Senior Council. I was a Plebe like you for my first summer, an Equite for my second, and team leader for the Senatores in my third."

He waved a hand. "Don't worry about all these terms. You'll quickly get used to our HP speak. When in doubt, just say trainee. I am lucky enough to be helping to run this amazing summer academy."

Claps from the cloaked teens.

"So, the Equites and Senatores can concur that the food here is amazing. Chef Emilio plans awesome meals." Matthew moved easily across the stage. "We work really hard, but we have fun too. Every afternoon we have Interdisciplinary Activities, which are a chance to meet friends with other purposes. In IA, you can cook, do an obstacle course, learn about computers, or even play board games."

I found myself hanging on Matthew's every word as he described the logistics of living in the cabins, mealtimes, and activities. He made everything seem interesting and important.

"Let's take a look at how this process works," he said. "Phase One, which starts tomorrow, is baseline testing. Some of the tests, like low-level fitness and academics, will be for everyone." He waved his hand and a photo appeared on a screen behind him—trainees running on the track—sparking a mixture of cheers and groans.

"No worries. We're not asking you to run a marathon or bench press your body weight. But basic fitness is important for us all as it nourishes the mind. Phase Two, we start to home in on your special skills." Photos of football players colliding, a model posing for a photographer. Giggles from Britt's corner.

"What's your purpose, Matthew?" an older trainee yelled.

Matthew grinned. "Isn't it obvious?"

"Future NBA center?" the trainee called.

"Pop star," called another.

"Chosen One," the group chorused, bursting into laughter.

Matthew gave an exaggerated roll of his eyes and we all laughed, even though we were clueless. "Phase Three, your purpose is finalized, and you will receive advanced training in your area." A photo of swimmers hovering on starting blocks.

I noted that there were no photos of geeky kids at computers. Or freckled girls with no artistic abilities and so-so grades.

"If you are successful in your training this summer, you will be invited back for two more, where your skills will be perfected. In addition, you will become mentors and guides for those below you." He spread out his arms. "Welcome back to the Equites, our second-year trainees."

The teens on the left side of the auditorium put their right hands across their chests, then held them up as fists.

"And the Senatores, our fearless leaders!" The teens on the right side copied the Equites, then burst into cheers and high fives.

I tried to imagine myself in their shoes—at ease and thrilled to be with my fellow trainees, all of us knowing our ultimate purposes. A swell of jealousy welled up, followed by sadness. If only I had a purpose, I could stay and experience this kind of community and friendship. But even trying my hardest, there was no way I would even last here a week.

"And finally," Matthew bowed to the adults. "We are lucky enough to have a cohort of world-renowned tutors. You Plebes may not see much of them your first summer. But when you become Quites and Tores, you will benefit from their invaluable wisdom and teaching."

We clapped for the tutors who smiled and nodded.

"The Tores are in their final year and will serve as your counselors and team leaders." Matthew held out his arms to the group in a wide embrace. "Good luck tomorrow. Oh, and one more thing." The screen showed a photo of a grinning Hollywood superstar cradling his Academy Award. "Know that after finishing HP, you will be prepared to go into the world and shine, just like so many who came before you."

CHAPTER
FOUR

THE NEXT MORNING, a group of us waited at the edge of the track. I shivered and rubbed my palms over my arms. The mountain air had a cold bite, and I hadn't thought to wear a hoodie. Samantha had popped into our room with our HP training *uniforms*. Mine was black athletic shorts, a white sports bra, and a white T-shirt with a purple HP on the front and the number 42 on the back. I received four sets, along with sweats, a swimsuit, and an extra pair of tennis shoes. Britt's clothing was similar, although her shorts were cute cotton ones, and her shirt was a fitted tank top. Still, number 27 had whined about the clothing and pouted when Samantha told her she couldn't wear makeup and had to put her hair into a ponytail.

I had planned to quiz Samantha about the testing process, to get a sense of how quickly I would get booted out. I was surprised to realize a part of me wanted to stick around. Maybe it was Matthew and his charisma or the intrigue of the chanting and Blakewell's eerie floating head. I was curious what would happen next.

I was with about twenty Plebes—most looking athletic and confident. The serious girl from the night before was there, holding herself still, her head swiveling like an owl's back and forth as she studied the others. Her T-shirt was too big, and her shorts hung down almost to her knees. She wore a necklace with a crown-shaped pendant and gold stud earrings. With her tiny size, I figured her purpose must be gymnastics.

The woman from the check-in table, wearing a gray tracksuit with purple trim, strode onto the field. Older trainees followed her, carrying clipboards. They wore black shorts with two purple stripes down the side and purple T-shirts with emblems on their sleeves.

She blew a whistle. "I'm Crystal Macintyre, the director of testing. Your Tores leaders will be assisting me, so follow their directions carefully. First off, two laps on the track to warm up. Go." She blew the whistle again.

I sighed and trudged onto the track. Running was so incredibly boring, just putting one foot in front of the other for no reason. Dad had tried to get me to jog with him, but I was miserable after five minutes. I had pretended to twist my ankle so I could stop. I glanced at Crystal. Would that work today?

"Not a chance," the gymnast said. "She won't fall for it."

I jumped. Where had she come from? And how had she read my mind?

"I'm not built for running," I protested.

The girl regarded me with chocolate brown eyes. A smile played at the edge of her lips. "Try not to be so rigid. You're going to surprise yourself."

I stared after her as she took off running. Rigid? More like realistic!

I jogged my laps, finishing toward the back of the pack. Crystal gave me and the other stragglers a hard look, then consulted her clipboard. "We're going to break into groups and do a circuit. Push-ups, sit-ups, and pull-ups." She read out names and I ended up in a group with two other girls and two boys. Of course, one was the gymnast. I just couldn't get away from her.

She didn't seem surprised and held out her hand. "I'm Gabi."

I took her hand. "Lina."

The third girl had an olive complexion and spiked black hair with blonde tips. Apparently, she hadn't gotten the no-makeup message because she wore thick black eyeliner and mascara. On her wrist was a bracelet with dangling charms. Looking Gabi and me up and down, her lips curved into a smirk. Both boys smiled and nodded hello. The first, tan with tousled brown hair and a chiseled jaw, looked like he had stepped off Troy Bolton's basketball team in *High School Musical*. The other was a large, heavyset boy with dark skin, short hair, and bulging muscles—clearly a football player.

A Tore with red hair and a kind expression shook my hand. Theo was going to time how many push-ups I could do in two minutes. I glanced at my pale, skinny arms. I would be stronger if I had been able to get in more time at the climbing wall, but my parents were always pushing homework over fun. Kneeling and stretching out on the grass, I got my body lined up.

Theo knelt next to me holding a stopwatch. "Ready, set, go."

I began doing push-ups. After about ten, I was bored, just like with running. It wasn't that I couldn't do it, but why ...? I breathed in the scent of the dirt and grass. It was the same grass we had in California but more bristly with scattered poky pine needles.

"Faster, Lina," Theo urged. "Pick up the pace."

My chest muscles were burning. Out of the corner of my eye, Spiky's face was flushed and determined. She was doing at least two push-ups for every one of mine.

"And, stop," Theo said.

I collapsed onto the grass. My arms were achy and rubbery.

"Thirty-six," he said, scribbling on his clipboard. He offered me his hand, pulled me to my feet, and went to confer with the other Tores.

"Yes!" Spiky exclaimed. "Fifty-eight." She high-fived the grinning *Bolton*. He lifted his shirt to wipe his face, exposing a perfect six-pack. The warm scent of cologne wafted our way.

Gabi was pulling in deep breaths. She gave me a weak smile. I returned it. "I'm already beat."

Spiky whirled. She took in our sweaty faces, gave a snarky smile, and kissed her bicep.

Okay, no ego there. I was used to arrogance but the girls at my school were more subtle about it. They communicated their superiority with giggles or knowing looks. Channeling that clique now, I swept my gaze over Spiky with my best, *You are nothing but a piece of dog crap* look. Her nostrils flared and I suppressed a smile as I turned away.

The football player had his hands on his knees and was breathing hard. "You okay?" I asked.

He ignored me, his face tense, lips pursed.

I'm making friends all over the place.

Crystal blew her whistle. "We have the winners from this station. Number eighteen for the girls and number twenty-nine for the boys."

Spiky whooped and bounded over to high-five a boy who was over six feet tall and looked like he already played for the Lakers.

"Keep it up and you'll be in the running for Campio and Campia," Crystal said.

"What's Campio?" I asked, trailing Theo to the next station.

"It's the top Plebe in each purpose. Don't worry about that now."

Don't worry about that ever. This station was sit-ups and I managed to make it to forty-nine before fearing I was going to throw up.

At the pull-up station, I cracked my chin against the bar and only got to ten.

Spiky and the Laker were high-fiving all over the place. She shot me a triumphant look and I ignored her, turning and stepping away from my group. I didn't like failure being shoved in my face. Getting space from upsetting situations—and people—was one of the tools I used to prevent anger flares.

The next wave of trainees was on the track. A skinny boy lagged behind the rest, his knees bowing in and feet kicking out with each step. As he reached the halfway mark, he slowed to a walk, then stopped, cupping his hands behind his neck.

"Keep moving!" a Tore yelled from the side. "Number forty-one, finish your lap."

The boy's chest hitched, and I felt a wave of sympathy. He was an easy peg as a computer nerd who had probably never run a mile in his life. Even though Matthew had said physical fitness was important, why make everyone run on the first day? Wasn't that something they could work up to over the course of the summer?

"Come on, buddy," I murmured. "You can do it."

As if hearing me, the boy straightened and turned my way. His arms dropped to his side, and he cocked his head like Desi did when he spotted a squirrel.

My own body reacted weirdly. I had never seen this boy before but there was a sudden connection between us, like an invisible rope of energy pulling us together. And I knew—how I knew, I had no idea—so much about him. That he was an only child, and his favorite foods were chicken tikka masala and peanut butter cookies; that he spent days in the library curled up in an old armchair reading books; that he spied on people like I did, only he used computers.

I didn't realize I was moving until I had crossed most of the ground between us. He was moving too. Arriving up close, we stopped and stared at each other. He was a touch taller than me, his eyes the color of the ocean on a cloudy day, pale blond eyebrows matching almost-white blond hair.

I knew him. That recognition was mirrored in his stunned expression.

"Number forty-one, get back on the track." A Tore was jogging over, waving her arms.

Our hands reached out and met. His fingers were longer than mine, but thinner and more delicate. I felt an overwhelming urge to protect him like I did with Emma Claire.

"How do we," I whispered. "What is ..."

"I don't know." His forehead wrinkled. "Do you like licorice?"

I did my best thinking when I had something in my mouth—gum, straws, fingernails, the sleeves of my shirt. My parents were constantly yelling at me to stop chewing on things. And my absolute favorite was red licorice twists.

The Tore, a muscular girl with frizzy, bleached-blonde hair, clamped her hand on the boy's shoulder, "Forty-one, finish your warm-up. Now."

My urge to protect swelled. "Hold on," I said to her. To him, "I love licorice. And you like chicken tikka masala?"

His eyes grew bigger and he nodded.

The Tore scowled at me. "Plebe, return to your group."

"Give us a second. We're trying to figure out ..."

"That was an order," the girl barked. She yanked him backward and he fell, yelping as he hit the ground.

My anger flashed. I lunged forward and shoved the Tore hard. The girl fell, landing next to the boy who cringed away from her. She sprang back up, eyes flashing, fists clenching. I clenched my own fists. The girl was at least six inches taller, and it had been a while since I had hit anything besides the punching bag in the basement. But with hot blood pumping through my system, I craved the feeling of my fist connecting with flesh and bone.

Theo ran up, planting himself between us. "I know emotions are high," he said firmly, "but this needs to end now." He looked warningly at the girl as she started to protest. "Becky, you are a Tore, the mature one here. Lina is a Plebe and is still learning her place."

The girl's jaw bulged, and her face grew pink. I imagined steam shooting out of the top of her head, like a cartoon character. Finally, she let her hands relax and stalked off, pulling the boy behind her like a chew toy.

"Everybody is waiting for you," Theo told me.

The rest of the world flooded back into my consciousness—the mutterings of the other Plebes who had watched the whole thing, the screech of birds in the trees, the bright sun overhead. It was all too much noise and activity. My heart was racing, my breath coming in fast pants, and I felt a surge of panic. Once my anger came, it was hard to calm back down. I needed to find a quiet place where I could *hush*, return my body to normal.

I managed to nod at Theo, turn, and hurry toward the gym. A

few minutes in the bathroom alone should be enough. As I passed my group, a smirking Spiky stepped in front of me. "Forty-two, was that your crush?" she sneered. "Did he reject you?"

I was used to stupid insults from girls at school, so I ignored Spiky and started to go around her.

She grabbed my arm, "Giving up already? Do you need a good cry?"

"Get your hand off me," I said, heat flooding my face. I had passed the yellow zone and was speeding toward the red.

"Whoa, so sensitive." She started to let go then reached back and poked me with her finger.

I tackled her onto the grass. Before she could react, I drew my arm back and punched her in the face. Ah, I had missed that feeling—part pain, part exhilaration. The punching bag was a poor substitute for hitting someone who really, really deserved it. Pulling my arm back again, I felt strong arms around my waist, lifting me into the air. I flailed, but the grip was tight.

"Please calm down," a deep voice said. "I don't want anybody to get hurt more."

I was in the clutches of the football player. His gentle tone didn't match his enormous strength. I struggled, but he held me easily.

Spiky leaped to her feet. "What's wrong with you?" she yelled, jabbing her finger at me. Blood oozed from her lip and dribbled onto her T-shirt. "You're an entitled rich bitch like all the rest. I'm going to kick your ass." Bolton put an arm across her chest to restrain her.

"Yeah, you just try." I tried to free myself so I could pound the smirk off her face.

The pierce of the whistle and Crystal strode over. She jabbed it at us. "Any more screwing around and you're both doing ten laps." She jerked her chin at Spiky. "Number eighteen, trade places with fifty-four. We're moving onto the obstacle course."

Spiky shrugged off Bolton's arm and shot me a death stare before stalking away toward her new group. Well, that brought the total up to two girls I had managed to piss off in five minutes. I was still breathing hard, adrenaline flooding my system. The football player must have sensed my agitation because he set me down but kept his hands on my shoulders. The pressure helped me to calm down and my heart rate to slow.

"Thank you," I finally said, examining my hand. Bruised, red knuckles but nothing broken.

"You could thank me, you know," the deep voice said.

"I did." I turned and instantly realized my stupidity. Up close, I could see the hearing aids tucked behind his ears. He hadn't been ignoring me earlier—he just hadn't heard me. "Thank you," I said clearly.

He smiled and his face crinkled like a little boy's, creating deep dimples in both cheeks. "Happy to help. I'm Charles."

"Lina." I glanced at Gabi who must have thought I was a total freak—throwing tantrums and getting into fights like a toddler.

"I try not to be entitled," I said apologetically. "I just have these anger issues sometimes." I blew on my knuckles.

Gabi glanced toward Spiky. "She's actually quite wealthy herself. Family lives on the Upper East Side."

I dropped my hand. "What? How do you know?"

"I just know," Gabi said simply.

I just know. I would hear that phrase a lot from Gabi in the weeks to come, and it would prove to be true, over and over.

This time, I was skeptical. "*How* do you know?"

Gabi gave a small sigh. She raised a finger. "Her accent is upper-crust Manhattan." A second finger. "Her haircut and highlights are pricey." Third finger. "The bracelet she is wearing is Lavignes. Sold exclusively at an upscale boutique on the Upper East Side. Fourth finger. "Pretty sure she's the daughter of an Italian American entrepreneur who made a fortune in frozen dinners."

I gaped. To me, Spiky's hair just looked ... well, spiky, and I hadn't noticed any accent.

"The family was featured in the *Times* several years ago," Gabi said. "The company is worth at least fifty million."

"So ... what was that crap about kicking my rich bitch ass?"

Gabi shrugged. "Who knows? Maybe she has guilt about being a trust-fund baby. It could even go back to the struggle between the Italians and Irish in the 1880s."

"Huh? I mean, my ancestors were Irish but ..."

"The Italians and Irish have a long history of conflict. When the Italians began immigrating in the 1880s, they clashed with the Irish who were already here and felt as if their barely achieved success was being threatened."

Charles and I exchanged confused looks. Who was this girl? My favorite subject was history, but I didn't know any crazy details like this. And how did she recognize accents or know about a bracelet sold in a New York boutique?

"That can't be why she picked a fight with me. Because she's Italian and I'm Irish?"

Gabi laughed. "No, she wouldn't know her American history that well, or care. She is fiercely competitive and views you as a rival. Maybe for that Campia award."

I snorted. No way was I competition for anyone, let alone Spiky.

I wanted to confess that I would be leaving soon anyway, but hesitated. I now hoped I could get to stay long enough to figure out the connection between me and that boy. I wanted—no I needed—to talk to him again.

Gabi tapped a finger against her lips. "Also, she is an opportunist, so I assume she was trying to curry favor with that Tore you knocked down. Brownie points so to speak."

Charles shook his head at me. "You're a tough little Irish scrapper. You always cause this much trouble?"

I laughed, "You have no idea."

CHAPTER
FIVE

AT THE EDGE OF THE WOODS, Crystal brandished her whistle like a scepter. "This is a timed obstacle course. Your assessment will be based on both accuracy and speed. If you cannot finish an obstacle within the set time limit, you will move on to the next."

"This body isn't going over walls," Charles grumbled. "These feet stay on the ground."

"You'll do fine," I said, being sure to face him and speak clearly. "Look how strong you are."

He grimaced. "Exactly. Give me an obstacle to tackle. Give me a strength challenge."

"They must have all the athletes do similar physical testing," Gabi said. "To get a baseline."

Was she saying I was with the athletes? What a joke! My parents had stuck me in many sports—soccer, softball, lacrosse—and I had bombed them all. They had finally given up and let me count hiking and the climbing wall as *sports*.

"I don't like heights," Charles said as we moved forward. "Do you think we have to do anything up high?"

I hope so. Way better than jogging or push-ups.

"Ma'am," Charles said to Crystal when we reached her. "I'm here for football, so I'm hoping I can skip this and do some strength testing instead?"

Crystal gave him a hard look. "The testing challenges are not optional."

Charles heaved a sigh. "It's just that ..."

She blew the whistle and pointed toward the trees.

Charles reluctantly began jogging.

Soon it was my turn, and I took off down the path, easily avoiding the jutting tree roots and rocks. After a few hundred yards, the path opened into a clearing. A dirt pit had a thick net of ropes strung across it. A Tore stood to one side, holding his clipboard.

"Go under," he directed.

I dropped to my stomach. Crawling like a crab, I thrust with my arms and legs, the earth sucking around my body, smearing into my clothing and between my fingers.

And I loved it. I had never admitted this to anyone, but I loved getting dirty. At age four, I had rolled around in the backyard dirt and lain on my belly in the weeds, watching my mom grow increasingly frantic as she searched for me. By dusting my skin with dirt and climbing our tree, I could spy on the neighbors. I had learned Mr. Foster was having another woman over when Mrs. Foster was at yoga, Mrs. Wilson liked to dance around the house naked, and teenage Bobby Patton wore Marvel underwear.

At the end, I crawled out, shook off the dirt, and took off again, a huge smile on my face. Around the next bend was a wooden platform with a hanging rope connected to a jumbo set of monkey bars. A bored-looking Tore sat on a tree stump, pressing the button on his stopwatch as I spit on my hands and grinned. Rope climbing was a breeze and I had calluses on my hands from the climbing wall. A few shimmies up the rope and I was at the top and swinging across.

The next obstacle was a giant wooden ladder. The bottom rung was taller than me. I bent my knees, leaped straight up, and wrapped my arms around it. Drawing my legs up to grip the beam, I twisted my body around until I was on top of it. Standing, I did another jump to reach the next beam and repeated the movements. The rest of the world fell away at the sensations of the coarse wood under my hands, the tensing of my abs, the timing of twisting. At the top, I let out a whoop of triumph.

"Very nice," the Tore said. "That's the best time yet today."

Getting down was similarly easy and we high-fived before I headed down the path, my body zinging with adrenaline.

I rounded the next bend and skidded to a stop. Charles was caught in what looked like a massive spider web. Thick white ropes were staked to the ground at the bottom and wove across each other as they stretched up diagonally to a platform anchored by two trees. The task was clearly to start at the bottom and crawl up the web to the platform.

Three-quarters of the way up, Charles dangled upside down, his leg tangled in the ropes. A Tore stood under him, hands on hips. "Buddy, can you work that leg out?"

"No," I yelled, running toward them. Charles' head was fifteen feet off the ground. A fall would badly injure him. "Don't pull your leg out!" I glared at the Tore.

"He tried to climb up underneath," he said, looking annoyed. "That's wrong, but I'm not allowed to say anything."

Charles tried to lift his upper body. The net creaked, and his fingers brushed the ropes before he fell back and groaned.

"Stay still," I called, hoping he could hear me. I didn't say what I had noticed when he tried to grab the ropes—his leg had slipped. If it came out, he would plummet straight down.

The Tore had unclipped a walkie-talkie from his waistband and was muttering into it.

"I can't breathe," Charles said, his voice rasping. "I dropped my inhaler."

I scanned the ground, spotted the small canister, and ran to scoop it up. A classmate had asthma and I knew it got worse when she was exercising or scared.

"Just stay calm," I called, knowing how ridiculous it sounded. My thoughts raced. Charles weighed over 200 pounds. He would land on his head, breaking his neck or crushing his skull. There was no way the Tore and I could catch him. I could climb up the web and try to pull him up. But the swaying of the ropes during my climb could dislodge his leg, and I wasn't strong enough anyway.

"Help is coming," the Tore told me.

"When?"

He shrugged.

"Don't you have some sort of safety plan? He needs help now!"

Another shrug.

I had to do something. I wedged the inhaler inside the band of my sports bra. "Give me your sweatshirt."

"What are you ... ?"

"Just do it," I grabbed at him.

"Okay, okay," he said, pulling off the sweatshirt.

I tied it around my waist and ran around to the other side of the platform, a wall with a rope dangling from the top. I climbed up and was quickly on top of the platform. Charles' section of the web was about twelve feet down.

"I'm right here," I yelled. "Don't move."

There were squeaks, like helium escaping from a balloon— the noise my classmate had made right before the paramedics rushed her to the hospital.

No time for panic. I tied the sweatshirt to my ankle, dropped onto my stomach, and used my knees and toes to ease my body onto the ropes. My heart pounded and adrenaline flooded my body, but I forced myself to move slowly. With the help of gravity and the weight of my limbs distributed evenly, I was able to inch forward without causing any sway.

When I got close enough, I reached back for the sweatshirt. "Grab this sleeve and wrap it tight around your wrist," I called. "I'll pull you up." I pushed the sweatshirt through a gap and waved it until the sleeve brushed against Charles. He reached for it but couldn't grasp it.

A commotion below as Crystal and her Torres rushed into the clearing. "Number forty-two, get down immediately," she bellowed.

I ignored her. Charles' squeaky breaths were fading, and I knew time was running out. I closed my eyes and debated the options. I could tie the sweatshirt around his leg, anchoring him more tightly to the rope, then wait for the others to help. He wouldn't fall and crush his skull. But the asthma would kill him.

I could tie the sweatshirt to his ankle and try to lower him down myself. But we were too high, and I wasn't strong enough.

"I'm right above you," a voice interrupted my thoughts. I jerked and the ropes swayed. Pressing my fingers into their rough fibers, I forced a deep breath.

"Name's Hayden." The voice was a boy's, with an unusual accent. "I'm a Joe, and I'm here to help."

I had no clue what a Joe was but didn't hesitate. With two of us, I had one last idea. It probably wouldn't work, but it could give Charles a chance.

"Are you strong?" I asked.

"I am."

"Get down here and hold my legs."

The ropes shifted, then a form eased just next to and behind me. Glancing back, I saw an older boy with dark brown eyes and a serious, determined expression.

"Can you just tie the jumper around his leg and secure him to the rope?" he asked. "Then we can wait for the medics?"

"No, he's got asthma. I've got to get him his inhaler before he stops breathing."

"Crap," he muttered. "We need an EpiPen and hurry up the medics," he yelled to the group below. He wrapped his fingers tightly around my ankles. "All right then, go on. I've got you."

I tied Charles' leg to the rope. Taking another deep breath, I eased myself through an opening and stretched my arms toward him. Inching my body further forward, I wrapped one arm around his back to keep our bodies close.

"Nice," Hayden said. "Keep going."

Once my waist was through the hole, the only thing keeping me from falling would be him holding my ankles.

"I've got you, I promise," he said.

I thrust myself forward. Blood began rushing to my head in pounding pulses. Ignoring the image of my skull bursting open like a smashed pumpkin, I ran my fingers up Charles' chest, locating his chin and then mouth. Puffs of breath tickled my fingers, and I felt a rush of relief.

I carefully pulled out the inhaler, gripping it tightly. If I dropped it, there was no plan B. Focusing all my mental energy on the canister, I pulled the cap off with my teeth. Tugging at Charles' lower lip, I brought the round opening to his mouth, hoping it would dispense the medication upside down.

"How's it coming?" Hayden's voice was calm but had an edge. "You 'bout finished?"

I pressed the top of the canister, and its faint puff seemed like a good sign. I pressed it over and over, releasing the medication into Charles' mouth and—hopefully—lungs, until it was empty.

CHAPTER
SIX

THE OINTMENT THE PHYSICIAN ASSISTANT smeared on my scrapes smelled like Desi's liquid vitamins but instantly began to soothe my skin.

"What is this?" I asked.

"It's a blend an HP grad created," Dylan said. He picked up the purple jar and studied the back. "Has all sorts of herbs in it. Calendula, aloe vera, and other stuff."

"Okay. Well, thanks," I said. I had resisted going to the infirmary because I wasn't hurt, but Crystal had ordered me here, probably to get me out of the way.

"No problem." Dylan threw his gloves in the trash. I had been waiting for him to scold me, to tell me I could have been killed, that I had—once again—rushed into a situation without thinking. Instead, the lanky man with a tattoo of Ms. Pac-Man on his bicep and black plugs in his earlobes had gotten me a clean uniform, examined my skin, applied the ointment, and patted me on the back. He hadn't even asked if I had been scared.

And the weird thing was that I hadn't really been scared. Hanging up there by my ankles, confronting death, I had never felt so elated or alive.

As Dylan was leaving, a trainee entered. He had tousled brown hair, dark eyes, and a scar that ran across the bottom of his chin. His T-shirt had an eagle emblem on the sleeve. "Nice work up there," he said, eyes twinkling.

I recognized the accent and felt an instant connection—not like the supernatural one with the boy from the track, but a bond of having achieved an amazing feat together. I fought the urge to jump off the exam table and hug Hayden—the last thing he would want was contact with that stinky ointment. Instead, I held up a palm and slapped him a high five. "How did you hold onto me that long?"

Hayden stretched out his arms and wiggled his fingers. "They're a bit tired. Luckily, you're a wispy thing. And these babies are strong."

Strong was an understatement. Those tendons, muscles and bones had held my weight until the inhaler was empty and a rescue crew arrived. By the time they lowered Charles to the ground and I scrambled down the web, Hayden was gone.

"How is he?"

Hayden hesitated and I dug my nonexistent nails into my palms.

"I haven't heard anything yet. But I'll come find you straightaway at your afternoon testing when I do."

I gaped at him. "Testing? Seriously? I couldn't care less about that now."

Hayden crossed his arms over his chest and leaned against the wall, regarding me. I knew he was a rising senior in high school like the other Tores. But his attitude was more like an adult's. "You should care," he said finally. "You ought to take this seriously."

I tried to hold his gaze but ended up looking down at my clenched hands. I suddenly wished the snobby girls at school could see me talking to this cute guy. Hanging upside down with him holding my ankles had been like being in an action movie. Nothing that exciting was ever going to happen to me again.

I rubbed a dab of ointment into the back of my hand. "I'm not a model," I said quietly. "I'm not a musician, an athlete, or a computer geek." Shame swelled in my chest. "Being good at a ropes course is going to get me, what, a prize on some stupid reality TV competition?"

Hayden gave a surprised laugh. "Don't be daft," he said, pushing himself off the wall. He leaned his back against the table and opened his hands. His fingers and palms were muscular, the skin on them covered with thick calluses that had tackled more than monkey bars. "We're not talking reality TV or some boring science lab, Luv." He clenched his fists and the muscles on his forearms bulged. "We're talking Special Forces. And who wouldn't want to be part of that?"

"Special Forces?" My mind shot to the poster of my Army Ranger and a rush of excitement rolled through me. "Like as in the military? That guy last night didn't mention anything like that."

"The celebrities are more glamorous, you know, like actors, athletes, Nobel Prize winners. But many of the top military leaders in the world are HP'ers."

"Is that what the eagle is for?" I gestured at the emblem on his sleeve.

He nodded. "The eagle is the symbol of strength, both in the pursuit of peace and, if needed, for defense."

I stuck my arms out next to his. Scrawny by comparison, the only bulges being knobby joints. I swallowed hard then forced myself to say it. "Really, I'm not good at anything, Hayden. Getting invited to HP was a mistake."

Hayden was silent for a moment then shook his head. "What you did today shows guts and ingenuity," he said. "That's what's key. The rest will come." He stood and walked to the door. "Sit tight until your mater comes to fetch you and we'll talk more later."

After he left, I thought of my Ranger. I had spent hours staring into his fierce eyes, imagining the discipline and work it had taken to get there. But I had never imagined I could be like him.

Special Forces? Being able to get through an obstacle course or hang upside down for ten minutes didn't mean I could be military. When Seal Team Six assassinated Osama Bin Laden, I had been obsessed with the reports and news coverage. But as far as Mom and Dad were concerned, the military was either for kids who couldn't hack it at college, or incredible athletes who wanted scholarships. Even if I had the skills buried somewhere deep inside me, how could HP know that? I had never been on a competitive sports team or even done well in gym class.

Jumping off the table, I paced the small space. Special Forces? Should I at least try for it—really try, not just the minimum needed to satisfy my dad? It might be too late. I hadn't done great on the physical tests, especially the chin-ups. And I hadn't even finished the obstacle course. Time was ticking by, and the other Plebes were out there finishing their physical tests.

I tried the door. Locked. I chewed on my thumbnail, ignoring the bitter taste. Hayden had said to sit tight, but why had he locked me in? I opened the cupboards under the sink. Bins of wrapped packages like gauze and ace bandages.

It was 11:34. I had an innate sense of time, which drove my parents nuts because I was always late. I tried the door again—still locked. I noticed the panels in the ceiling were like the ones at my middle school. After watching *The Breakfast Club*, I had been determined to sneak through the ducts like the rebel Bender did in the movie. During lunch one day, I had sneaked into the guidance counselor's office, put a chair on her desk, and gone for it. Unfortunately, I had barely been able to squeeze my frame into a space that was too narrow to move in without getting stuck. She had returned just as I was dropping back onto the desk. My lame explanation—that I thought I had heard a mouse and was trying to catch it—had earned me two days of detention and no TV for a month.

The infirmary was at the back of the athletics building that housed the gym, the pool, and offices. The building seemed pretty new, which might mean it had a bigger space—or smaller. Gabi could probably lecture me on duct sizing if she were here. I removed the exam table's sheet of paper, set it on the floor, and hopped onto the table. Jumping straight up, my fingers pushed up the panel in the ceiling. It came back down askew. After several more jumps, I pushed the panel to the side, leaving a two-by-four-foot opening.

From the cupboard, I grabbed two plastic bins, dumped their contents, and stacked them upside down on the table. I stared up at the hole. Even if I could get up there, the ceiling might not hold my weight. What was I doing? There was absolutely no good reason for me to go crawling around the air ducts. I should put everything away and wait for Samantha.

Special Forces, I heard Hayden's voice in my head. Then Gabi's— *try not to be so rigid.* Why not at least see if I could make it up there? I could come right back down.

Resting the ball of one foot on top of the bins, I swung my arms, bounced with my other leg, pushed hard with my toes, and reached above me. The bins clattered to the floor, but I was up, elbows braced, legs dangling. I scooted back on my elbows, swung my legs up and rolled onto my stomach.

The space was bigger than at the middle school. Okay, I had proved to myself I could get up here, now I should hop back down.

Sounds of yelling and whistles echoed through the duct. Curious, I rested my weight on my knees and elbows and began wriggling forward. I would just take a quick peek.

After a few minutes, a warm, chlorinated breeze wafted from a metal vent in the side of the duct, along with the sounds of voices and splashing. Through it, I glimpsed the expanse of an Olympic-length pool.

A male version of Crystal held a clipboard and barked orders to Tores holding stopwatches. I prayed swimming was not going to be part of my testing. There was no way I was getting into or across that pool.

The man strode over to a woman at a computer. "Are these results accurate? I expected a bit more from sixty-seven."

"Let's double-check," she said, tapping at the keys.

The swimmers had numbers in block letters on their caps. Sixty-seven skimmed through the water, easily ahead of the girls in the other lanes. At the end, she pushed herself out of the pool, stood, and stretched her arms over her head. With a thick neck, wide shoulders, and long legs, she had the same body type as the swimmers on our state-champion Green Hills team.

The woman rattled off a bunch of numbers with the words *free* and *butterfly* mixed in.

"Hmm," the man said. "Not much improvement from last year."

"Those are solid times."

"Mother won gold, father silver." He sighed. "I'm looking for a bit more than solid."

"This is only the beginning of her second summer. She'll be another Ledecky when you finish with her. I have confidence."

"Let's try it again after lunch," he said.

Lunch. I jolted. It was 11:53. Going backward was harder, and I was sweaty and covered in fresh scrapes by the time I returned to the hole. I slid onto the table and settled the panel into place.

Voices and footsteps in the hall. The plastic bins and their contents were all over the floor. There was a scraping of a key, a thunk, and the door opened.

Samantha's expression morphed from cheery to shocked. "What is going on in here? What have you been doing?"

CHAPTER
SEVEN

I DID THE ONLY THING I COULD THINK OF—burst into tears. Grabbing the paper, I clutched it to my chest. "Don't look at me," I moaned. "I'm a total mess. I thought I was okay, but then I was trying to get splinters out and I made it worse." I stretched out an arm. Dust from the vent clung to the ointment, making my skin a messy gray with flecks of blood. "I tried to find band-aids, and there was all this stuff, but no band-aids, and I have to go to the bathroom."

After a moment of stunned silence, Samantha knelt next to me. "It's okay," she soothed. "I didn't realize how traumatized you were, or I would have been here sooner." She rubbed a hand across my back. "Do you want me to get Dylan?"

"No," I said quickly. "I just want to finish my testing."

"All right." She helped me stand.

"Can I," I hiccupped. "Can I take a shower?"

"Of course. I'll give you a pass so you can be late to lunch. Hurry though because you'll have the afternoon testing right after."

As we walked from the gym toward the cabins, a group of girls joined us, wrapped in oversized purple towels and talking about how they couldn't wait for Chef Emilio's brownies.

Samantha glanced at her wrist. "Be sure you're at lunch by 12:40. I'll check in with you later."

I fell in behind the swimmers, who looked curiously at me.

"Number forty-two ... aren't you the one who saved that Plebe on the ropes course?" asked a girl.

I gave a small shrug. "I helped. Just in the right place at the right time."

The girl grimaced, showing a mouth full of braces. "One of my friends broke his arm on that course last year. I was so happy I didn't have to do it."

I mirrored her expression. "It's not as bad as the pool. Swimming terrifies me."

"Seriously?" said a blonde girl with legs as high as my shoulders. "Swimming is all I know how to do. Luckily after today, you'll get more focused on your purpose."

This was the girl who had been windmilling through the water like she was strolling. "Are you an Equite?" I asked.

She nodded. "Equites summer is much easier than Plebes so don't get too freaked out."

"Yeah, but you knew that swimming was your purpose before you came? I still don't ..." I trailed off.

The girl shook her head. "No, I didn't. I was an athlete, but I grew up in Winnipeg, so my parents are seriously disappointed I'm not a hockey player, or at least a figure skater." She looked down at her legs. "But I'm too tall for skating and not coordinated enough for hockey."

I was pretty sure this was the girl I had seen getting out of the pool and stretching her arms over her head. "Your parents aren't swimmers?"

She flashed me a curious look and I added, "I mean, I thought my mater mentioned that someone here had parents who were Olympic swimmers. I just assumed ..."

The girl snorted and shook her damp curls. "Not me. My parents' idea of swimming is drinking margaritas in a hot tub."

I shrugged. "Must have been talking about someone else." I headed toward Madison as the girls cut down the path to their cabin. That was the second thing today that made no sense—the first being the boy from this morning.

After a shower, I hurried to The Chalet. Lunch was ending so I only managed to grab a brownie. It was yummy and I wished I had taken two. Crystal arrived, wearing a gray pantsuit with a lilac scarf, the whistle replaced by a little bell. She ordered a group of Tores to hand out booklets, Scantrons and pencils, rang the bell, and told us to start.

The first section had us pick between two options, like salty versus sweet, compromise versus disagree, and cold versus warm. I blew out a breath. What was the point of this, or any multiple-choice test? When, in real life, would I ever have multiple-choice options? I had tried to use that argument with my parents when I had gotten a C- on an English test. Dad had looked amused, but Mom had made me sit in my room until I read *Bud, Not Buddy* cover to cover.

"Is there a problem?" Crystal appeared next to me. The scarf around her neck had what looked like dancing llamas on it. Before I could stop it, a snort of laughter erupted.

Crystal's eyes narrowed. "Get working. You won't get extra time."

I went through the questions—trying to pick what I thought

someone in the military would choose—hard over soft, cold over warm, spicy over plain. Section Two was a typical standardized math test full of equations and diagrams. Section Three was reading comprehension, with questions related to written passages. Section Four went back to being bizarre, with true–false questions like, *I often think people are talking about me*, and *My hands and feet are warm enough*. Afterward, the Tores collected the materials and handed out juice boxes and slim booklets. Feeling like a kid at a birthday party, I sucked down my berry punch and debated asking for another.

"In this last part of the testing, you will be freewriting your answers," Crystal instructed. "There is no right or wrong, only your interpretations."

I opened the booklet and stared. Was this a joke? A cluster of colored blobs, like one of the abstract paintings DJ had hanging in her office. She paid thousands for artwork that looked like it had been finger-painted by kindergartners. The instructions below the blob read *Describe what you see*.

A child's finger painting, I wrote, then flipped to the next page. Another finger painting. If I used my imagination, I could visualize a pair of foxes ice-skating and wrote that down. Image three had intertwined sinewy black figures. *Ninja warriors battling*. Image four was blue and green figures with a splash of red. *Pool party massacre*. This was kind of fun! I kept turning the pages, allowing my imagination to go wild.

The bell tinkled. "Congratulations on finishing your testing day," Crystal said. We erupted into cheers. "Return to your rooms and wait for instructions." She nodded at the Tores. "Collate the tests and deliver them to the computer lab for processing."

Back in my room, I flopped on my bed, my brain spinning. Soon we'd be going to dinner and I could find that boy. Brittany breezed in and froze, her eyes widening. "What happened to you?" Her hair was in a bun and the HP athletic wear had been replaced by a leotard, tights, and ballet shoes. She looked like the figurine on Emma Claire's music box.

I felt a twinge of longing for my sister. "I'm guessing you didn't do the ropes course?"

She glided across the room and peered at me. "Holy cow, you look rode hard and put up wet. Don't tell me you were part of that accident?"

"Um, yeah," I said, my gut clenching at the thought of Charles. Hayden had said he would come with news, but nothing yet. I filled Brittany in on the disaster. Her mouth was hanging open in a very unladylike way by the time I finished. I debated getting her take on the girl from the pool but held back. I needed more time to think about it myself. "How was your testing?"

Brittany shrugged. She ran a hand along her tights, frowned, picked off an invisible speck. "It was fine, I guess. They gave us a weird free write test."

"With funky finger paintings?"

"Yes! Just what does my modeling career have to do with frogs kissing?"

Frogs kissing? That must have been the picture I thought was of ninjas fighting. Hmm ...

"They had us jog a bit, which was easy because I do two miles a day at home. Then they took our measurements, got us in heels, and had us walk the runway."

"Wait." I gestured toward the bulletin board. "You had to walk like that as part of your testing?"

Britt smiled. "I do a good strut. And I've been wearing heels since I was knee-high to a jackrabbit. My mama made sure of that."

"I can't imagine you with one of those ugly pouts."

"Oh yeah?" She stood up and walked to the door. When she turned, her expression was fierce. She strode across the floor, fixing me with a dark, penetrating gaze.

I laughed and clapped. Brittany had gone from Southern Belle to Angry Urban in a flash. "Can you act too?"

Britt relaxed and smiled. "Some. A better dancer than actor though. HP's lessons will help fix that."

Our speakers let out a series of tones. "Plebes, proceed to the meadow for a social hour," Samantha's voice said.

As I stood, I handed Brittany the handbook, opened to the rules page.

"What's this?" She studied the page, then looked up, eyes shining. I had put a checkmark next to several items: *Follow leaders' instructions at all times*; *No physical altercations*; and *Stay in designated areas.*

"Nice work," she exclaimed. "I'd better get my butt in gear."

Picnic tables with fruit, cheese, and crackers were set up at the edge of the meadow. For the first few minutes, we crowded around the tables, then settled into respective groups. Brittany had informed me on our walk over that the cliques, or purposes, had nicknames. The Jocks (obvious choice) ribbed each other and laughed loudly in that easy way athletes have. The Angels—gorgeous actor/model types—floated over to the meadow, nibbling on pieces of fruit. The techie Geekits and academic Einsteins huddled under a tree, locked in intense conversations.

Each purpose also had an emblem. The horseshoe symbol on Samantha's shirt was electrical power, meaning she was a Geekit, the Einsteins had atoms, Jocks Olympic wreaths, and Angels swans. Hayden had said he was a Joe, so the Eagle must signify the military.

Grabbing a handful of crackers, I walked around, growing

frustrated when I didn't spot the boy. *You should have at least asked his name. What if he's already gone?*

Sensing a presence, I spun around. Gabi stood there, holding a giant apple in one hand. "Charles is okay. He is staying overnight at the hospital and will be back tomorrow."

My gut unclenched. "That's great. You really think he'll stay? After this ...?"

Gabi took a delicate bite, chewed, swallowed. Then her face broke into a beaming smile, and I could imagine her on the podium at the Olympics accepting a gold medal for the vault. "He will. He's got a great future here."

"How do you know?" Maybe he had fantastic tackling or blocking skills, but would he last here long enough to show them?

"I told you. I know things. Don't you?" She took another bite.

"No, I don't think ..." I paused. I *did* know things often, but I got my information by watching, listening, and blending into the background. By crawling through air ducts and eavesdropping. Did Gabi think I just knew things, like some sort of mind-reader?

Gabi looked over my shoulder. "Hello there. Lina's soul brother."

I spun around and felt that instant zing of connection. The boy's hair was slicked back with water and his eyes were seafoam green in the rays of the setting sun. He seemed taller than he had earlier, with delicate limbs that jutted out from his clothing. The only part of him with any sturdiness was an angular jaw and chin.

"I'm Lina," I said. "And this is Gabi."

"We met during our computer testing," Gabi said. "See you later, Eric." She strolled away.

Eric smiled and dipped his head, which made him look like a bashful second grader.

"How did you know I love licorice?" I blurted.

"And hiking and collecting rocks?" Eric shrugged a shoulder. "I've dreamed about you. For years." He ran his eyes over my face, studying each feature. "I always assumed you were from a movie or a computer simulation." His brow furrowed. "I never considered that you might actually exist."

"You dreamed about me," I repeated, trying to recall if Eric had appeared in my dreams. No, not that I remembered. I was frustrated that I hadn't had any sense that he existed. But I also felt a growing warmth, a thrill over having a strong connection to another person.

"Do you have any game tags?" Eric asked. "Are you on YouTube?"

I shook my head. Just the fact that DJ was posting videos for her followers made me stay away. "There's got to be something though. Where are you from?"

Within moments of playing the *who, what, where* game, it was obvious we wouldn't find a connection. Eric and I came from different worlds. I had been born and raised in Southern California, while he had grown up in New Hampshire. My parents worked in real estate and medicine while his were foreign language professors. An only child, he had spent his days roaming a college campus. When he showed up in computer science courses, the professors had initially found the serious boy amusing and let him observe. Later, while I was scraping by with C's, Eric was assisting in graduate-level research.

My only trips out of California had been to see my grandparents in Arizona and my cousins in Pennsylvania. Eric had traveled to Europe, where his parents criticized him for holing up in the hotel with his computer instead of touring cathedrals and museums.

"Do you believe in past lives? Or ESP?" I asked.

Eric looked surprised. "Of course not." He scuffed the pine needles with his toe. "Do you?"

A bell at The Chalet started ringing. "No, not really," I said as we began walking. "How else do you explain this?" I gestured between us.

"There's always a rational, scientific explanation. We just don't know what it is yet."

"There is a lot to figure out about this place." I agreed.

Eric rubbed the tips of his fingers together. "Let me share something," he said. "Statistically, graduates of HP go on to earn salaries more than five hundred percent above what would be expected from their demographic categories."

"Isn't that the point? They're fulfilling their ..." I made air quotes, "purpose?"

"HP graduates are also five times more likely to die prematurely."

I thought of myself hanging upside down from the web. "That's because a lot of them end up in risky careers."

The aromas of garlic and tomato wafted from The Chalet and my stomach growled. The handful of crackers hadn't made up for a missed lunch.

Eric shook his head. "I did statistical analysis of the data, controlling for types of employment. There's less than a .05 percent probability that those death rates could be explained by chance."

"Shrimpy and scrawny sitting in a tree," a taunting voice called. Spiky sat cross-legged on one of the picnic tables. "K-i-s-s-i-n-g." Hearing her, Bolton nudged another lax bro and tilted his head in our direction.

That girl just doesn't give up! I could feel Eric shrink beside me. Clearly, he was used to being teased. A flare of anger shot through me, along with the urge to slug Spiky in the other eye. I took a deep breath, telling myself that another fight was just what the insecure, wannabe was aiming for.

I channeled my disinterested face and clapped my hands slowly. "Very original. What are you, five?"

Spiky pushed off the table and strode toward us. Her cheeks flushed, making the skin around her right eye appear even more bruised and puffy. "I'm going to make your life miserable." She stabbed a finger toward Eric who flinched. "And your boyfriend's too."

My expression was neutral, but if she touched Eric with that fingertip, I would flatten her again.

Footsteps crunched. "Evening Plebes," a cheery voice said. "Ready to head on in and get some dinner?" It was a smiling Matthew Drexler, wearing a crisp purple polo and jeans. He nodded at me. "Lina, your save on the ropes course today was inspiring." He turned to Spiky. "And Barbie, I heard you almost beat the record on that course. Fantastic."

Barbie? I felt Eric jolt next to me. I grabbed his wrist to keep myself from laughing.

Although, if Bolton's real name turned out to be Ken, I would lose it.

Spiky—Barbie?—melted under Matthew's praise. She tilted her head, lowered her chin, and gazed at him from under her thick mascaraed eyelashes. "I'll get that record next time."

Matthew flashed his perfect smile. "I'm sure you will." He turned his attention to Eric, lightly cuffing him on the shoulder. "Sounds like you're going to give our CS tutors a run for their money."

Eric ducked his head. "I hope."

"Let's head to the dining room," Matthew said. "I hear Chef Emilio prepared four-cheese lasagna."

"Oh, lasagna, my favorite. Fresh or frozen?" I shot Spiky a look. Her nostrils flared, but with Matthew next to her, she stayed silent.

At the dining room, a Tore directed us to sit with our cabins. Eric and I exchanged unhappy looks. "Let's talk more later," I said. "Which cabin are you in?"

"Jefferson, room 210."

"I'll come meet you."

"My pater said that we go straight to our rooms after dinner. And lights out is at ten thirty."

I spotted Samantha waving me over. "I'll figure something out." Stupid rules were not going to stop me from finding out more about Eric—and the information he had to share.

CHAPTER
EIGHT

AFTER A DELICIOUS DINNER, Brittany and I returned to Madison to find clothing laid out on our beds—a lilac sundress for her and a silky purple shirt and flowy black pants for me. Samantha had informed us that, after tonight, we would need to dress properly for dinner.

"Did you hear there's a dance at the end of week four?" Brittany held the dress against her body and frowned.

Saying nothing, I shoved my clothes in a drawer. Even if I were still here at week four, I would not be attending a dance. Not my thing.

At lights out, I lay motionless. My body craved the heavy unconsciousness of sleep, but my brain wouldn't slow down. So much had happened today that the jog around the track felt like forever ago.

Charles was in the hospital, but doing okay? At least that's what Gabi had said. Still, I would feel a lot better when I saw him in person.

Hayden thought that my purpose was Special Forces. Could I even begin to hope that he was right?

And Eric. The connection with him felt unworldly. He had scoffed at the idea of past lives, but maybe we should consider it?

I sat up. I wasn't going to be able to sleep until I talked to him. If my parents were here, they would remind me to be patient and point out that I could see him tomorrow. But patience was a skill I had never mastered. I needed to see Eric now.

The speakers were playing a flute melody that supposedly enhanced REM sleep and cellular growth. Brittany was snoring softly, a mask over her eyes, hair gathered on her head and face smeared with white cream.

The moonlight was enough for me to pull on a hoodie, sweatpants, and shoes. I pushed open our window. It slid easily to six inches and then stopped. I felt along the top of the frame. Wooden pegs were preventing it from opening further. I tried tugging at the pegs, but they were hammered in tightly.

I moved to the door and tried the handle. Locked. I went into the bathroom, closed the door and turned on the light. There were no panels in this ceiling. There had to be a way out, didn't there? Locking us in at night was a fire hazard.

An idea sparked. I turned off the light and stood in the doorway, letting my eyes adjust. Padding over to Brittany's desk, I grabbed a can of hair spray. I placed my desk chair in the center of the room and stepped onto it. I shook the can, uncapped it, and sprayed the smoke detector.

A lavender-scented cloud filled the air, followed a few moments later by the piercing whoop of a fire alarm. Jumping down, I shoved the chair back, returned the hair spray and pressed my palms to the door, I grinned when I felt the thunk of the lock sliding back.

"The fire alarm has been activated," a voice from our speakers said. "Remain calm, walk to your closest set of stairs, and exit the building."

I entered the hall, hurried to the stairs and ran down them and out the exit, taking a hard left across the path and into the trees.

I moved swiftly toward Jefferson, trying not to trip on tree roots or rocks. If it had the same layout as Madison, Eric's room would be second from the end on the second floor. Stopping across from his cabin, I peered out from the forest. The only noise was the faint sound of the alarm whooping. Taking a step, I fell flat into a ditch that had been hidden by leaves. Jumping up, I ran across the path and stopped under Eric's window. Picking up a small rock, I threw it at the glass where it made a cracking noise. I waited a moment then threw another. A faint light came on. A few moments later, the window slid open, and a flashlight beam played across the window ledge.

"Hello?" came Eric's hushed voice.

"It's me," I whispered.

There was a scuffling noise and Eric's pale face appeared looking down at me. "My window's stuck."

"I know," I said, kicking off my shoes and running my palms over the cabin's surface. Fortunately, it was full of knots and bulges. Finding secure spots with my fingers and toes, I began climbing.

"What are you doing?" Eric blinked. "That's not safe."

I worked my way up, thankful for the climbing wall practice. At his window, I propped my arms on the ledge and found rests for my feet. "What did you mean about the list? And all the deaths?"

Eric stared, clearly stunned by my spiderlike abilities.

"I only have a minute. They'll notice I'm gone. What do you have?"

Eric glanced toward his sleeping roommate then cleared his throat. "I've been researching HP since I got the invite. Some of the most powerful people in our history came here."

"I know, the Kennedys, senators, scientists, blah blah blah." From DJ's nonstop jabbering, I had heard all about famous HP grads. I was sure she prayed that I would return home with a BFF with the last name of a major hotel chain.

"Yes, but those are the good guys. Do you know who else went here? Bernie Madoff, Lee Harvey Oswald, Jim Jones. And more. We're talking serious bad guys."

Lee Harvey Oswald had killed JFK and Bernie Madoff had stolen millions of dollars in a Ponzi scheme, but I didn't recognize the third guy. "So those grads used their skills for the dark side. That sucks but so what?"

"The question is, did they go rogue or did HP purposely train them to carry out horrible deeds?"

"Why would HP do that? My dad always says that power corrupts, so HP probably just made these guys powerful and then they became bad."

One of my calves twitched and I shifted my weight. "Let me tell you about this other weird thing." I rushed through the story of the girl who supposedly had Olympian parents but claimed they didn't swim.

"What were you doing in an air vent?"

"Long story. But isn't that crazy?"

"Maybe it was a different girl. You probably couldn't see her that well."

"I heard them say her number," I insisted. "Sixty-seven."

"So, could she have been adopted?"

"Maybe ... but wouldn't she have said?"

Eric was silent for a moment. "It is suspicious. Give me a few days. Once I can hack into their system, I will locate her health application. The family history section will show if she's adopted."

My calf twinged again. If it cramped, I could fall two stories. Not good. I grimaced. "What about us? How does HP fit into the way we know each other?"

Eric blinked. "I don't know. But you'd better get down before you fall. Please. We've got plenty of time to figure this out. It's only day one."

Clearly, my soul brother had the patience I lacked. I felt his concerned gaze as I worked my way down, slipped on my shoes, and returned to the forest. The Madison trainees were huddled at the edge of the trees. A fire truck, lights flashing, sat in the visitors' lot.

"There you are," Brittany exclaimed. "I was worried."

I feigned innocence—a skill I had mastered. "I had to pee. I tried The Chalet, but it was locked so I went to the gym." I grimaced. "I'm so *not* peeing in the bushes. Embarrassing!"

Brittany nodded approval. "Totally. I can't believe y'all are seeing me practically naked and all a mess."

I noted that, except for a smear around her hairline, the white cream was gone, Britt's hair was in a neat ponytail and—was she wearing lip gloss?

"Okay folks, it's all clear," a pater announced. "False alarm. Please remember we do not allow incense or candles in your rooms."

There was a collective sigh of relief, and we trooped back inside. In our room, Brittany climbed into bed, pulled on her eye mask, and went back to snoring. I got into bed and tossed and turned. Finally, I pulled off the comforter and pillows, shoved them under the bed, and arranged them into a nest. Eric was right—depending on how long HP let me stay, we had time to figure things out. Curling up with Cairo in my arms, I heaved a sigh and fell into a deep sleep.

CHAPTER
NINE

IN KINDERGARTEN, DJ had enrolled me in gymnastics, likely so she could dress me in a sparkly leotard and matching bows. I loved the class, at least the six sessions I got to do. I quickly mastered the somersaults, walked across the balance beam and bounced across the long trampoline. The problem was that I got bored and wanted to swing from the rings hanging from the ceiling or jump into the pit with foam blocks. After refusing to sit with the group and taking multiple running leaps into the pit, the teacher called me a "liability" and I was kicked out.

The HP gym was like the one from kindergarten but on a whole new level. Mats covered the floor, topped with all sorts of beams, ropes, rings, and ladders. Multiple trampolines, foam pits, and scaffolding were positioned throughout. The towering walls were angled, curved, and jutting in all directions, with deep cracks and molded handholds. A giant flag hung from the ceiling. In its center was an eagle with a circle of stars above its head and an American flag over its middle. It held a branch in one claw and a bunch of arrows in the other.

"This is so cool," a muscular girl with cropped black hair exclaimed. "Are we going to get to climb that?" She pointed at what looked like a giant claw with spikes on the end."

"I hope so," I breathed. This made Denali at the rec center seem easy. "When do you think we're going to start?"

"Soon, I hope." She smiled and held out her hand. "Sakura. I'm from Japan."

Sakura had a firm grip. "Lina, California. Wow, Japan? That's far."

Sakura raised her arms over her head and yawned. "Very far. I'm still jet-lagged."

"Hey, I'm Ryan," a boy exclaimed, pushing in between us. "I'm from Santa Claus."

Ryan was like an oversized puppy with lanky limbs and shaggy reddish hair. "Indiana," he supplied, seeing our confused looks. "Santa Claus, Indiana. It's where Abe Lincoln grew up."

Unfortunately, Spiky was there too, shooting me death stares. A set of identical twins, wiry girls with straight black hair and severe bangs, was tagging along with her.

A whistle blew. A group of Senatores strode toward us. Becky, the Tore I had shoved, was at the front, her hair cinched into a bun on her head. Spotting me, her eyes darkened. Likely, she was one of those girls who would hold a grudge forever.

Stopping in front of us, the Senatores swiveled and clasped hands behind their backs. "Baby Joes, sit," Becky ordered.

We sank to the floor.

"Baby Joes?" Sakura whispered.

"I think it's like G.I. Joe," Ryan said.

I had loved G.I. Joe but had hardly had the chance to play with one. My friend Spencer had gotten a 1,000-piece military set, so I would go over there and spend hours setting up and carrying out battles. DJ had absolutely forbidden "boy toys" for her daughter. She had bought me a Cinderella Barbie instead. I had chopped Barbie's luscious blonde locks, stripped her naked, and brought her to Spencer's to be a prisoner of war.

I scanned the row of Tores. Theo was standing next to Becky. Hayden was at the end of the line and winked at me, which made me feel less nervous.

"I am Becky Hunter, a Tore lead for your summer training, under the supervision of Captain Carl Hansen, Head Tutor." She gestured toward a man on the other side of the gym who was wearing a tracksuit and talking to a group of Quites. He nodded at us and saluted.

Becky saluted back, then gestured to two Tores who wheeled over a whiteboard. She rapped a knuckle on the board. "I don't know what life is like at home, but here there will be no coddling. No wasted time hanging out with your friends, stuffing your faces with junk, or scrolling through social media. Starting today, you adopt the mindset of discipline and hard work." She wrote *Discipline* and *Hard Work* on the whiteboard and underlined them.

Those two words were usually associated with the words *disappointment* or *consequences* in my home. A slew of teachers, coaches, and parents could attest to that. I bit down hard on the piece of gum I had sneaked after breakfast.

"At seven a.m. sharp, you will report for breakfast. At seven-thirty, you will report here for your daily assignments. We conclude at five p.m., at which point you will shower and then proceed to your IA."

Ryan's hand shot up. "What's an IA?"

Becky scowled. "Read your handbook. It describes the Interdisciplinary Activities. Building community is an important part of the HP program. It is your opportunity to nurture connections with other cohorts."

"It's stupid stuff like berry picking and sculpture," Spiky muttered.

"Dinner is at seven p.m.," Becky continued. "Studying from eight p.m. to ten thirty p.m., then lights out."

This schedule left little time to meet with Eric, except at meals or during this weird group time.

"Prior to breakfast, you are expected to complete a two-mile run."

A run before breakfast? Not a chance!

As if reading my thoughts, Becky said, "You will be fitted with a tracker to monitor your compliance. All Baby Joes are required to achieve an optimal level of fitness. This means that by the end of the session, we expect you to complete your two miles in sixteen minutes or less."

I swallowed a groan. I was pretty sure that I had clocked in at about twelve minutes for that one mile I had been forced to run in gym class.

"During this first week, you will not need to run before breakfast."

"Mors Week," Ryan murmured, the redness on his cheeks deepening.

"Mors?" I whispered. "What's that?"

"It means death in Latin." Sakura looked more intrigued than scared. "Death week."

"You also will not have IA this week," Theo said.

"When do we get to climb?" Sakura asked, gesturing to the claw.

"Make it through the week and then we'll talk," he answered.

"What about the solo?" Sakura persisted. "I heard we get to spend the night in the woods by ourselves?"

My head whipped toward her. "Really?"

Sakura nodded. "It'll be awesome."

I pondered the idea. On the one hand, a solo did sound interesting. I spent a lot of time alone so that part wouldn't be hard. On the other hand, during our family's only camping trip, the tent had fallen over, the hot dogs burned, and Emma Claire was convinced she heard a bear. By the time the sun had set, we were checked into a motel, watching American Idol and eating pizza.

The gym door opened, and Matthew entered wearing a purple T-shirt with a wolf emblem. He stopped next to Hayden and they bumped fists. "Just ignore me. Sorry to interrupt you, Becky."

"Are you joining us for training, Matthew?" Becky flashed a sparkling smile. The girl actually had teeth.

"I thought I'd hang with you for the beginning. Don't forget, I trained with you Joes a fair amount last summer."

Hayden eyed Matthew critically. "Do you still have what it takes? I think being the Chosen One has made you soft."

The Chosen One? I remembered the older kids yelling that last night. It made me think of Mufasa holding Simba up over his head in *The Lion King* while all the other animals bowed down.

Matthew sighed dramatically and poked at his stomach. "You may be right. Too many meetings, not enough exercise." He gestured at us. "I'm counting on these Baby Joes here to help me out. Can you guys do that?"

We all chorused a yes.

"Speaking of chosen, let me know when a good time would be to," he touched his shoulder.

Becky took a step back. "Please, go ahead."

Matthew nodded. He walked to the front of our group and pressed his palms together. "Hopefully, I was able to impart to you last night that we work hard and play hard here at HP. We are both individuals honing toward our purposes and part of a team. Our group training and IA activities are collaborative, yet we also recognize the importance of individual achievement and success."

He pulled two objects from his pocket and held them up. Round medallions with a black insignia of an eagle. "One girl and one boy from each purpose is designated the Campio or Campia for that week. These are Plebes who have shown exceptional traits in their areas. The medallion is worn so that all of HP can recognize and celebrate their achievements. At the end of the summer, whoever has received the medallion the most weeks will receive the official title and earn a spot on the Youth Council."

"That means Council meetings four times a year in posh locations," Hayden said. "Like Hawaii."

"Hey, Mr. Murray," Matthew protested. "We work hard at our Council meetings. It's not all sand and surf."

"You're looking pretty tan for all that hard work."

"Jealous," Matthew stage-whispered, and we laughed. "We are going to honor the start of training by naming our two Campiones. It's a hard choice since you all have only just arrived and had one day of testing. But we got a sense of your potential yesterday."

If it hadn't been Matthew talking, I would have zoned out by now. I had never liked competition, so I didn't care which overachiever got to wear the medallion and feel superior.

"For the boys, we had a clear winner on the physical tests and the obstacle course." Matthew called up a muscular boy who looked like a mini version of The Rock. He clapped him on the shoulder and handed him the medallion.

"And for the girls, this was a tougher decision. But core values of our program are courage and loyalty, and one of you demonstrated both yesterday in your actions on the obstacle course."

My head snapped up.

"Lina Jamison, please come up." Matthew beckoned to me.

My jaw dropped. I got unsteadily to my feet, feeling like I was in a dream. Soon it would turn ugly and morph into everyone pointing and laughing.

A gasp behind me. "She didn't even finish," Spiky exclaimed. "And her fitness was nothing compared to mine." The twins mimicked her gasps and murmured support.

Matthew took my hand and placed the medallion in it. "Keep it up," he said warmly.

I was so overwhelmed by Matthew's touch and the weight of the eagle in my palm that I'm not sure my gaping mouth ever closed. I managed to wrap my fingers around the medallion and stumble back to my spot, where Sakura and Ryan both slapped my back. "My pater said that the Plebes on Youth Council are set for life," he exclaimed. "Having all those connections is the fast track to a primo career."

"Thank you, Matthew," Becky said, her tone indicating she was not pleased with his choice. She clapped her hands together. "All right, we're headed outside. At the end of today, you will receive your textbooks and syllabus. Some skills we will work on during training, others you may need to learn on your own." A glower toward me. "If you do not meet the minimum requirements in all areas, you will not be retained."

The fitness tracker was a sleek bracelet that fit snugly around my wrist. According to the strawberry-blonde Tore who fastened it on, the tracker would gather all sorts of data about my activity and vital signs. It also had a built-in GPS to provide accountability for the morning runs.

"You'll like wearing it," she said. "It was awesome to see how my fitness level and times improved by the end of Plebe summer." She wrote 42 in Sharpie on a water bottle. "Make liquids a priority. We're at a high altitude so you can get dehydrated super easy. Alternate two waters with one electrolyte solution."

"Like Gatorade?" I asked, accepting the bottle.

"Similar, but it's a drink that a grad invented." She gestured toward the row of giant coolers at the side of the track. "Less sugar and more specific to teenagers' needs." She patted me on the shoulder and gave me a knowing smile. "Good luck with Mors Week."

That was the fifth person, including Samantha and some older girls from my cabin, who had wished me luck. I soon found out why. We started with a two-mile jog around the track. The Equites joined us, taunting us and saying how slow we were.

We moved on to *ladders*, which involved starting at one end of the football field, with flags placed at four intervals. When the whistle blew, we had to sprint to the first flag then back to the beginning, then sprint to the second flag and back, and so on until we had run across the entire field to the last flag and back. I did okay with the first two flags, but then my heart started to pound, and I couldn't get enough air. On the third flag, the girl in front of me stuck out her leg, sending me flying onto the grass. After it happened a second time, I realized it was one of Spiky's twins. The Quites didn't care and screamed that I was pathetic, the slowest Joe they'd ever seen and would never survive.

After my third face-plant, a panting Matthew appeared, like an angel. His dark hair was soaked with sweat, but his smile was still bright. "Come on, Lina," he urged. "You can do anything you put your mind to. Actions define identity."

Gasping and trying to ignore the searing pain under my rib cage, I dragged myself up and trailed Matthew, who had run off to encourage another Plebe. Holding onto his words of encouragement, I managed to make it through the rest of the exercise.

After ladders, it was another two-mile run that felt like slogging through mud. I drank from my water bottle and then vomited it all up during the second mile. "Twelve!" a group of ecstatic Quites cheered, counting the number of times one of us puked.

By the end, where a tired but cheerful Matthew was patting each of us on the back, I questioned whether I might have a heart attack and die. When Matthew left to visit another cohort and Becky ordered another round of ladders, I was sure of it. My only consolation was that Hayden hadn't stayed to watch. I couldn't stand the thought of him seeing me failing on the first training day.

During the second round, even the physically fit Plebes struggled. Spiky's face was tomato red, her hair plastered to her head. She and her gang gave up trying to sabotage me and focused on their own survival. I tried to put myself on autopilot and ignore my burning, shaking muscles. At one point, Becky got out a high-pressure hose and sprayed me and other Baby Joes who were not keeping up.

By lunchtime, my muscles were noodles. We shuffled silently to The Chalet and collapsed into chairs in the dining room. Lunch was smoothies that looked like sludge but tasted like Reese's Peanut Butter Cups. Despite the delicious flavor, I was barely able to choke down half a glass and doubted it would stay down the rest of the afternoon.

CHAPTER
TEN

AFTER LUNCH, we were herded onto white vans and driven on bumpy roads for ten minutes. We stumbled out to confront a steep hill with patches of grass, tree stumps, boulders, and a spindly metal chairlift snaking up the middle.

"Meet Black Hole Hill." Becky pulled a stopwatch from her pocket. "You will have fifteen minutes to get to the top. If you make it, you can ride the chairlift." Her lips curved wickedly. "If you don't, you will have to walk back down."

I don't remember getting from the van to my bed. Brittany woke me and I debated skipping dinner but knew I needed food. I also debated staying in my grimy clothes but, even though I was trying to break some rules, I couldn't handle more conflict tonight.

I took a quick shower, letting the water run over me as I was too tired to apply soap. As I slowly pulled on my dinner clothes, I noticed Brittany had a white swan medallion pinned to her dress.

"Haute Couture Girl of the Week," she trilled. She glanced

around, as she often did, automatically searching for her phone. "How can I not post this?"

Crap. I was supposed to wear the eagle medallion. After today, I knew I didn't deserve it. Again, to avoid conflict, I rummaged in my gym bag, found the eagle, and pinned it to my shirt. Britt started to gush then stopped when she noticed my scowl. We walked in silence to the dining room where she hurried to join her fellow Angels at the salad bar.

Standing motionless in line for the grill, I questioned if I had the strength to hold a tray. Someone bumped me and I stumbled, my muscles screaming in protest. Another bump and I whirled, expecting to see Spiky's taunting face.

Charles stood there, eyes twinkling, dimples popping. He grabbed me into a bear hug. "My guardian angel. This girl saved me and she's just a little scrapper."

I felt a simultaneous rush of relief and pain as he lifted me into the air and spun me around. He set me down then frowned. "Hey, what happened to your face?"

He was referring to the bruise blooming on my chin, caused by tripping on my way down Black Hole Hill and colliding with a rock. Of course, my fall had been witnessed by Spiky and the twins who were coasting back down on the chairlift. They let out loud whoops of laughter and pointed so all the Baby Joes could witness my shame.

"I had my own version of the ropes course today. But I'm fine. What about you?"

Charles whooshed out a breath. "Hospital got me all fixed up. Got a bunch of meds and a better inhaler. Plus, no more ropes courses." He waited for me to carefully pick up a tray and place a cheeseburger on it, then piled four burgers and two cups of fries onto his tray. "The coach promised me just straight football from now on."

Noticing my arms trembling, Charles grabbed my tray and nudged me toward the dining room. Gabi and Eric were sitting together and Charles, ignoring calls from his football buddies, took our trays over to them.

Gabi's face lit up. "Welcome back, Charles. You look great!" Her gaze turned to me, and she wrinkled her nose. "So, Hell Week really is a thing?"

I nodded as Charles pulled out a chair for me. "It's actually called Mors Week. The Latin makes it even worse."

Gabi spotted the medallion. "And you're the Campia." Her gaze flicked toward Spiky. "That's going to present a challenge, isn't it?"

"It already has," I muttered, lowering myself into the chair. "Crazy, because the whole thing's meaningless."

Gabi and Charles exchanged a look. "You have a lot to learn, little scrapper," Charles said, patting me on the shoulder.

"Getting Campiones means prestige," Gabi added. "And prestige means power. Both of those are what the trainees here want, especially that wannabe over there."

Eric was staring at my bruise, his brow furrowed. "I hear they make you run until you throw up."

"Four times." I gazed longingly toward the ketchup bottle. "Pass that please?"

"You threw up four times?" Eric's face contorted. I knew he had a fear of germs and lived in terror of getting food poisoning or the stomach flu. I felt flattered that he didn't bolt from the table.

Charles grabbed the ketchup and covered both of our burgers.

"It wasn't that bad," I reassured Eric. "I'm proud of myself for surviving the first training day." I didn't mention my fall or that I had been one of the last ones down Black Hole Hill. "And don't the Geekits have some sort of hell week too? Don't all of you?"

Eric blinked and picked up a carrot stick. "No, not really. I mean, if you don't already know C, Python, and Java, you're going to be spending a lot of time cramming. But no," he shuddered, "physical pain or anything like that. Worst thing I've had to do is that running yesterday."

"Football practice is going to be tough," Charles mused. "But me and my boys do double workouts at home, so it won't be too bad." He picked up a burger and devoured half of it in one bite.

"My boys and I," Eric corrected, then reddened. "Sorry, I'm working on not being the grammar police."

Gabi's plate was piled high with melon, pineapple, and berries. She forked a strawberry. "I have a few thousand pages of journal articles to read. But I love science so it's not a big deal." She popped the strawberry in her mouth. "And I've read most of them already."

"Why so much reading?" I reached a shaky hand toward my plate, willing the hamburger to leap into it. "I would think your workouts would be your main focus."

Gabi's forehead wrinkled. "Workouts?"

"Yeah, for gymnastics?" I pressed my fingertips against my plate and attempted to pull it toward me. "Isn't that your purpose? I mean you're little, you were testing with us yesterday and ..." I eyed the mound of blueberries on Gabi's plate. "You eat only fruit."

Gabi tilted her head back and let out a belly laugh that was much deeper than I expected from someone so small. "I like fruit," she exclaimed. "We don't have much fresh fruit at home so I'm taking advantage." She tossed her head, her ponytail swinging back and forth. "Gymnastics? I can't even do a cartwheel."

Eric took my plate and cut my burger into neat quarters. I picked one up and took a bite. It tasted amazing. Suddenly, I was starving.

I took more bites while Gabi explained that her purpose had been unclear, so she had done testing for several cohorts. It looked like she would mainly be an Einstein, but cross-train with the Geekits, do some physical fitness with the Joes, and learn at least two more languages."

"Oh, and I love history, so I might help with the museum they're building onto the back of The Chalet."

Eric stopped wiping up the ketchup that had dripped from my burger. "So, your purpose is to be a spy?"

Gabi started another belly laugh, then noticed Eric's expression. "A spy? You're serious?"

Eric folded the napkin, careful not to get ketchup on his fingers. "It's only logical. You have a perfect memory, a deep understanding of human motivation, and you are being cross-trained in science, computers, languages, and history."

Gabi sat back in her chair and fingered her crown pendant.

"Is being a spy even a purpose?" I asked. I put my elbow on the table and propped my head in my hand.

"Like James Bond?" Charles raised an eyebrow.

"Women make excellent spies," Eric said. "They have better emotional intelligence and arouse less suspicion."

Gabi thought some, then her face brightened. "You're right, Eric. I've got too many talents to be pigeonholed in one area. Being a spy would allow me to utilize many more skills."

Eric nodded. "Even though we are currently segmented into cohorts, HP actually has a lot of variability when it comes to purpose. If you think about it, when the program started, many of the key purposes we have now didn't even exist. There weren't supermodels or famous athletes or computers. The Geekit group wasn't formed until the early eighties when John Kemeny brought CS here. Now, it's a large percentage of trainees."

Gabi twirled her ponytail. "Makes sense. HP's mission is to funnel grads into positions of power and influence. There are some obvious big categories, but many smaller, specialized areas as well."

I yawned and crossed my arms on the table, resting my chin on them. "Eric, tell them about what you learned. What we were talking about with all the bad guys."

Eric hesitated.

"Was it that HP grads have been deeply embedded in the military during all of the United States' acts of aggression?" Gabi asked. "Or that a large percentage come from disadvantaged backgrounds and are the first in their families to attend college?"

Eric's eyes widened. "You've been researching too?"

"Of course." Gabi leaned across the table. "You think I didn't question why this poor Mexican chica got invited to a fancy academy?"

"Did you know that an HP grad has been in every Super Bowl since the game started?" Charles said. "And there are at least six head coaches who went here."

I wished I could teleport myself back to my bed, but instead let my eyes close. The last thing I remembered was my hoodie being draped around my shoulders.

CHAPTER
ELEVEN

MORS WEEK RESEMBLED the movie *Groundhog Day*, where the second day and the next and the next were nightmare replays of the first. Mornings began with laps on the track, ladders, torture workouts and—when I didn't think I could take another step—Black Hole Hill. Captain Hansen came by occasionally to check in, but we were mostly at the mercy of the Tores. By evening, I was a mess and relied on Brittany to drag me to dinner, where Eric and Gabi made sure I ate. Even while vomiting up my electrolyte drinks and slogging my way down Black Hole Hill, I reassured myself I was getting better. Sakura and Ryan had helped me trip the twins back during ladders, so they had stopped targeting me. By the end of the week, I was even in sight of the top of the hill when we hit the fifteen-minute mark.

On the last day of Mors Week, we were told to change into camouflage. Putting on our brown and green uniforms, we seemed to go from awkward teens to young adults and I exchanged excited, proud looks with the other Baby Joes.

The straps of the backpack felt strange tightened to my shoulders and hips and contributed to the thrill of something new and different. Strutting in our stiff boots, we followed a trail behind the gym to a stretch of ground about the length of two football fields. The area was flooded with water, creating what looked like a swamp. The left half was mostly thick grass and mud, while the right half had obstacles, like fallen trees, tangles of bushes, and boulders.

My happiness began to fade when I saw that Becky was heading up the exercise. Why was she always in charge?

"Line up Babies," Becky ordered, tapping her pen against her clipboard. She read our names off, arranging us in a row at the edge of the field. When she came to me, she pointed to the far-right side. "Ready to prove yourself today, Jamison? Personally, I don't think you have what it takes. Remember, actions define identity."

I found Becky way more intimidating than Spiky. She and the twins had moved on to targeting other girls who were real competition for Campia. With Becky, I sensed a deep, enduring anger. I had slighted her once and she would never let it go.

No big deal, I told myself as I walked to my spot, fingering the straps of my pack. Wading through muck would drain my energy, but I could handle it after a week of ladders and Black Hole Hill.

"You've got ten minutes to get across," Becky said. She nodded toward a Tore who held up a starter pistol. "On your mark, get set ..." The pistol blasted.

I skimmed my gaze over the swamp, designing a path that would avoid the largest tangles and boulders. Taking a breath, I plowed forward, my first goal a pile of rocks halfway across. Mud sucked at my boots and, after a minute, I was breathing hard. The water got deeper, soaking my calves and spilling into my boots.

Reaching the rocks, I put my hands on my knees and took gulping breaths. I was tired but had made good progress. It had only been two minutes and I could see a Tore waiting on the opposite side.

When my heart rate had returned to normal, I set my sights on a mushroom-shaped boulder and took a step. A sharp crack of a branch and I was falling. Breath whooshed out of my lungs as I plunged into cold water.

In eighth grade, I had been forced to go to Eleanor Allan's birthday party—her mom and DJ were "besties". The theme had been *Legally Blonde*, so everything was decorated in pink, and Ellie's bikini was a replica of Elle Woods' in the movie.

Ellie was the prettiest girl in the class. She would smile to my face, then say horrible things to her friends—that I still wore Pull-Ups at night (not true) or that I had gone to urgent care to get a huge blister on my butt drained (true—from poison ivy—but private!).

DJ forced me into the pool and stayed to drink cocktails with other moms. Wearing a shiny pink suit that made me look like a glob of gum, I hovered by two of the nicer girls who were in the middle doing handstands.

"Lina, try this," Bailey said. She dove forward, thrusting her legs out of the water and into the air. She surfaced wearing a giant grin, water streaming off her face.

I shook my head. I hated putting my face in the water, hated swimming in every way. One summer, I had thrown such a fit at lessons that DJ had been forced to switch to privates and pay triple.

"Come on, it's easy," Macey encouraged.

Ellie and her gang were in the deep end watching. "No peeing in the pool, Kitty Cat," one of them called.

My face flushed. If we had been on land, I might have gone after her. But in the pool, I was helpless, and they knew it.

"We'll help you," Macey said. "You can borrow my goggles." She held them out. "Put these on, then jump forward and ..."

Hands grabbed my ankles, yanking me under. Stinging water gushed up my nose and panic hit me. I began thrashing, trying to get my ankles free, to pull myself up to the surface.

Finally, one of my frantic kicks connected with bone, and my ankles were released. I burst out of the water, spluttering and screaming. The moms turned in horror, while Ellie's clique slapped on innocent faces. DJ dragged me out of the pool and to the car. I had been grounded for two weeks and had not gotten into a pool since.

The same panic slammed me. I flailed my arms and legs, managing to get my head briefly above the surface for a breath before I was sucked back down. The pack dragged me toward the bottom, where my boots touched the dirt. I tried to push off, but my legs weren't responding. My heart pounded and my chest felt incredible pressure to take a breath. I tugged at the pack's straps, but they felt melded to my shoulders. I was getting dizzy. Finally, I was able to wrench the pack off and let it drop. Kicking as hard as I could, I fought my way back up and took a huge, gulping breath.

My brain was sending the message to my limbs to move, but the wet clothing and boots made it impossible. I tried another breath and ended up inhaling dirty water. The forces dragged me back under.

The water was winning the battle, growing thick and warm around me. My panic eased, and I felt weightless and suspended in the murkiness. Opening my eyes, I saw a figure next to me. It stretched a hand toward me. Unafraid, I reached out and touched the outstretched fingers. A feeling of warmth and love enveloped me.

Something hard wrapped around my shoulders. I thrashed,

wanting the sense of peace back. Struggling, I was pulled through the water, then lifted and slammed onto a hard surface.

"Breathe," a voice yelled in my ear. A weight slammed into my back and I coughed, expelling water and dirt. I managed a breath and then vomited water. Choking and gasping, I fought to suck in air.

"What the hell was that?" an angry voice demanded. "She could have drowned."

"We're supposed to push them to the limit," a female voice responded.

"And what would that limit be? Death? Just when would you have intervened?"

"When I felt it was appropriate. It's a judgment call."

My head spun. Where was I? What had just happened in that water?

I managed to open an eye. Two pairs of muddy boots were facing each other.

"You've crossed the line, Becky," Hayden said. "I'm reporting this to Hansen."

A harsh laugh. "Go right ahead. And how will you explain your presence here? Aren't you supposed to be running the high-wire course for the Quites?"

I opened my other eye then pushed myself onto my elbows. My chest hurt and I hacked out a wad of water and dirt. I lifted my head to see Hayden and Becky facing off against each other. Hayden's jaw was clenched, his hands balled into tight fists. His hair was plastered to his head and muck dripped off his clothes.

Becky, totally dry except for her boots, had a smug, satisfied expression. She eyed me as if I were a dead mouse a cat had dropped on the front stoop.

"Number forty-two, I'm going to have to mark this course as a fail." A smile played at the edge of her lips. "A major fail."

Shame enveloped me. I was twelve years old again, being mocked by Ellie and the popular girls. Then anger flooded in—who was Becky to judge me? This wasn't a poolside party with mean girls. What kind of insane academy was this to send a teenager wearing fatigues and a backpack into a water pit? I could have died! First Charles, now me? Rage boiled inside and I felt an overwhelming urge to scream.

I would die before letting Becky know how terrified I had been. How ashamed I was that I had needed to be rescued. I struggled to my feet and jabbed a finger at her. "You're a sadistic narcissist," I hissed. I didn't know what that meant, but it was what my mom called Uncle Bartholomew who had lost Aunt Sally's wedding ring in a poker game and driven Gramp's new car into the side of a hill.

"Watch your mouth," Becky said, slapping me hard across the face.

"Cut it out, Becky," Hayden yelled.

With my emotions roiling, I hardly noticed the sting of the slap or the way my head whipped back. "Go right ahead," I yelled. "Give me a major fail. I could care less because I quit."

I spun and stormed off—if tripping and stumbling my way through the mud could be called storming. The anger morphed back to humiliation. Hot tears rolled down my cheeks. *You're an idiot*, I told myself. *You are a stupid Kitty Cat. Not soldier material, let alone Special Forces.* How had I been stupid enough to let myself think I might end up staying here? I was as bad as DJ for hoping this elite academy could be the answer to my pathetic future.

"Lina, wait," Hayden called. He skipped across the mud like it was a sidewalk and caught up, grabbing my arm. "Are you okay?"

I wrenched my arm away and ducked my head so he couldn't

see the tears. I had gone from impressing this older boy on the ropes course to being a whiny baby who needed saving. "I'm fine," I muttered. "Thanks to you."

Hayden grunted and fell into step next to me. "That part of the course is advanced. You shouldn't have been sent that way. Definitely not without more training."

All those years of swim lessons, where I had thrown tantrums instead of learning basic skills. Had I known then that swimming would matter, I would have tried. But at the time, it had just been something else DJ wanted me to do. Now it was too late. I focused on my boots. Step, lift, step. We were almost at the edge of the swamp.

"You're not quitting," he said.

I took a last giant step and felt the lovely firmness of hard dirt and grass beneath my boots. The waiting Tore stared, making no move to write on her clipboard.

"Nice job," a taunting voice called. Spiky and the twins, dry and relaxed, were eyeing me with delight. "Real star performance." Spiky gave me a thumbs-up and an exaggerated wink.

I felt a gut-wrenching punch of shame and began walking as fast as my rubbery legs could go. There was nothing HP-worthy about me. It had been a fantasy that I could end up being a Joe with Hayden, or even his friend. "I didn't ask you to help me. And I'm not asking your permission to leave."

Hayden snorted in frustration. "Lina, that's not what I meant. It's only ..."

"Find someone else to save," I snapped.

CHAPTER
TWELVE

BACK IN MY ROOM, I pulled off my filthy camouflage and stood under a hot shower, scrubbing with shampoo and soap until the muddy water ran clear. Toweling off, I pulled on jean shorts and a T-shirt and retrieved my duffel from under the bed. My parents would be disappointed, but wasn't this what they had expected? None of us had thought HP would uncover a hidden genius. And Dad couldn't claim I hadn't tried. I had almost drowned I tried so hard!

Stuffing toiletries into my bag, my thoughts turned to Eric. Not getting to figure out our connection would be my main regret. But I knew where he lived—his parents were language professors at Dartmouth—and I would find him again, somewhere outside of this crazy place.

Anyway, Gabi could help Eric figure out the mysteries of HP better than me. I would miss hanging out with brilliant Gabi, and Charles who was like a protective, silly big brother.

Hefting my duffel, I took one last look at the room. My side was empty, the other half a pink explosion. I would even miss Brittany, who was teaching me that some beautiful girls could be decent. The halls were empty as everyone was in their morning sessions, so at least I wouldn't have to explain myself to the other Plebes or Samantha.

Exiting Madison, I paused and closed my eyes, inhaling the warm scent of pine.

"I won't ask you if you need help with your bag." Hayden stood a few feet down the path, arms folded across his chest, eyes burning.

Now that my anger had cooled, I felt terrible for having yelled at him. Hayden had just saved my life and had been nothing but kind to me. I knew I should apologize, but what was the point? It would just make leaving harder. Stepping around him, I headed toward The Chalet.

Hayden followed. "Let me just ask you one question," he said in a low voice. "What is the Council's top priority?"

What a weird thing to ask me right now. "What council?"

"The Council," he repeated. "For HP. What is its top priority?"

I was confused. Had the time in the water deprived my brain of oxygen? I had absolutely no idea what Hayden was talking about. Was it a military organization? Matthew had mentioned something about councils a few times so maybe it was a student council?

"No clue. Trainee safety?"

Hayden blew out a breath. "That's what I thought. Look, you need to stay at HP. I need you to stay."

I sighed. "Hayden, I appreciate all you've done for me, but I don't belong here."

"You can't let one bad experience shape your whole view of your potential."

"Actions define identity, right? What did my actions tell you today?" I held my fingers in an L shape up to my forehead.

"Where did you hear that phrase?"

"Matthew told me that during Mors Week. And Becky said it before ..."

"You can do this, Lina. Accept there will be setbacks. We all have setbacks."

"But I can't swim," I muttered.

"What?" Hayden grabbed the duffel's strap, forcing me to stop. I reluctantly faced him. "Like at all."

He stared at me. "You can't swim?"

"No," I said, heat moving up my neck.

Hayden's jaw clenched. He looked up at the trees, as if trying to summon patience.

"I didn't know there would be swimming," I protested. "Not today."

"You had no business being out on that course if you couldn't swim."

Red shame stained my face. "What choice did I have?"

The tendons in his neck bulged. "You always have a choice, Lina."

"Really?" I gestured around us. "What choice have I had in any of this? Nobody asked me if I wanted to come to this place. Nobody asked me if I could swim. Just like no one asked Charles about his asthma before ordering him to do the ropes course. How can we choose if we don't have enough information?"

"But swimming, it's just a ..." Hayden rubbed his hands over his face. "It's a basic life skill. Like reading or riding a bike. And you're from California. I shouldn't have to explain that to you."

I clenched my fists and kicked at the ground. No way was I going to share my humiliating swim story with Hayden.

"Okay." He pressed his hands together. "So, I can teach you to swim. It's not that hard, you'll pick it up quickly."

Shame and helplessness washed over me. I couldn't explain the terror I felt at the idea of being in water. After this morning, just thinking of dipping a toe into a pool made me panicky. Continuing at HP was pointless. Thinking I could eventually be in the military had been a fantasy.

"Come on," he pressed.

"No! I can't explain, but I just ... I just can't."

This time when I walked away, Hayden didn't follow me.

My raging emotions swept me up the stairs and into The Chalet. The entryway was empty, and there were sounds of clinking from the dining room. I turned left, passing the auditorium, conference rooms, and a set of stairs before I dead-ended at a wall of plastic sheets. There was a sign with a hard hat symbol that read *Future HP Historical Library*.

There had to be admins who worked in this building. Someone had to order the food, get transportation, pay the employees. And I had seen Edmund Blakewell in a second-floor window, so it wasn't empty.

I returned to the stairs. Leaving the first floor of The Chalet was against the rules. Fantastic, I was thrilled to break one more rule on the way out. If I ran into Blakewell, who cared? He was incredibly creepy, but at this point, what could he do—kick me out?

I set my duffel in an alcove, took the stairs up and walked down a carpeted hall toward doors that looked like they could be offices. As I got closer, one was ajar and I heard voices. I raised my hand to knock.

"So, number twelve will be coached further in chemistry to see if she can get up to speed," Blakewell's deep voice said. "If not, she will be denied next summer."

I froze. This was definitely not an admin office.

A rustle of papers. "The emergent case. I'm not convinced there is a problem here."

"We need to trust our Tores leads," an indignant voice said. Crystal. I shuddered and dropped my hand.

"Besides the debacle this morning, her initial physical testing was mediocre, and she ranked high in paranoid and antisocial traits."

"Her actions on the ropes course were impressive," Blakewell said. "That's the kind of gumption we want in our trainees. Time will tell as far as the other traits. Those can be molded to our advantage."

I pressed myself against the wall. They were talking about me!

"Now is not the time to take risks," Crystal said. "She needs to go."

"Give it a few more days," another voice said, his tone bland. "We've seen this before. A few more days and she'll fall into line like the others."

I peered through the crack in the doorframe. Crystal stood by the corner of a wooden desk with scrolled edges. Aside from the loafered shoe of a man sitting in a leather chair, I couldn't see anything else.

"This summer is crucial," Crystal said. "We can't have any upsets."

"We won't," the man said. "Sending her away this soon could affect morale and we don't want that."

"We must carry on as always," Blakewell agreed. "Our plans will take time and patience and HP must stay consistent. Until our key players are in position, we adhere to tradition."

"But from what the lead Tore described ..." Crystal persisted.

"Enough." The sound of a fist slamming the desk. "Stop wasting my time with inconsequential issues. Give it a few more days and reevaluate then."

"Yes, sir," Crystal said. She smoothed her hands against her skirt. "Thank you for meeting with me."

She was leaving. I turned and ran down the hall. I debated trying a door but didn't know if they were unlocked. There was an alcove with a small table and plant, and I squished inside the best I could.

Crystal was muttering as she advanced down the hall. Fortunately, she was so consumed by her annoyance that she passed me without a glance. I heard Blakewell's door shut, waited a moment, then peeked around the plant. The hall was empty. I ran down to the first floor and grabbed my duffel. Questions bloomed in my mind about what I had just heard, but I popped them like bubbles. I was leaving, so the mystery of this place didn't matter anymore.

I followed another hallway and came to an office. A woman sitting at a desk and sectioning an orange eyed me. "Can I help you?"

"I need to call my parents."

She removed a segment. "We don't allow contact with families. It can interfere with the process."

"Well, my process is over. Please give me a phone."

The woman set the orange down and wiped her fingers on a napkin. "Let me just check ..." she picked up a phone.

The last thing I wanted was Crystal or another difficult adult trying to stop me. "It doesn't make sense that you won't let me call my family," I said, channeling DJ's icy tone—the one that meant a manager needed to be summoned. "How's that going to make HP look? Keeping a sixteen-year-old girl hostage?"

Her eyes flashed, but she stopped dialing and tossed the phone on the counter between us.

I put in Dad's number, hoping I could explain the situation to him and avoid my mom's hysteria. The phone rang multiple times and I worried I was going to get voicemail.

"Walker Jamison," my dad's deep voice said.

"Hi Daddy," I said, feeling like bursting into tears. Suddenly I wanted nothing more than to be in Aspen with my family, even if it meant fighting with DJ and watching Emma Claire's endless rehearsals.

"Lina? How did you ..." a pause, " ... it's Lina."

I could hear my mom's voice in the background.

"Daddy, can you come pick me up? I can't stay here."

"No, I didn't call Haverford. I don't know, Darcy. Why don't you talk to her?"

"Wait, Dad," I said. "Let me just—"

"Lina?" my mom's voice blasted in my ear. "Oh Lina, it's so terrible. It's too awful."

I walked away from the desk, hoping the woman couldn't overhear. True to form, DJ was majorly overreacting. Disappointing, yes, but awful?

"I'm sorry Mom," my voice trembled. "I didn't want to let you guys down. But ..." I paused. Did she already know that my failure was related to swimming? She would never forgive me for that.

"We didn't want to worry you," my mom said. "How did you ... Walker, let them know I'll be right there ... look, Lina, she's going to be fine. Aspen has excellent doctors."

I froze. Something was wrong. DJ knew nothing about my problems at HP. The awful thing that had happened was not my swamp disaster. "Wait, what? Doctors? Is Emma Claire okay?"

"Honey, it was just a little accident," my mom's voice broke. "They were doing a lift. Her partner tripped and she landed pretty hard."

"So, she's hurt?" I pressed my hand to my chest. "How bad?"

"She needs surgery to put the bones in her arm back in place. But first they are doing an MRI to make sure there is no bleeding in her brain."

Bleeding in her brain? "I need to be there. I'll take a bus, I'll ..." I glanced toward the woman, who was typing at her computer, pretending not to listen. "I'm sure there's a bus from here to Aspen."

"No, Lina, you need to stay there where you're safe and sound. You'd only get in the way."

"But Emma Claire," I protested, imagining my little sister in pain and scared. She would want me there, to bring her popsicles and read *Harry Potter*. "I'm coming."

"You are not," my mom snapped. "Stop being selfish, Lina. Think about Emma Claire. Do you want her to know she's why you left HP? That she's the reason your entire future was derailed?"

"Except I'm already—"

"I need to go. They're taking her for the scan."

"Wait, just, tell her I'm sending her a big hug."

"I will. Now you focus on making us proud."

My mom hung up and I stood, staring at the phone in my hand. Now what was I going to do?

CHAPTER
THIRTEEN

I HEADED BACK TOWARD MADISON. I was terrified. Emma Claire needed surgery. And she might have a brain bleed? Did it mean she would be brain-damaged? Could she die? I wanted to sprint to the end of HP's drive and hitch a ride to Aspen. But what I wanted didn't matter, and shouldn't. I needed to stay here so my parents could focus on my sister. There was no other option.

"Whoa, where you going, Scrapper?" a voice boomed. Charles was waving from the deck next to the dining hall. I ducked my head and kept walking. The next thing I knew, he was clamping an arm around my shoulders and taking my duffel. "Me and Gabi saved you a seat," he said, steering me toward the stairs. "After this morning, you need ice cream."

"I'm not hungry," I said.

He propelled me into the dining hall to a table where a smiling Gabi gestured to a tray piled with chicken sandwiches, fries, and fruit salad. I didn't have the energy to fight or explain, so let Charles lead me.

Her smile faded as I slumped across from her. "Uh-oh. What's wrong? What happened?"

"Don't tell me you haven't heard yet. Hayden had to rescue *me* this time." I could feel the eyes of the other trainees on me and hear their snickers.

"That boy's gutsy," Charles said, putting three sandwiches, fries, and a giant scoop of fruit salad onto his plate.

Gabi waved her hand dismissively. "Of course, we heard about that."

"Everyone did." Charles patted me on the shoulder. "We all have off days, right? Don't I know it."

"But there's something more," Gabi said.

I propped my elbows on the table and put my face in my hands. "It's my sister," I said between my fingers. I described the call, leaving out the part where I was going to beg my parents to come get me.

Charles, who had his head leaned in close to hear me, rested his hand on my back. "Emma's going to be okay. Dancers are tough."

"I agree," Gabi squeezed my arm. "And you know I have feelings about things, right? I feel like Emma Claire is going to make a full recovery."

My chest loosened a bit. "I hope you're right."

Charles put a sandwich in front of me. "Now eat."

Pesto chicken with tomato and melted mozzarella. I felt a flicker of hunger. "Charles, didn't you want to go home," I asked tentatively, "after what happened?"

Charles finished his bite. "You mean the ropes course? And my asthma attack?"

I nodded, avoiding his eyes as I reached for the mayonnaise.

Charles barked a laugh. "Go home? Leave HP? Are you kidding?" He waited until I put mayo on my sandwich then took it and covered his fries. "Would take a lot more than a little embarrassment and a night in the hospital." He grabbed dripping fries. "Did you know there are at least eight NFL Hall of Famers who went here? And lots of players who got full rides to places like Alabama and USC. Straight to the pros after that."

He shoved the fries in his mouth, chewed, and washed them down with a gulp of water. "Nobody from my high school has ever been recruited by those big boys. And if I don't get a football scholarship to college, I don't go."

I wouldn't exactly call Charles' episode on the ropes course a *little embarrassment*, but clearly, he had gotten past it. Would he judge me if he knew I had been trying to quit? That I was on my way out—would have been—if Emma Claire hadn't gotten hurt? I took a bite, chewing slowly. Shame was filling me again, and not because of the swimming. Charles had almost died a week ago, yet here he was, cheerfully digging into his food and thrilled to remain at HP. In my selfishness, I hadn't ever considered the opportunity HP presented to my fellow Plebes. It could be a huge boost in their lives, leading to college and success in future careers.

"Nobody in my family has ever gone to college," Gabi said.

"No one?" In my house, going to college was not a question. Jamisons went to college, and usually graduate school. My parents would send me anywhere I could get myself accepted, even a ridiculously expensive private school.

"You'll be the first," Charles grinned at Gabi. "College is made for nerds like you."

Gabi's eyes lit up. "I know right? My family calls me the walking Wikipedia and I'm already taking college classes." She picked a grape from the fruit salad. "My mom cleans houses, and my dad is a manager at KFC. In my family, graduating high school is an anomaly, let alone attending college."

I had so many questions for Gabi. How did she know all these big words? How had she ended up at HP with parents like hers? What did her family think of her finding her purpose here?

As I tried to figure out how to ask, Eric walked up and hovered next to our table. "Would it be all right if I sit here?"

I imagined years of Eric alone at a table in the cafeteria, too timid to ask the other students if he could sit with them. Or—my heart ached—asking but being rejected.

I patted the chair next to me. "Always."

Eric set his tray down. The food on his plate was neatly separated into sections: cucumber salad, Asian noodles, four pieces of sushi, and one dumpling. His hand brushed against mine and I had a flash of realization. "It was you with me in the water," I exclaimed. "You were next to me, and I wasn't afraid anymore."

They all stared at me.

"Are you talking about this morning?" Gabi asked.

"Yes. In the swamp."

"Eric was with you in the swamp? This morning?"

"I was nowhere near a swamp," Eric shuddered.

"When I was trapped earlier," I said, remembering the figure floating next to me. How it had erased the panic and brought a feeling of peace and love. I grabbed Eric's hand.

He twitched but then relaxed and let me hold his hand. He looked me up and down. "You all right? You look a little ..."

"Beat up?" I let go of his hand and reached for a fry.

"Well, yes," Eric said, picking up his chopsticks. "What happened?"

Apparently, Eric was the one Plebe who hadn't heard. "I had a fight with a water pit. Guess who won."

Eric paused, a piece of sushi halfway to his lips. "A water pit? But you can't swim."

"How did ..." I stopped. Eric knew I couldn't swim the same way I knew he was a decent swimmer, having grown up next to the Connecticut River. I described my disaster, including the confrontation between Hayden and Becky. I stopped before my tantrum, embarrassed that I had behaved like such a brat when HP was the golden ticket for kids like Charles and Gabi.

"Is that why you were leaving?" Gabi tipped her head toward the duffel.

"Sort of, but I'm not now," I said quickly. "At least not yet. But Becky's out to get me." *And Crystal too* I thought, remembering what she'd said in Blakewell's office.

"That's messed up." Charles shook his head. "Lucky that Hayden was there."

Eric gathered noodles in his chopsticks. "I'm sure Becky was just trying to follow Council instructions. She came into the CS lab to run scenarios and she's actually pretty nice."

I froze, a fry halfway to my mouth. There was that Council again. I stared at Eric. "I could have drowned."

Eric chewed then swallowed. "That's being a little dramatic, don't you think?" He blotted his mouth with a napkin. "I can't imagine HP letting something bad happen to a trainee."

Gabi turned to him. "What if Hayden hadn't been there? What do you think would have happened?"

And what about with Charles on the ropes course? I wanted to add.

A burst of laughter as Bolton, Spiky, and the twins entered.

Hayden and Theo were just behind them. "Eat your lunch and be on time to your next activity," Hayden ordered. "Don't make me tell you again."

Spiky and Hayden spotted me at the same time. Hayden stared for a long moment then turned and strode toward the kitchen. I debated going after him. I needed to apologize for being such a baby, to fill him in on Emma Claire, to tell him I'd at least try to learn to swim, even if it terrified me.

Spiky's face lit up. She nudged Bolton and pointed. They both laughed and the twins joined in.

I ignored them, tired of dealing with Spiky, or my awful morning. "So, I know I've been kind of fading at dinner. What have I missed? Have you guys made any headway?"

"On what?" Eric asked.

"You know, about what we talked about. The grad list ... the deaths?" I was eager to add what I had overheard from Blakewell, a creep who wasn't even supposed to be here.

"Yeah," Charles said. "Eric, man, you were going to tell us more about those suspicious deaths."

"Oh, that." Eric set his chopsticks down across his plate. "I am convinced it's not a big deal. Just me getting overly conspiracy theorist on the internet." He shrugged. "I am a Geekit after all."

I frowned. "What about all the bad graduates from HP? Those statistics you were telling me?"

Eric blinked. "True, there are some HP graduates who have done horrible things. But sometimes purposes are used in a negative way. That's just the way the world works. Power breeds corruption."

I narrowed my eyes. That was what I had said. And he had disagreed. "Weren't you and Gabi talking about ..."

"Howdy y'all," Brittany sashayed over, holding a green smoothie.

I could feel Eric shrinking into himself. Pretty girls—girls in general—were way out of his comfort zone. "Guys, this is my roommate, Brittany," I said.

Brittany slid into a chair and gave me a puppy dog look. "Those french fries look so yummy."

I pushed the plate toward her. "Help yourself."

Brittany glanced around as if the diet police were going to swoop in, then grabbed some fries. "OMG, such heaven," she moaned, downing them in two bites and reaching for more. "Hopefully just a few won't bloat me."

Spiky reappeared, shot us an amused look and headed to the other end of the dining room. Hayden followed a moment later and joined some Tores a few tables away. He did not look in my direction.

"So, we were discussing the high death rate," Gabi prodded Eric. "But we never got around to the cause. What did you find in your research?"

Eric had been unable to look up since Brittany arrived. "Nothing statistically relevant," he said woodenly. He pushed his chair back. "Anyone want ice cream?"

"I do," Charles said.

I felt like I was in an alternate universe, where nothing made sense. I didn't know how or why, but between our initial talks and now, Eric had changed his mind. He had been so certain that something sinister was going on at HP. He had been determined that we were going to figure it out.

"Let me ask you guys a question," I blurted. "Do you know what the Council's purpose is?"

"To create space and provide tools to unleash potential," Eric and Brittany replied in unison.

"Jinx," Brittany said with a laugh. Eric flushed and looked pleased. A chill ran down my spine. "How did you know that?"

Brittany shrugged and reached for the last fry. "Didn't Matthew say it at the thing?"

Eric picked up his tray. "I think it's on the website."

Charles tilted his head and pointed toward his hearing aid. "Must have missed something. So, what's new." He piled the napkins and fry cups onto his tray and followed Eric.

"See ya," Brittany said, popping the fry into her mouth and getting up.

Gabi watched Brittany glide off. "Not true," she said, tugging at her ponytail. "Matthew did not say that and it's not on the website."

Our eyes met and I saw my confusion mirrored in Gabi's.

"I have a perfect memory," she said. "And I've never heard that expression before in my life."

CHAPTER
FOURTEEN

I WAS RELIEVED MY AFTERNOON SCHEDULE had me in The Science Center. I didn't know how being a Joe related to science, but it was nowhere near a swamp or pool, so fine by me. I walked with Sakura and Ryan who chattered about the end of Mors Week and, thankfully, did not mention my failure.

The Science Center was nicknamed The Cube as it resembled a giant ice cube with strips of wood and metal dividing it into squares. A maple tree with thick branches and green leaves shaded the entrance. Cement steps led up to glass doors and a high-ceilinged open area with lounge chairs. Glass windows on either side revealed lab rooms with long tables and cabinets. In one room, a group of white-coated Quites was watching a tutor stir a solution in a beaker.

Our schedules had different room numbers, so we separated, and I followed a hallway to room 120. When I knocked, a gruff voice commanded me to enter. Unlike the spacious, sunny labs, this room was dark, small, and square. Two medical-looking machines were on a cart against a wall and a rectangular fish tank sat on a low table in the middle. Black hoses ran between it and a panel in the wall.

I recognized the tutor from our first meeting, with his disheveled black hair and perma scowl. Today, he wore a white lab coat. "You're late," he barked. His thick accent sounded German or Russian.

"Sorry, we just finished lunch."

"Sit." He gestured to a chair next to the table. "I am Doctor Volkov and will be doing this session of testing."

Feeling like I was in a bad sci-fi movie—with gloomy lighting and an evil Russian scientist—I perched on the edge of the chair and examined the tank. The water in it was clear, the surface rippling as the hoses added more. I was relieved to see nothing floating.

Doctor Volkov rolled over the cart with the machines. "These will measure your vital signs." He attached a black plastic clip to the end of my left finger. The machine started beeping and two numbers flashed in red: 94 and 74.

"What is that?" I asked.

"Your oxygen saturation and pulse." He wrapped a blood pressure cuff around my upper arm. "This will take measurements every minute." He pushed a button.

A whooshing noise as the cuff tightened and the doctor pointed to the tank. "Put your right arm into this water. It must be submerged up to your elbow. Keep it in there as long as possible. The water is very cold but do not pull your arm out."

"And it's just water?" I instantly regretted the question because I sounded scared and small.

A flash of scorn in his eyes. He must be wondering how this freckly girl had made it to HP. He had heard about my failure at the swamp and knew I was weak. "Just water." He put his finger next to a button on his watch. "When you're ready."

I plunged my arm into the tank. The cold water instantly bit into my skin. I gasped and fought the urge to jerk my arm back out. The beeping from the machine quickened, but I didn't need that to know my heart rate was shooting up. It was like my arm was being gnawed on by a school of tiny sharks. I tried counting in my mind—had it been ten seconds? Eleven? Twelve? I gritted my teeth and attempted to take breaths. The pain was deepening, into the muscles and tendons of my hand and arm, pulsing up to my elbow and shoulder. The whooshing noise began, and the cuff began to inflate. Did that mean I'd made it to a minute? Or was it a minute from when the doctor first put the cuff on? I wanted this to stop. That was it, I was going to pull my hand out. What did it matter how long I could keep my arm in ice water? What was the point?

I caught a glimpse of Volkov's face. His condescending expression was the same one Ellie flashed me in the halls. The expression of someone who knows they are better than you, that you will never amount to anything.

I closed my eyes and tried to *hush*. I imagined myself in my room, gazing into the Ranger's eyes, drawing strength from his intense stare. He could submerge his entire body in freezing water for as long as it took to get the job done. He would ignore the knives jabbing into his skin, the icicles forming on his brow, the urge to quit. I pictured myself next to him, allies in the fight, gaining courage and warmth from each other.

As if from a great distance, I heard the beeps slowing. I was centered in my body, and all was warm and still. My arm felt a distant tickle of pain, but it was as if it belonged to someone else. I was one with the slow beat of my heart, the gentle swish of air in and out of my lungs.

A jerking on my shoulder snapped me back. The doctor was shaking me. "You must remove your arm now," he commanded, his voice harsh and loud in my ear. "Number forty-two, listen to me and do it now."

An enormous wave of pain rolled up my arm and exploded into my chest. I screamed and flung myself backward. The chair toppled over, and I landed on the floor. A heavy weight fell into my lap, searing my bare legs. Realizing that the weight was my frozen right arm, I screamed again. I tried to lift it, to move it off my legs, but couldn't.

A warm towel landed in my lap. I grabbed it with my left hand, fighting with the expanding blood pressure cuff, and wrapped the towel around my injured arm. It was starting to throb as it began to thaw. "I'm sorry," I told it, cradling it against my body as if it were an injured puppy. "I didn't mean to hurt you."

The doctor was talking into a phone on the wall. "Don't give me that nonsense," he barked. "I should have stopped it sooner, but you didn't give me any parameters. The expectation was 180 seconds max." He paused. "275. So don't tell me ..."

I lifted the edge of the towel. My arm was a whitish blue with angry red streaks starting to appear. I tried to move my fingers and was relieved to see them wiggle.

The doctor slammed the phone down. He swiftly crossed the room and ripped the cuff off my left arm. "Let me see," he said, unwrapping the towel. His fingertips probed the bones along my arm. He rotated my wrist and felt and moved each finger. Finally, he placed his fingertips against my wrist and nodded. "Your pulse is strong. I don't think we need the medics." His eyes met mine and the smugness had been replaced by relief, concern, and even a touch of admiration.

The ice water test was the scariest of the afternoon, but not the only weird one. At the next session, a friendly woman in a lab coat directed me to a chair in the middle of a circular platform. She strapped me in and then pressed a button which caused the platform to begin turning. I closed my eyes, pretending I was on the Mad Tea Party ride at Disneyland. After a minute, she stopped the platform, unclipped me, and told me to walk across the room and tape a picture to the center of a mirror. Luckily, I never got dizzy, so had no difficulty with that task. In other rooms, I built structures from random assortments of materials, determined what flat shapes would look like when folded, and identified patterns from a series of numbers and shapes.

By the time I got back to my room and changed for dinner, the shame from the morning had faded a bit. I wasn't ready to celebrate, but I wasn't ready to crawl under a rock either. I would try to hold my head high and be proud of what I had accomplished, in Mors Week and my testing this afternoon.

CHAPTER
FIFTEEN

AT DINNER, the dining room had been transformed. The tables were arranged in rows and covered with deep purple tablecloths. Glowing lanterns hung on the walls and fat candles in glass jars bathed everything in a rich, golden glow. The Quites and Tores wore their cloaks, and the tutors joined us in their robes.

We waited behind our chairs until everyone had arrived. The Tores leads for the Jocks came to the front of the room. They pressed their fists over their hearts, then held them out in front of them. "Courage. Loyalty. Triumph," they intoned.

We copied them. "Courage. Loyalty. Triumph." It felt strange but also thrilling. The weight of HP's traditions permeated the room, in the formality of the setting, the cloaks, the saying that had been repeated for several hundred years.

Once we were seated, the kitchen staff and Tores brought in plates with roasted chicken, baby potatoes, and green beans. I quietly ate my food as the other Baby Joes chattered excitedly, quizzing the older trainees about the patches on their cloaks and what was next now that

Mors Week was thankfully over. Despite my attempt at confidence, I knew that doing well in the afternoon testing wouldn't count for much since I had failed the swamp. And the next time we had to cross that swamp, or any body of water, I would fail again.

I had been relieved to turn in my Campia pin that morning. While I had enjoyed the other Plebes' looks of respect, I hadn't deserved it in the first place, and it had made me a target. Tripping and sniping aside, Spiky—who acted like she had won an Academy Award when Becky proudly pinned it on her—had truly deserved it after kicking butt during Mors Week.

At nine fifteen, there was a brisk knock at our door. Brittany, at the mirror practicing facial expressions—serene, seductive, wicked—answered it.

Hayden stood there, wearing a sweatshirt and shorts.

"Well, hello there," cooed Brittany. "I don't think we've had the pleasure."

"Hayden Murray," Hayden politely shook Brittany's hand. He looked past her to where I was sitting on my bed, gnawing on a thumbnail. "I was asked to pass along a message. Emma Claire's MRI scan was normal. She just came out of surgery for her broken arm and is doing well."

I dropped my head into my hands. Emma Claire was going to be okay. Nothing else mattered.

"That's wonderful news." Brittany clapped her hands together. "Now you can stop being so mopey."

Hayden spotted the empty duffel sticking out from under the bed. "So, you're planning to stay?"

I nodded. "I'm going to try. My family ..." I stopped. I had a lot of explaining and apologizing to do.

"Then we have a training exercise. Put on your swimsuit and let's go."

Swimsuit? My head jerked up. Tightness squeezed my chest. "I've got all this reading to do," I sputtered, motioning to my books. "There's a test tomorrow."

"Leave it. Meet me downstairs in five." He turned and strode down the hall.

"What's his problem?" Brittany harrumphed. Flopping onto her bed, she picked up her *History of Fashion* textbook.

"Me," I said, not blaming Hayden for being angry. He should literally throw me into the deep end of the pool and let me sink or swim.

"Is he gay?" Brittany asked, clearly not used to a boy who wasn't falling all over himself to flirt with her.

I dug my swimsuit out of the drawer and headed to the bathroom.

"Wait," Brittany exclaimed, snatching a tiny bikini out of a bin and draping it over one finger. She gave me the wicked smile she had just practiced. "Wouldn't you rather wear something sexy? Find out if he's straight—he is awful cute."

"You can have him."

Britt swung the suit back and forth. "Maybe. But I've got my sights on someone else."

I went into the bathroom. "Please don't tell me it's Bolton."

Brittany giggled. "Bolton? Did someone's parents really name him that?"

I tugged up the suit, hating the rubbery feel against my skin. "No, it's actually, um ..." I struggled to remember. " I think maybe it's Finn or Phineas, or something like that."

A louder chuckle. "Like *Phineas and Ferb*, the cartoon? That poor doll."

I opened the door. " I think Phineas is also a character in some famous book."

Brittany frowned as I untwisted the straps. "That one piece has absolutely no oomph. Are you sure you don't want—"

"I'm good." I reached for my sweats. "So, if it's not Bolton, who are you hunting?"

Brittany's eyes lit up. "Matthew. I mean, obviously. He came into our modeling session today and was checking me out."

Brittany certainly didn't struggle with self-esteem. I could not imagine a boy like Matthew ever being interested in me. "Isn't he a little old? He's a graduate."

Brittany's lips twitched. "Hon, he's barely out of high school. And already on the Council. That boy is going places."

I pulled on my sweatshirt. "No relationships, remember."

Brittany made a checkmark motion with her finger. She had already checked off *no makeup, no perfume* and *no crop tops*. "I hear that rule gets way relaxed as the summer goes on. As long as you're discreet." She winked. "And I can be discreet."

Hayden was waiting by the entrance. "I checked you out with Samantha."

"Samantha is okay with this?"

He nodded. "She owes me a favor."

"I'm supposed to read like the entire history of the US military before tomorrow," I said, following him onto the porch.

"Priorities." Hayden pulled a flashlight from his pocket. "All that book knowledge won't matter if you drown."

I couldn't argue with that so followed him down the path, surprised when we continued past the turnoff for the gym. My unease grew as we neared the lake. In the moonlight, its surface was a smooth pearly green. A family of ducks glided next to the shore, and dragon-flies zipped in and out of the grass. I shuddered.

Cupping my elbows in my hands, my thoughts spun. I didn't have to go in the water—Hayden had just been lecturing me about choices and I could refuse. Except, I had also committed to staying, to trying to learn how to swim.

Hayden motioned me onto the dock. He pulled off his shoes and sweatshirt. I reluctantly copied him. The chilly night air felt good against my skin, which was flushed from nerves.

"Have you ever meditated?" he asked.

Murky water lapped ominously at the wooden poles of the deck. "Meditated? What do you mean? Like saying ohm and chanting?" There was a meditation club at school. The kids wore loose black pants and sat around a metal bowl making low-humming noises. "Not my thing."

Hayden sat and crossed his legs. "That surprises me, actually." He tipped his head indicating I should join him.

I sat, the rough wood tickling my legs. Something splashed behind me, and I whipped my head around, scanning the darkness. "Do I look like a Buddha to you?" I managed.

Hayden smiled. He pressed a palm to the center of his chest. "Do this."

I placed my palm on my chest. The swimsuit fabric was slippery against my fingers and my heart thumped frantically underneath. I had the sudden urge to start singing the Star-Spangled Banner and let out a nervous snort.

Hayden leaned toward me. "Tell me, Lina. Do you ever feel like you can go inside yourself? Like you can leave everything behind and center yourself within?"

I did do that—had done it that afternoon in fact to tolerate keeping my arm in the ice water. But how did he know?

"Sometimes ... I guess."

Hayden rubbed his palm in a circle. "Can you block out everything, everyone, until there's nothing there but your center, your heartbeat? Your breath?"

I tried to keep my jaw from dropping. How could Hayden know about the way I could wall myself away from the world? Away from hunger, away from cold, away from any senses and emotions?

He was watching my face and nodded. "I thought so. That's a kind of meditating, you know. And I'll bet you can do it really well."

One time, I had been upset after my parents took away all my electronics for spying. I had crawled into a cardboard box in the basement and withdrawn for so long that they had almost called the police. "I call it hushing."

"Hushing," Hayden repeated. A smile played on his lips. "I like that. Do it now."

"Here?" I wasn't used to hushing out in the open, especially with someone watching. This afternoon had been an exception—usually, I was tucked away in a safe spot, like under my bed.

"Here. Don't worry, I've got your back."

Nervous, I closed my eyes and began to *hush*. First, the small muscles—my fingers, my toes—then the larger muscles, working from my arms and legs inward to the core muscles of my stomach and back until all were relaxed. Then I moved to the organs and blood vessels, the nerves, until nothing was left but the beat of my heart and the rise and fall of my lungs.

I don't know how long I sat that way, in a suspended stillness. When I opened my eyes, Hayden was in the lake, pulling himself through the water with smooth, swift strokes. He went under and surfaced a few moments later next to the dock.

"You feel centered. You feel strong," he said—a statement, not a question.

"I do," I said, realizing that I felt more at peace than I had since arriving at Haverford Pines.

"Keep that feeling," he said, reaching out his hand. "And come in the water."

In a dreamlike state, I crawled to the edge of the dock, hung my feet over the side, and took Hayden's hand. When I slipped into the lake, I noticed the coolness of the water against my skin and a mossy smell. The familiar sense of panic was there, but it was far away, like a distant voice calling. My arms and legs moved gently in a circular motion, supporting my body on the surface.

"Brilliant," Hayden said. "Now float on your back." He rested his hand on my spine and guided me until I was staring up at the sky. We spent the next half hour acquainting me with swimming. It turned out that I was a natural. I could float, swim freestyle, and even perform a decent dive. Hayden instructed me to swim fifty yards away and back and I found myself enjoying the feeling of my muscles gliding through the water.

When I returned, he was lying on his stomach on the dock, grinning at me. "Nice work." He extended a hand to pull me out.

I sprawled next to him. "Swimming is tiring."

He laughed. "Wait until you try it with your pack."

I groaned. "We already know how that one ends. I'll sink like an elephant."

"Elephants can swim," Hayden corrected. "And now, so can you."

I propped myself up on my elbows, feeling like I might cry. What

Hayden had just done for me—nobody had ever been that nice. "Thank you ... I don't know how you did it, but ...".

"How do you think I learned how to rock climb? I'm dreadfully afraid of heights."

I snorted. "Yeah right."

He scratched a fingernail against a spot of peeling wood. "At boarding school, we had to climb a ladder and walk across a log stretched between two platforms. Let's just say, it was not my finest moment. I ended up with my arms and legs wrapped around the log, bawling like a baby."

I laughed, trying to imagine a terrified Hayden clinging to a log.

I found the birthday party story spilling out of me, ending with me never getting into a pool again.

"Dreadful," he said. "No wonder you have been petrified."

"Well, I eventually got them back."

Hayden turned on his side.

"I let it go for a long time. I was used to kids being jerks. Then they did something terrible, and I couldn't ignore it anymore."

I described how Ellie, her boyfriend Max, and their group, after ignoring the new, shy boy for most of the year, had suddenly acted friendly toward him. During lunch one day, they had encouraged him to drink a bunch of soda, then blocked him from the bathroom.

"Noah kept running to the different bathrooms. All blocked." I cringed, describing the hurt expression on his face when he realized his new *friends* had tricked him, followed by the stricken one when he couldn't hold it any longer and wet his pants in the hallway. As everyone laughed and jeered, urine stained the front of his khaki pants and pooled in a puddle on the floor.

"Bastards," Hayden said. "That poor kid."

"Noah was a lot like Eric. He wanted to fit in and have friends, but he was awkward and didn't get how social stuff works. It was cruel what they did."

"So, you paid them back?"

I knew that nothing would ever make that moment better for Noah, but he deserved revenge. My initial instinct had been to pound their laughing faces in, but I had already gotten in trouble for Mason's dislocated finger and there were too many of them. So, I had to plot something else.

"Every year before spring break, our club throws this big party with a performance by the synchro and diving teams. Ellie and Max are the self-appointed king and queen."

"Is synchro the water dancing thing?"

I nodded. "The girls spend thousands of dollars on fancy costumes and makeup. Ellie makes a special pink punch, and they do a toast with champagne glasses before they perform. Max likes to brag about the bottle of Absolut he adds to the special punch—the Pink Stink."

Hayden raised an eyebrow.

"Yep. I too added something to this year's Pink Stink. Liquid laxative. I wasn't sure about how much to use or the right timing, but I got lucky. In the middle of the grand finale of the dancing and diving extravaganza ... boom."

Hayden's eyes widened. "How bad was it?"

"Let's just say the pool had to be closed for deep cleaning and those $800 swimsuits went in the trash."

Hayden tipped his head back and laughed. "They deserved it, the sick lot of them. But they must have figured it was you?"

"You know, I wasn't even there. I was at home watching TV and eating pizza—so nobody could blame me."

He waited.

"Okay, I ..." I made air quotes, "'borrowed' the car to drive over to the club, which is about ten minutes away. It was easy to wait until everyone was eating dinner, climb over the fence, and find Ellie's jug of Pink Stink."

"Brilliant," Hayden said. "There's a future Joe for you."

"Yeah, except I ran a red light on the way home and a photo ticket was mailed to my dad. I was busted big time. Actually, that's how I ended up at HP. But that's a whole different story."

"Remind me not to cross you."

I clapped my hands. "The best part was when we got to school the next day, there were swim pull-ups taped to Ellie and Max's lockers."

"Clever and appropriate. Nice touch."

Hayden seemed okay with me breaking rules to punish bullies, but would he approve of my sneaking around The Chalet this afternoon? He did seem to sense HP's weirdness too. Why else had he asked me about the Council?

"When you asked me before," I said, "about the Council. What did you mean?"

Hayden stiffened. He slid an arm under my thighs and lifted hard, somersaulting me into the lake. I inhaled and got a lungful of dank water. Coming to the surface, I coughed and spat, flailing my arms and legs. He grabbed me, pulling me against him so my back was pressed against his chest. "Quiet," he whispered in my ear. "They haven't turned off the microphones yet. And they're everywhere, even on the dock."

CHAPTER
SIXTEEN

I FLOATED THROUGH the rest of the week in a cloud of happiness and confusion. Happiness because I could swim—a skill I had never thought would be possible! With my newfound confidence, I had thrown myself into training, finally making it up Black Hole Hill in time to catch the chairlift. We were starting to use the equipment in the gym, working on flexibility, basic tumbling, and climbing, and I eagerly attacked the exercises.

Confusion because of what I had learned from Hayden. Microphones all over, listening in on us. Seemingly part of a system to make sure we stayed in line and followed the rules? Weird because even though Britt and I griped about the rules, they didn't seem serious enough that HP would need to spy on us. In normal conversations, I now found myself trailing off in the middle of sentences, wondering if someone was listening.

Sunday night, we gathered for a celebratory assembly. The other Plebes and I proudly wore our new T-shirts, complete with emblems. While not as impressive as the cloaks—only given if we were asked back for Equites summer—I was thrilled to sport the eagle on my sleeve.

Gabi sat between Charles and me and I wondered if I could confide in her. Her shirt had a wolf emblem like Matthew's, which we had learned meant she had cross purposes. Charles' had the Jock's Olympic wreath and Eric's the Geekit's power symbol. He was sitting with other Geekits in the front and I was happy he was fitting in, probably for the first time in his life. Except, I felt a growing distance between us, and something else had changed—his curiosity about HP had dulled and he seemed content to go along with the group.

Brittany swept into the seat next to me. She wore a purple tunic, tied with a sash, and stiletto heels.

I gave her a questioning look and she winked.

Matthew walked onstage wearing an HP jersey and jeans, a guitar hanging from a strap around his neck. "Good evening HPer's," he called.

I felt the familiar thrill as Matthew's presence amped up the energy. Brittany leaned closer. "He's gorgeous, am I right? Do you think he has a girlfriend?"

"Most definitely," I murmured, admiring the sweep of his dark hair.

"He certainly has an ego," Gabi muttered.

Matthew strummed chords, sparking more cheers. "Plebes, give yourselves a huge round of applause for making it through the first two weeks!"

Cheers and hoots.

"You've accomplished so much and now you can start digging into your purposes."

"Sing for us, Matthew," an Angel called.

Matthew grinned. "Trust me, nobody wants that." Fortunately, I have skilled trainees here, and learning to support each other is part of what HP is all about. Tonight, we celebrate our unique talents and what brings us together."

The room darkened as a black-and-white photo filled the screen. Trainees spilling out of a bus, wearing T-shirts, shorts, and laced canvas shoes. "Not much has changed at HP over the years. When you first arrive, you are separated into groups by your strengths. Our training is intense and specifically geared toward cultivating your purposes."

A photo of boys wearing V-neck sweaters and tall socks. "But our true power comes with synergy, when we use our connections and talents to work together for a higher purpose. It starts with the Interdisciplinary Activities." A photo of trainees at the lake, examining vegetation.

"During the second summer, Equites work on honing their purposes but also have combined history sessions and other trainings. Senators form Coalition Cohorts that are intended to create a close community before and after graduating."

A gangly boy with his arm draped over a sturdier boy sticking his tongue out at the camera. "Ivan and Tom met at HP when they signed up to plant a vegetable garden. Even with their different talents and backgrounds, they became close friends at HP and continued that bond afterward."

A stern man with unruly black hair in a lab coat, next to a uniformed muscular man.

I gasped. "That's the doctor I told you about. With the ice water!"

"He does look creepy," Gabi said.

"Both these men moved on from HP to more than fulfill their purposes. Ivan received his MD/PhD from Johns Hopkins, teaches neurobiology at Stanford, and is an illustrious tutor for us in the summers." There was scattered clapping. "Tom obtained a PhD in history from Yale and is currently a leader in the US military. The friends you are making and members of your Coalition Cohort will be lifelong colleagues. Because why?"

"Strength in connections," everyone chorused.

I stared straight ahead, pretty sure I hadn't heard Gabi or Charles chime in.

"Hey ladies," Charles leaned toward us. "We've already got our coalition. Eric can be our Geekit, so we just need an Angel! Brittany, you wanna join?"

"Maybe," Brittany said coolly. "You gonna get me fifty-yard line seats to your games when you go pro?"

"Definitely. I'll even let you borrow my Super Bowl ring."

"I'm in," Brittany said, holding up her palm for a high five. "Ooh, but let's snag him too, shall we?" She gestured to a boy wearing jeans and a black T-shirt who had come onto the stage. "JJ's voice makes me melt."

Matthew handed him the guitar. "If you haven't met Jake Joslin, you're in for a treat. I expect we'll see his name at the top of the music charts in a few years." He winked at Jake and strode to the side of the stage.

Jake strummed on the guitar and began singing. His voice was low and mellow but held immense power. Everyone quieted and I could practically hear Brittany's heart fluttering. Maybe he would give Matthew some competition.

Jake clapped his hands together over his head and we all copied him. Suddenly, three guitarists and a drummer appeared onstage. Spotlights swiveled to light up the newcomers. The trainees roared in surprise then began clapping. Some rose to their feet and started dancing.

Gabi jumped up and pointed. "It's the Beatles. The Beatles!"

"What?" I peered at the stage. The men had messy hair and wore black suits. They could have been the Beatles, or four guys from my high school marching band as far as I could tell.

"John Lennon," Gabi squealed. "He looks so real!"

"Thanks to our CS trainees for the holographic images and sound," Matthew said.

"Geekits!" everyone chorused.

The Beatles vanished to insane applause. A trainee in denim shorts and a flowered top skipped onto the stage. She joined Jake and began singing with him. Her voice was like warm honey.

"Elise Higgins, another future star," Matthew said. "Here at HP, we are lucky to have numerous Grammy-award-winning songwriters and musicians as graduates."

Jake and Elise finished the song, bowed, and exited the stage.

"We have had four HP grads become Miss America. And the number who have won Academy Awards is in the double digits."

"That's my cue," Brittany whispered, slipping out of her seat and making her way down the aisle. She joined two other girls wearing tunics.

"Next week, we will have our actors perform," Matthew said. "In the meantime, here is a demo from the Angels."

Spotlights hit the center aisle and music thumped. One of the girls began strutting down the aisle, her expression fierce, her hips swaying. Reaching the end, she paused, untied her tunic and let it fall. Underneath, she wore a cropped HP jersey and tight white shorts. On her abdomen were temporary tattoos of a football and basketball.

Charles and the rest of the Jocks jumped to their feet, hollering and cheering. The girl pumped her arm, turned, and strutted her way back, dragging the tunic behind her.

The next girl followed and, when she dropped her tunic, wore a mini white lab coat and rolled-up scrub shorts. From the pocket, she removed a pair of safety glasses and put them on.

"Please, no," Gabi said, burying her face in her hands.

Brittany was next and I couldn't believe how easily she moved in stiletto heels. Her body was like a wild cat prowling across the floor. At the end, she shrugged off her tunic, exposing a snug camouflage crop top and matching Lycra shorts. She pretended to hold up a rifle, aim, and shoot. The Joes howled and clapped.

I hooted, and Brittany winked at me again as she went by.

"Look for these gorgeous, talented ladies on the runway and covers of top fashion magazines." Matthew held out an arm toward Brittany as she got closer. Beaming, she snuggled in next to him.

"Let's have a fun night, and here's a thought to leave you with. We write our own destiny. We become what we do. So, get out there and work hard."

"They do look good together, don't they?" I commented to Gabi, watching Matthew murmur in Brittany's ear.

In the aisle, Charles was pretending to strut like a model, cracking up the trainees around him. Gabi remained silent, her attention focused on Matthew and Brittany.

I nudged her. "Can't you see them posing together on the red carpet?"

"No, that's not it." Gabi fingered her pendant. "That phrase about writing our own destiny. It's Chiang Kai-shek."

"And that is ...? I'm not the walking Wikipedia, remember?"

"He was a Chinese dictator in the first half of the twentieth century. A controversial figure. Seems an odd choice."

"But writing our own destiny is a good thing. Isn't that what we're supposed to be doing at HP? Maybe Matthew didn't know who said it."

"Maybe," Gabi mused. We joined the other trainees streaming out of The Chalet and heading to the meadow. The setting sun made the tops of the trees glow like candles. A grinning Chef Emilio and the kitchen staff were handing out ice cream sandwiches. Music began blaring from speakers and everyone started dancing.

"Courage, loyalty, triumph," a few of the trainees started chanting, and soon everyone was jumping and thrusting out their fists. "Courage, loyalty, triumph."

Gabi looked around, a confused expression on her face. I decided to chance it and put my mouth next to her ear. "Microphones are listening to us. They'll go off soon, but until then we have to be careful."

Gabi stared at me. I jumped up and down a few times and pumped my fist in the air.

Gabi bounced on her toes, angling so her mouth was close to my ear. "Why turn them off? Does something happen so they don't need them?"

Interesting that she wasn't asking me why there were microphones in the first place. Her brain had jumped immediately to the confusing part—why have them only to turn them off?

"Yes, something happens. Look at Eric. His suspicious thoughts have vanished."

"True," Gabi said slowly. "And others added. Like that weird nonsense about the Council's purpose."

I swayed, trying not to avoid bumping other trainees. "And tonight. Strength in connections? Everyone knew it but us."

"How?" Gabi swayed her hips and waved her arms over her head. "And why?"

"Hayden says it's some kind of brainwashing. You don't even know it's happening then suddenly, any bad thoughts about HP are gone."

"And new ones planted in their place." Gabi continued to sway half-heartedly. "That's creepy."

The music stopped and there was the long blow of a horn. Everyone groaned.

Gabi linked her arm through mine. We got behind some rowdy Jocks whose jabbering would cover up our voices.

"Does Hayden have any explanation?" she said.

"Yes, but he didn't have time to say."

Gabi was silent for a long moment, then snapped her fingers. "I know what it is." She let out one of her belly laughs. The Jocks turned, laughing when they saw such a big sound coming from petite Gabi.

"I never would have thought that would work," she exclaimed. What do you know ..."

"What? What is it?"

Gabi tugged at my arm, pulling my face closer to hers and spoke quickly and urgently in my ear.

CHAPTER
SEVENTEEN

I TRUDGED UP THE STAIRS, a pile of manuals in my arms, a bulky bag slung over my shoulder. Barely noticing my aching muscles anymore, I wrangled open the door, dumped the bag, and brought the manuals to my bed.

I slid a stick of gum out from under my mattress. Popping it into my mouth, I chomped and tried to collect my thoughts. My brain had zero interest in reading about how to pitch a tent. A quick break wouldn't hurt.

After Brittany had fallen asleep last night, I put my ear next to my speaker and listened hard. Boring classical music—lots of piano and violins—nothing more. No whispered words, no garbled messages. I couldn't believe that the music was doing anything to the trainees. If it were, why were my thoughts still normal?

It wasn't until I tossed and turned and finally sought out my nest that I got it. Under there, curled up with Cairo in my blanket and pillows, I couldn't hear the music at all. I ended up there most nights, so the messages weren't getting to me.

Gabi had said that for her the subliminal implanted messages would be incompatible with her perfect memory. Her brain would reject them as there would be no memory associated with learning them. She was still skeptical that something so basic would work, but I thought of creepy Volkov—if anyone could figure out how to brainwash people, it would be him.

At lunch, Charles had stopped by our table before joining his football buddies. As he walked away, Gabi locked her gaze on him. "I hear the Baby Joes have a solo challenge," she said, tugging her earlobe. "Do you really have to stay out overnight all by yourself?"

I shrugged. "It can't be that hard. Not compared to Mors Week."

Gabi tugged her earlobe again. "True, I'm sure you'll be well prepared."

"Gabi, do you have an earache?" Eric asked. "My sinuses have been bothering me with this dry air. Saline spray helps."

"My earring is stuck." Gabi twisted the gold stud. She waited until Eric looked down at his plate before glaring pointedly at me, then over to where Charles was sitting.

I screwed up my face. Charles didn't wear earrings. Charles didn't have an earache. What was Gabi going on about? Then—a lightning bolt of understanding. Charles did have something on his ears. He wore hearing aids. And at night he must take them off—without them in, he wouldn't hear the music either!

I walked over to Britt's bulletin board where she had hung the list of HP rules and checked off *no gum* and *no perfume*. I also noticed she had checked off *no interfering with the fire system or smoke detectors*. My roomie was no dumb blonde.

On her desk were two frames. The smaller had a quote, "*Style is a way to say who you are without having to speak. Rachel Zoe.*" The larger held a photo of a smiling Brittany wearing a blue sash and a crown. A couple flanked her, beaming with pride. The woman was short with blond hair that poufed high on her head and fell over her shoulders in waves. She wore heavy makeup and red lipstick. The man was the woman's height but seemed taller with the giant cowboy hat perched on his head. He had a thick mustache and deep-set brown eyes.

Scuffling noises outside the door. I returned to my bed as Brittany burst in, holding an HP tote. "I got it," she exclaimed. "I got the shoot with Anders Jorgensen tomorrow!"

I picked up my manual. "Yay? Congratulations?"

Britt pulled out a magazine and thrust it in front of me. On the cover, a tan woman was stretched on the beach, hair flowing, breasts barely contained by a red bikini.

"Isn't he fabulous?" Britt gushed.

"He's basically naked."

Brittany snorted. "He's the photographer, you silly, not the model." She clutched the magazine to her chest. "He's like world-famous and has shot the *SI* Swimsuit Issue twice. Our tutor only chose two Angels and I'm one. You need to help me decide which bikini. If I do good enough, the photo might be in *Glamour*!"

As she rushed into the bathroom, I stared at a diagram of a tent. Before tomorrow, I had to be able to pitch one in under three minutes.

She opened the bathroom door and stuck her head out. "I think I might look a little bloated."

"What do you expect eating all those salty fries? Only celery sticks from now on."

Britt stuck her tongue out. "You sound like my pageant coach." She walked to the center of the room and gazed in the mirror. "OMG,

I need my phone. How can I know which of these will photograph the best?" She turned to me. "What do you think?"

I looked Britt up and down. Much to DJ's disappointment, I had never bought into trying to look a certain way. I avoided fashion sites and their perfect, airbrushed models and couldn't care less about my mom's latest diet. But I knew that Britt was perfect. The right combination of soft skin, hard muscle, and curves. The cobalt bikini made her skin glow. I couldn't help but feel self-conscious about my pale skin, messy brown hair, and skinny limbs.

"It looks amazing." I reminded myself that Britt's purpose was modeling while mine was a more athletic, mental domain.

She tugged at a strap. "Do you think I need one that pushes up my boobs more?"

I burst out laughing. "You'll rock anything you put on."

"Maybe I need another opinion. I should see if Matthew's available."

I rolled my eyes. *No romantic relationships* would be going down soon.

"What about a belly button piercing? Lots of models have them and they look hot." Britt sashayed over and stuck out her abdomen. "I could put it in right here," she squeezed the skin above her belly button. "Do you think the swelling would go down by tomorrow?"

I stared at Britt's fingers, at the swirl of her belly button. A blue tinge darkened the center where it dipped like an inverted seashell. I felt a chill run up my spine and knew I had to find Gabi.

CHAPTER
EIGHTEEN

I LEFT THE TENT BAG OUTSIDE the door and tiptoed into the computer lab. Geekits hunched over computers staring at long strings of symbols and letters. Gabi and Eric sat next to each other absorbed in their screens.

"Hey guys," I whispered. Gabi looked up and Eric raised a hand in greeting.

"Um, Gabi? Do you have a sec to help me with my tent?"

"Your tent?" Gabi screwed up her face.

"IA time today is for finishing our coding," Eric said.

"In the spirit of IA cooperation then? I need to put it together in under three minutes and hoped you could help my efficiency."

Eric stopped typing. "I can help you. I worked with the Dartmouth rowing team on their stroke efficiency. It significantly improved their times."

Of course you did. I gave Gabi a pointed look. I needed her right now, not Eric.

Gabi got it. "How about if I help Lina then you join us? I need practice assessing human dynamics."

"You can fine-tune things at the end," I added.

Eric swiveled and regarded me. I was sure he would know I was lying—but he just shrugged.

The string of code on his computer suddenly lit up in different colors and began twirling around the screen. The other Geekits erupted in murmurs.

Eric spun back around as the symbols twirled and coalesced into a cartoon pig wearing ballet shoes and holding a bottle of lemonade. The pig smiled, belched, and took a puff from the cigarette in his other hand.

The Geekits, who all had the pig on their screens, burst out laughing. Their tutor jumped to his feet and came over. "Not funny, guys," he nudged a Geekit out of the way and tapped at keys. "Who did this?"

Gabi and I left the lab and headed to the football field. The Jocks were running drills at one end, so I strode to the other, loosened the string on the tent bag and dumped its contents. "Time me," I said loudly. Hayden had said the field was free of mics—they could get stomped on—but I still didn't want to rouse suspicion.

Gabi looked at her tracker. "Ready? Go."

I unfolded the tent canvas so it lay flat. Picking up the disjointed metal poles, I snapped them together. I hadn't felt like I had absorbed the directions, but the next thing I knew, the tent was standing.

"Two minutes, thirty-nine seconds," Gabi said. "Not bad."

I stepped back and inspected the lopsided tent. "Is this right?"

"Not sure. Let's take a look at the inside." Gabi lifted the flap, and we crawled in. It smelled like stale plastic and dirty feet.

Gabi wrinkled her nose. "I've tried testing out Eric a few times. You know, little comments about HP and its suspicious history. No response, he's definitely brainwashed."

I pulled a flashlight from my pocket. "Lift up your shirt. I need to see your belly button."

Gabi's eyes widened and she lifted her T-shirt. I shone the light on her belly button. Her skin was darker than Britt's but deep in the center it had the same dark blue tint.

Sweat formed in my armpits. "Why is your belly button blue?"

"It's not blue," Gabi said, ducking her head to try and see. "It's just a darkening of blood vessels close to the skin surface. It's hardly ... why? Is yours blue too?"

"Mine and Britt's." I sat back on my heels. "Gabi, doesn't that seem strange? Blue belly buttons? I always thought mine was weird, but ..." I shrugged. "Lots of things about me are weird."

"I guess I don't know," she said slowly. "How many belly buttons have you looked at?"

The tent flap flew open, and we both jumped. "Hey ladies." Charles' beaming, sweaty face appeared.

"Get in here," I said, grabbing his hand and tugging. It was like trying to budge a slippery boulder.

"Nah, I gotta keep running. Just wanted to say hey."

"Seriously. Get in here now."

Charles' smile faded. He dropped his helmet and squeezed into the tent, his padded, sweaty body instantly upping the stench.

"Lift up your shirt," Gabi said, reaching for his jersey.

"What?" Charles recoiled like Gabi had asked him to drop his pants.

"We need to see your belly button. It's important."

Charles pulled up his jersey and I shone my flashlight on his belly button. His dark skin made it impossible to see if he had the blue tint.

"I can't tell," I huffed.

Charles yanked his jersey back down. "That's just rude. I don't like anyone messing with my belly button. I'm going now."

Gabi grabbed his sleeve. "Wait! Why are you sensitive about your belly button?"

Charles looked sheepish. "It's stupid. But if I poke in there, I can feel something, like a little rock. I made the mistake of telling my brothers about it and they called me Pebble for like four years."

Gabi and I stared at each other for a beat, then our fingers flew to our bellies, poking and pressing. I lay down on my back—I had never mashed my flesh this way. And then I felt it—a tiny, hard object embedded deep inside my belly button.

My wide eyes met Gabi's and she nodded. The tent suddenly became overwhelmingly claustrophobic. We pushed through the flap and tumbled onto the grass, sucking in breaths of mountain air.

"There's got to be a rational explanation," Gabi insisted. "There's always a rational explanation."

I propped myself on my elbows. "Okay, so what is it then? I'm sorry, but having some weird thing in your belly button is not normal."

"You think it's a tracker, like a dog chip?" Charles said. "You know, Leo got one of those at the vet." He gripped my arm. "What if they flooded our rooms with sleeping gas and stuck them in?"

Desi had also been chipped at the vet. Considering HP was manipulating trainees' thoughts through subliminal messaging, I wouldn't put it past them.

"Charles, you've had yours for a while," Gabi said. "And Lina noticed the blue before HP too."

I gnawed my thumbnail, fighting the urge to claw at my belly button. I couldn't stand the thought of an object inside my body. Was it to monitor my location? Was it releasing some sort of chemical into my bloodstream?

A group of Jocks jogged by, yelling for Charles to join them.

"Asthma break," Charles held up his inhaler.

"Why the belly button?" Gabi said. "That must have some significance."

"It's hard to find," Charles said. "A place nobody would notice."

"True," Gabi said. "It doesn't serve any purpose. Just a remnant of the connection between the fetus and the placenta."

"Gross," I said.

"When a baby is born, a piece of its umbilical cord is still attached. There's an entryway into the body where someone could implant something."

"No way," I recoiled at the idea that this pebble had been in my body my whole life and I hadn't realized it. "Are you saying the doctor or someone at the hospital shoved it in? That's crazy."

Charles stood up. "This whole thing's crazy."

"And we haven't even told you about the brainwashing," I said.

"What?" He cupped a hand behind one ear. "Don't think I'm hearing you right."

"We have to consider all possibilities," Gabi said. "Including the medical staff."

"None of us were born at the same hospital," I protested. "Or even the same state. What? There was some troupe of evil nurses working together to chip us?"

Charles grabbed his helmet. "Maybe lots of people have these weird pebbles in their belly buttons. Coincidence?"

"No, no," Gabi jumped up and started pacing. "Think about it." She held up one finger. "First, we've got the daughter of Olympians who says her parents don't even swim." A second finger. "We've got a practically albino computer nerd whose parents are dark-skinned language aficionados."

"Eric told me his mom is Italian and his dad Chilean," she added when Charles and I looked confused. "I'm assuming they are not blond and blue."

"I've got another one," I exclaimed, describing the photo of Britt's parents who were both a foot shorter than their daughter.

Gabi held up a third finger triumphantly.

My head was spinning. "I agree that this is all creepy. But what does it mean?"

Charles readjusted his shoulder pads. "That swimmer must have been adopted. Her birth parents won medals, not the folks who raised her."

"Unlikely," Gabi said. "How would HP know about her biological parents? And, what are the odds two Olympic swimmers would not only have a baby together but also put her up for adoption?"

Charles frowned. "So, are you saying she was kidnapped?"

I shook my head. "That would have been a major news story."

"What if HP had her kidnapped?" Charles' voice rose in excitement. "They knew she was going to be a champion swimmer. And they wanted her for themselves. There could be a whole kidnapping ring!"

Gabi regarded him. "What's the name of the hospital where you were born?"

"Concordia in Cleveland. Me and my sibs were all born there."

"Lina?"

"Scripps in La Jolla. You?"

"Denver Health." She pressed her hands to her forehead. "We need Eric's help."

"For what?" I asked. "Pretty sure he was born in New Hampshire."

"We need him to get online and dig up information."

"We can't trust him right now."

"I know," Gabi huffed. "So, neither of you were adopted?"

Charles tugged his helmet on. "I've got two brothers. If my parents wanted to adopt, they would have picked a girl." He clipped his chin strap, waved a hand at the Jocks running by, and jogged away to join them.

"I'm not adopted," I said. "Only ..." I hesitated.

"Only what?"

"It's just," I paused, a lump in my throat. I was about to admit something that I had never told anyone. My parents and Emma Claire just made everything in life seem so simple. They could talk easily with other people and always looked attractive and confident. They had "good social graces" as my mom called them. I was the opposite with my lanky limbs, plain features, and social awkwardness.

"I've always felt like I didn't fit in my family," I blurted. "Like I got dropped in from another planet or something. If it turned out I was adopted, I don't think I'd be surprised."

Gabi was nodding. "Me too," she breathed. "My family doesn't know what to do with me. My sisters are all about social media and makeup and hanging out with their friends. I just want to be studying or taking online classes."

My uncertainty and confusion were mirrored in Gabi's eyes.

"We'll figure this out." She took a deep breath. "We've got four more weeks."

"And at least one Tore to help us."

CHAPTER
NINETEEN

SPEAKING TO HAYDEN without attracting attention was tricky as the Tores alternated time between their own training and working with the younger trainees. It took me a few days of waiting until I ran into him as he was leaving the gym, supervising four Quites carrying a torpedo-shaped boat. "I need another swim lesson," I murmured, holding open the door.

"Take it to the dock and set it down," he told them. To me, "Nine o'clock at the lake. I'll work it out with Samantha."

After dinner, I rushed to change into my swimsuit and, at nine, Hayden and I were floating on our backs in the lake admiring the blanket of stars.

I told him about the pebbles. He was bemused then alarmed when he located the object in his belly button. "Brainwashing is one thing," he said. "But chipping us. That's a whole new level of bizarre."

"Agree. How did you even figure out the brainwashing?"

"Our Plebe summer, my mate Nick and I couldn't figure out why the others were getting wonkier and wonkier as time went on. Saying stuff about the Council and achieving our destinies, like robots." He pointed. "Ursa Major. See the tail?"

"Why doesn't the messaging affect you?" I squinted but only saw a bunch of bright dots.

"Je parle plusieurs langues."

"Huh?"

"Hablo muchos idiomas."

"You speak like an idiot?"

Hayden chuckled. "I speak about seven languages."

I squinted again. I couldn't imagine being fluent in one other language—my Spanish grade was a consistent C+. "How does that matter?"

Hayden pointed again. "Ursa Minor, the Little Dipper. I've got so many multilingual phrases running through my brain that the messaging must get distorted. Every once in a while, I find myself thinking the Council will nurture my purpose, but then I say to myself, that's crap."

I was still awed by seven languages. "Did you grow up traveling all over? Were your parents diplomats?"

Hayden chuckled again. "Hardly."

Suddenly some stars merged into the figure of a bucket with a long handle, and I squealed. "I see it. One of the Dippers."

"Finally," he said and gestured toward the far shore. As we paddled, he described his childhood growing up in London. His run-down neighborhood had swarms of kids speaking different languages and parents who worked multiple jobs.

"I picked up the languages easily. Hindi, Arabic, and a mish-mosh of others. It's why I've got a quirky accent. Part English, part mutt."

We reached the shore and waded out of the water. "When I got to boarding school, I added four more," he made air quotes, "proper ones. French, German, Spanish, and, of course, Latin."

We sat on a log. "We can only rest here a moment," he cautioned. "Samantha said back by 10:30."

"It's 9:41," we said in unison, then laughed.

"You've got that too," Hayden said.

"Yep, and yet somehow I'm always late. Another thing that my parents love."

"I'm guessing you're on time when it matters."

He had a point. I had never been late to sessions on the climbing wall or to a meal. "So how did a mutt like you end up at HP?"

Hayden rubbed his fingertips over his scar. "It's a miracle that mailing even made it to me. My family had a good laugh, thought it was a fine joke. Find Your Purpose? As in which crap job was I going to get once I was old enough to drop out of school and go to work? Went straight into the bin."

"And?"

Hayden traced his toe in the mud. "It was like something out of a Dickens novel." When I stayed silent, he peered at me. "Don't tell me you haven't read Charles Dickens?"

I shook my head.

"Oliver Twist? Great Expectations?"

Another shake.

"Okay," he rubbed his hands together. "How about Cinderella? Or Snow White? Familiar with them?"

"You're really a princess?"

"No," he laughed. "But it felt that way. One night, this posh car pulled up. A uniformed driver opened the door for this distinguished man in a long overcoat. My friends and I were outside playing, and all stopped to stare. My brother raced over to ask for candy."

I guessed Hayden and his sibs had never been warned, like Emma Claire and I had a million times, not to take candy from strangers.

"The man knocked on our door and I was afraid he was there to collect money. My parents let him inside and we stayed on the street. After twenty minutes, he came out, got in the car, and they drove off. At dinner, my parents told me that I was coming here."

"That gentleman was an MP, a Member of Parliament," he explained before I could ask. "Like a congressman here. He told my parents he sponsored a young lad every year to attend HP. And if I did well, he would subsidize all three years and even put me up for a scholarship at Saunders."

"Is that a college?"

"Boarding school. You know, where you wear a blazer and study classic literature." He nudged me. "Like Charles Dickens."

"Did your parents ask this MP guy why you? How he had found you?"

Hayden snorted. "Have you heard the expression, don't look a gift horse in the mouth? My parents were damn sure it was a mistake, but they weren't going to do any correcting."

"So do you ever go home?"

"Of course. I love my family. I try to make it home for holidays a few times a year."

I thought about living away from home and was sad for him. "Didn't you want to stay home with your family and friends?"

"Part of me did. But that was never an option. When the glass slipper fits, you don't turn down the prince."

I nudged him back. "Nice."

He stood and gave a small bow. "Thank you. Shall we?"

We waded into the lake and started swimming. "I'm my family's future," he said. "With HP's guidance, I will be a success. Nobody else is going to pull them out of poverty. Nobody else is going to help my siblings go to uni, let my dad stop laboring or my mum have a day off, even buy herself some new clothes."

Like before, I felt ashamed of having taken HP for granted. DJ had a closet full of designer clothing and worked because she wanted to. My family had everything money could buy, whether I went on to fulfill a purpose or not.

"So, you had asked about the microphones. I enjoyed a bit of trouble before I came here. Smoked, drank, cut school. Nick too, and when we first got here, we were getting busted constantly—for sneaking out, for smoking, for meeting girls. We figured out they could only nab us every single time if they were somehow spying."

"Did you get punished?"

"Yeah. Extra calisthenics, restricted IA activities, nothing too bad. We shaped up for a bit. Then, when we started up again, we weren't getting caught anymore. And the other Plebes we had been making mischief with weren't interested. No more spying needed since the brainwashing had made everybody else mellow and obedient."

"How come it didn't get Nick?"

"That pasty Scot," Hayden chuckled. "He got terrible sunburns here but wouldn't wear a hat because it mussed his blond locks. For an Einstein, he was shockingly obsessed with his appearance."

He paused and sighed. "We figured it was a concussion he had gotten as a kid. Knocked him out and he spent months with headaches and blurry vision. Something must have been shaken loose that kept the brainwashing from working. Once we figured things out, we kept waiting for it to do more—to make Plebes do strange things. But nothing, so we chalked it up as one of HP's traditions. Some weird bonding tool."

"And Nick ..." I ventured.

"He's dead," Hayden said flatly. "Last fall, he was working in a lab and there was a fire. The fumes knocked him out, and the fire brigade didn't get there in time."

"That's awful. I'm so sorry ..." I hesitated, thinking of the suspicions Eric had brought up the first night. "Do you think it was an accident?"

Hayden gave me a hard look. "Of course, what else could it have been?"

Eric had mentioned some grim statistics and I couldn't hold back the thought—*could Nick have been murdered?*

CHAPTER

TWENTY

AFTER OUR WORKOUT the next morning, we gathered in the gym, perking up when Captain Hansen joined us.

"Good morning," he said.

We chorused a hello.

"The ability to blend into your surroundings, to sneak up on your enemy, is an important skill." His serious expression reminded me of my bio teacher, who had gray temples and a constant frown. Normally this would have made me nervous, but I was too tired. Pretending to adjust my shoelaces, I yawned into my elbow.

Last night, I had been unable to fall asleep, even in my nest. Every time I started to drift off, my thoughts jolted me awake. What would happen if I moved to my bed and heard the music all night? Would I become obedient like the others? Did all the trainees have implanted pebbles? How did Eric and I have this connection? Could we use it to bring him back to reality? And how had Nick died? At 4:12, I had drifted into an unsettled sleep and woke with a clenched jaw and stiff neck.

"Today, you will be engaged in an exercise with the Equites." The Baby Joes around me stirred and I straightened. We hadn't done any training with the Equites so far.

Hansen smiled and his expression softened. "Let's just say we're going to play a massive game of hide-and-seek. You will get the chance to practice your camouflage skills."

We looked at each other, wide-eyed.

"I suck at hide-and-seek," Ryan exclaimed, throwing out his hands and knocking over a water bottle. "I always get found."

I ducked my head, hiding my smirk. Finally, a skill I excelled at. Hiding was something I'd been getting in trouble for doing my whole life.

When I raised my head, Sakura was looking at me. *Let's kick ass*, she mouthed. I grinned and gave her a thumbs-up.

"All right, listen carefully," Hansen said. "You have fifteen minutes to change into your gear. Then fifteen minutes to find a hiding spot."

"Anywhere?" Ryan asked.

"No climbing trees or going inside. And you must stay within the borders of the buildings, meadow, and athletic fields. After fifteen minutes, we release the Equites and they have thirty minutes to find you." He clapped his hands together. "Let's go."

Sleepiness gone, I raced with the other Baby Joes toward the locker rooms. A table had a pile of camouflage uniforms, baskets with makeup sticks, and boots underneath. Grabbing supplies, I went into a locker room, kicked off my shoes and pulled on the camouflage over my clothes. The makeup sticks were two different colors: tan and dark green. I had no idea what to do with them. Ryan was making circles around his eyes with the tan, then moving to his upper lip. I copied him as he made splotches on his cheeks, down his neck, and on the backs of his hands.

"How do you know how to do this?" I asked as he switched to the green. His eyes met mine in his locker's mirror. With makeup, he looked older and less goofy. "Hunting. Been doing this since I was a kid." With easy motions, he finished his forehead and blended the edges with his fingertips. "Don't forget the backs of your hands," he advised.

Imitating Ryan, I managed to apply an assortment of blotches and smears. When Hansen called time, my pale skin, including the backs of my hands, was covered.

Released outside, the other Baby Joes scattered in all directions. I took a moment to ponder my choice of hiding spot. Climbing a tree would be too easy so I could see why that was forbidden. Where could I go that the Equites would not think to look, or see me?

It hit me. I sprinted toward the cabins. The ditch I had stumbled into the first night was still full of dead twigs, leaves, and pine needles. It was right on the edge of the allowed borders and not noticeable—unless you had accidentally tripped into it. I moved the debris to the sides, creating a space where I could lie on my back. After settling my body, I used gentle sweeping motions to gather the stuff back over me until my legs and chest were hidden. I rocked my head back and forth until a layer of leaves drifted across my face. It was not perfect, but I hoped the makeup would make me difficult to spot.

I began to *hush*. Being able to remain completely still was key—twitching, sneezing, or even loud breathing could give me away. It helped that I was sleepy as, within moments, fatigue took over and I drifted off.

I was curled up in the cupboard under the microwave. Sometimes the space was full of machines—a big bowl with a paddle to mix dough, another with a curved knife that spun and chopped up veggies. But today was Thanksgiving and the machines were on the counter so Mommy could make a feast.

The kitchen was the best place to hide and listen to grownups. The phone was in there and, if Mommy had a friend over, they sat at the counter and talked. I listened to the chopping noises and clank of dishes as Mommy and Aunt Lulu cooked.

"My back is killing me," Mommy said. "With Catalina, I never had pain like this."

The sound of the oven door opening and closing. "You were on the go so much with her that I'm not sure you would have even noticed," Aunt Lulu said. "And look where that landed you. Darcy, you need to take it easy this time. Why don't you go lie down for a bit?"

"I'll be okay. The doctor said it was the infection that caused Catalina to come so early. I'll be fine."

"That's what I mean." The machine with the blade whirred. "You didn't even realize you had an infection, you were so busy. Just promise me you won't travel."

Mommy laughed. "Don't worry. Not a chance we're going to get stuck at the Boston NICU again for a month. That was a nightmare." Another whir of the machine. "Everything is going to work out fine."

I woke with a start. The dream felt so real—could it actually be a memory? I had been five when my mom was pregnant with Emma Claire, so the timing could fit. And I had loved hiding in that cupboard.

What had she meant about the Boston NICU? I knew from my dad that NICU stood for Neonatal Intensive Care Unit, a place in a hospital for really sick babies. I had always been told I was "a little premature," but it had never sounded serious. And I had been born in San Diego, not Boston.

There were crunching noises and I hoped I hadn't dislodged my covering. "Now the best place to do this is in natural light." A girl's voice was coming from the direction of the cabins. "The lighting inside is different so be sure you come outside and check. After you cleanse and moisturize, you apply foundation. That will even out your skin tone."

I was relieved—these were not Equites on the hunt for Baby Joes. I consulted my internal clock. It was 11:17, meaning the exercise had ended. My hiding place had worked!

"How long should this take?" a second voice asked.

"Ten to fifteen minutes. Once you get it down, it's pretty quick."

I pushed up on my elbows, feeling triumphant at having outsmarted the Equites. Too bad I had slept through the debrief.

A flash of sunlight reflected off a metallic object. An eagle medallion, pinned to Spiky's shirt. She and Becky were standing next to Jefferson, and she was rubbing cream onto Becky's face. A mixture of fear and humor swept through me. Becky was getting a makeup lesson. From a girl whose eyeliner made her look like a raccoon?

"Make sure you blend the foundation where your jaw and neck meet," Spiky said. "Otherwise, you might have a line." She held up a small mirror. "Take a look."

Becky tilted her face to one side and then the other. "I like it."

"Great. We'll move onto eyes and lips."

I watched in fascination as Spiky used a black pencil to outline Becky's eyes, then handed her a slim tube. "You apply the lip gloss. Next time, we'll add mascara."

"Do you think it will help?" Becky asked in a tone I didn't recognize. They both sounded like normal girls—which was why I hadn't recognized their voices right away. She unscrewed the cap, pulled out the wand, and dabbed at her lips.

"Definitely," Spiky nodded. "You just went from drab to fab. He'll notice you now."

I pressed my lips together. *Drab to fab*? Sounded like the title of a bad reality show.

Becky examined herself again. "I don't know. He's got Angels throwing themselves at him. I can't compete with that."

Spiky waved her hand. "Matthew will want a woman with looks *and* brains."

Matthew? Becky was trying to snag the Chosen One? She thought she could compete with Brittany? Before I could stop it, a snort of laughter erupted.

Spiky and Becky froze, then swiveled in my direction.

I remained still, hoping the camouflage would somehow keep me hidden.

It didn't. Becky's face darkened. "You, Plebe!" she commanded. "Come out now."

I stood and brushed off my clothes. It was two against one so running was my best option. But I needed a moment for the blood to circulate back to my feet.

Becky's eyes narrowed. "You," she hissed. With the black eyeliner and fierce expression, she resembled an evil witch from a Disney movie. "You think this is funny, Jamison?"

Spiky smirked, clearly enjoying the moment.

I wiggled my toes. My feet were awake, and ready. "Hilarious," I called before turning and sprinting away. If I could get with the other Joes, Becky wouldn't dare hurt me.

"Let her go," I heard Spiky say. "She's just jealous. No amount of makeup could make that face pretty."

CHAPTER
TWENTY-ONE

AFTER RUNNING A LOOP AROUND the edge of the buildings, I felt confident Becky wasn't coming after me and snuck into the locker room to change. Skipping lunch, I met the other Baby Joes in the computer lab for our afternoon training. No one seemed to have noticed that I had missed the debrief, except for Sakura who gave me a thumbs up.

"You too?" I asked.

"Piece of cake," Sakura said, and we fist-bumped. "I could have been out there for hours, and they wouldn't have found me. Next year, we'll team up together and hunt down all the Babies."

"Absolutely." I was pleased that Sakura thought I would be a worthy partner.

Spiky flashed me a dirty look. She likely wouldn't retaliate, as that could put her Campia at risk. Becky certainly would though and I would need to watch my back even more.

When we woke up the computers, the dancing pig appeared, swigging lemonade and puffing away at his cigarette. The Geekit tutor let out a strangled curse, and the rest of us cracked up. While an amused Theo lectured us for being unprofessional, the tutor rebooted the system and pulled up our training.

At IA time, I hurried to the meadow where Gabi and Charles were waiting, yoga mats spread at their feet. I jumped onto the center of a mat and held my arms up like I was holding a bow and about to release an arrow. "It's warrior time."

Gabi raised an eyebrow. "You've never done yoga in your life, have you?"

I tried to raise one eyebrow back and failed. "And you have?"

"Maybe," Gabi said, switching eyebrows. "Maybe not."

"I'm up for it. Rangers practice yoga. It helps with focus, flexibility, and stress management."

"That's what Coach says too," Charles said. His weight was crushing the thin rubber mat into the grass. He wrinkled his nose. "But don't you sort of have to know what you're doing?"

"How hard can it be?" I put my hands on the mat and stuck my butt in the air. "Downward dog?"

"Hey, that's pretty good," Charles said. "Now can you lift your knee to the side?"

I bent my knee and lifted it.

"Peeing dog!" Charles exclaimed. He and Gabi let out matching belly laughs. I was trying to think of a sarcastic reply when Charles looked past me, his face lighting up.

"Hey man," he loped across the field to meet Hayden who was carrying a mat, a small cooler, and a speaker. "Even tough guys do yoga, right?"

"Absolutely," Hayden grinned. "You've got your inhaler, I hope?"

Charles patted his pocket. "Right here. Hey, are you any good?

I'm not sure we," he gestured toward us, "quite know what we're doing."

"He's teaching us," Gabi informed Charles.

Hayden held out his hand to Gabi. She took it and held it as they studied each other. Then they both smiled.

"How's Emma Claire?" Hayden asked me.

"Good. Samantha got me a message that the surgery went well and they're headed back home."

"Great news." Hayden set the speaker down, pushed a button, and classical music started playing. Rolling out his mat, he sat cross-legged and had us face him. "Welcome to the IA for those with their sanity still intact?"

"Swimming in the lake, the rope swing, and cookie decorating were good distractors," Gabi said.

"Plan worked then," Hayden said, winking at me. I had urged him to arrange this session so we could compare notes. "Take two cleansing breaths."

"What about Eric?" Charles asked. He took a loud, slurpy breath and huffed it out.

"He's doing some robot-building thing," I said.

Hayden moved to his hands and knees. "Curve your back up like a cat, then relax it down and stretch."

I copied Hayden. "I've got to tell you guys about this weird dream I had," I said, describing the kitchen scene. "What if it was a memory? It makes no sense that my parents wouldn't have told me."

"I'm not saying it's a memory, but it would make sense," Gabi said. "Your mom felt responsible for you being premature. She had an infection she didn't get treated. I'm guessing she can't ever admit her mistakes, so she pretends it never happened."

"Let's walk our hands out in front of us and lift our bums," Hayden said. He looked at me. "That seem right?"

I walked my hands out, feeling the usual frustration that accompanied thoughts of DJ. "Maybe. True that she will never admit she did anything wrong."

"What about your dad?" Charles asked, his voice muffled from being bent in half. "Wouldn't he have told you?"

My snort felt like a sneeze. I had more loving feelings toward Dad, but our relationship was also complicated. "No way without my mom's permission. Plus, my dad is obsessed with perfection too. Being premature means being not perfect."

"Perfection is not attainable," Gabi said. "You're amazing and they are missing out on it."

A lump formed in my throat. Nobody had ever stood up for me regarding my parents before. Regarding anything before. I smiled at Gabi and wondered if her family appreciated her. I doubted it.

Charles coughed. He pulled out his inhaler and took a puff. "Why does everyone say yoga is so relaxing?"

"How about a lemonade?" Hayden unzipped the cooler, pulled out a bottle and handed it to Charles.

Gabi also accepted a lemonade. "Hey, look," she tilted it to show me. "It's the dancing pig."

The bottle's label read *Paxton's Pub* and had the grinning chubby pig in ballet slippers.

"We just saw him again," I exclaimed. "He showed up on our computers this afternoon."

"What are you talking about?" Charles took a long swallow. "Man, this is good."

Gabi started telling Charles about the dancing pig virus and how angry the tutor had been. I glanced at Hayden who had gone pale. "What is it?"

Hayden ran a hand over his face. "You saw a cartoon pig on the computer. But not this exact pig."

"No, it was this exact pig. Drinking lemonade and wearing ballet slippers."

Hayden shook his head slowly. "Paxton's Pub is in London. Nick and I met up there a few times. They've got an amazing shandy, a beer, lemonade blend. They bottle it and plain lemonade, so I bought a case."

Gabi studied the label. "Your pig is popping up on HP's computers. Why?"

Hayden looked baffled. "I don't ... I can't ..."

"Could Nick have programmed the computers to do this as a joke? Before he ..." Gabi hesitated. I had already told them about Nick's awful death.

"No, Nick didn't program. His purpose was the traditional sciences."

I sat and folded my legs. "Hey, let's at least look like we're doing yoga. Just in case."

"Did Nick tell you what he was working on?" Gabi placed her hands, palms up, in her lap.

Hayden frowned. "He did talk about his research a bit. I wish I had paid attention. Pretty sure it was something about genetics. Unfortunately, I didn't ask good questions or listen that hard. Nick did seem ..." He rubbed at the scar on his chin.

"Seem what?" Gabi pressed.

"I don't know, he seemed upset by something toward the end of the summer. I was so busy being a hotshot Quite that I never really bothered ..." His face fell. "I've never told anyone about Paxton's Pub, and I can't imagine Nick did either."

"Could someone from HP have been following you?" I asked. "Seen you there together?"

"I guess so, but ..." Hayden waved his hand. "Why would they want to follow us? And what sort of sick joke would this be?"

My mind flashed to Becky, figuring it would be exactly the kind of sick joke she would enjoy pulling on Hayden, especially since their fight at the swamp. And if she knew Nick had been murdered, she would want to rub it in.

"I wasn't even in the computer lab this week," Hayden added.

I snapped my fingers. "But you were supposed to be. Theo told me he traded with you because he had sprained his finger."

Hayden's eyes widened. "That's true."

"I know this is going to sound crazy," Gabi said. "But could Nick still be alive? Could it be him?"

"Impossible," Hayden said. "He died in that fire. I went to his funeral."

I examined the label and imagined Hayden and Nick drinking shandy, talking about their purposes. "Hey, this one doesn't have a cigarette."

"Cigarette?" Hayden asked, an edge to his voice.

"On the computer, it was smoking."

Hayden jumped to his feet. "Well, that's just going too far." He scooped up the cooler and speaker and stalked off.

We stared at each other.

"Let him go," Gabi said as I stood. "He'll share more when he's ready."

CHAPTER
TWENTY-TWO

ERIC AND I STOOD ON THE PATH by The Cube. I was on my morning run and had "bumped into" Eric who was there for daily data collection. In reality, I had been watching out the window at the gym and waiting for him to pass by.

"I'm so worried, and they won't let me call her. I wouldn't ask you, but ..." my voice trailed off as I pretended to fight back tears. I hoped Eric couldn't tell that my emotion was not about Emma Claire, but about deceiving him. Guilt was an unusual emotion for me. Regret—yes, I had felt that many times after getting in trouble. But regret was about getting caught, getting punished. Guilt was a horrible feeling about doing something that could hurt someone I cared about.

Gabi insisted the email was our best next step. If there was any chance Nick was alive, we needed to try to reach out to him. Even more guilt piled on because we hadn't said anything to Hayden. I told myself it was because we didn't want to make him more angry and hurt if nothing came of this.

Two Einstein tutors walked past and I nodded hello, trying to look innocent.

Eric was twisting his fingers together. Breaking rules was not something he did, even before being brainwashed. "I'll try, but I can't make any promises," he finally said, accepting the piece of paper from my hand. "I've only accessed approved internet sites so may not be able to get it through."

Gabi said Eric could evade any HP blockades. It was only a matter of whether he would help, and how to keep him from acting suspicious.

The message was supposedly for Emma Claire or balletshoesEC@ gmail.com. If Nick were indeed alive and had invaded HP's system with a dancing pig, he could hopefully spot and intercept an email referencing ballet shoes on the way out.

Dear Cookie, last I heard, your health situation was serious, and I have been very concerned. Please let me know that my fears are unfounded and that you are instead healed and healthy. What can I do to help? All my love, Lina

Eric's brow furrowed. "Cookie?"

"A nickname," I said, again hoping he wouldn't sense the lie. Hayden had told me Nick's favorite food had been cookies. He and Hayden called them biscuits, but we had decided *Biscuit* was a suspicious nickname. I reminded myself that the real Eric, my soul brother, would have wanted to find the truth. He had been the one to spark my suspicions in the first place.

He pocketed the paper. "I'll do my best."

"Thank you." I wanted to hug him but settled for a hand on his shoulder. "Let me know as soon as you hear back?"

"I will. And Lina, I'm sure she's okay, so don't worry too much."

Eric's sweetness and caring were still there, even if his curiosity was gone. I gulped down guilt, turned, and continued my run. I would never admit this to my dad, but after three weeks of being forced to run every morning, I was starting to enjoy it. Something about being up early with the sun rising and the birds chirping made me content. And I had seen great progress toward the eight-minute mile goal—my time had already improved by two minutes.

I suddenly realized that in my hurry to watch for Eric, I'd left my tracker in the locker room. Without it, my run would not be recorded, and I would have to do a repeat run during IA, plus tack on an extra mile.

I turned back. If I hurried, I could retrieve my tracker and get in the two miles. The gym's back entrance was propped open and Crystal was leaving, holding a crate full of files. She turned toward The Chalet, and I sprinted to the door—going in the back would shave precious moments off my time.

The entrance opened to a hallway lined with storage rooms that held the boats and other large training items. One of the doors was ajar and I paused to look in. Instead of gear, the large room was full of metal file cabinets. I glanced up and down the hall, knowing I couldn't pass up a quick opportunity to snoop.

The room was dusty and smelled like my grandparents' house. I walked down a row, examining the cabinet labels. Some were date ranges, like 1920–1930, and others listed historical events or names—*Versailles, Pearl Harbor,* and *The Final Solution* were ones that sounded familiar.

Hearing footsteps, I crouched behind a cabinet just as Crystal reappeared. She picked up another crate and left, pulling the door closed behind her. I remained motionless for ten seconds, then got to my feet and continued down the row.

I stopped at *Apollo 13 Mission* and pulled the drawer open. I loved the movie and had spent weeks imagining myself as an astronaut, trapped in space fighting to get back to earth. Inside were several large photo albums, the old kind like my grandparents had with sticky film over the photos. I opened one. The first page had a photo of a boy with blond hair and a friendly smile. *Jack Swigert, age 6,* was written at the top. Flipping the pages, there were photos of him as he grew, mostly at HP, running, hurdling, and even doing the ropes course. Older, in a graduation gown, then a military uniform posing in front of a sleek jet plane. Finally, grinning and wearing a puffy white astronaut suit with an American flag patch on the sleeve.

"Whoa," I breathed. Jack Swigert was an HP grad!

Get going, my brain interrupted. Forgetting my tracker meant no one would know I was in here. Still, I needed to get my tracker and finish my run immediately.

One more minute won't hurt. I walked down the aisle, looking for a drawer that could have information related to Nick or any of the unusual deaths. My brain was niggling at me, telling me that I had missed something important. I spun and walked back, pausing at *The Final Solution.* It sounded like a math equation. I pulled it open. It held albums and several large envelopes. Taped to the front of an album was a photo of a fancy, cream-colored building. Three stories high, it had rows of arched windows, balconies, and statues, and was surrounded by a grassy circular drive. *Wannsee* was written in black pen at the top. The first pages of the album had black-and-white photos of a stern-looking man wearing a military uniform with multiple pins and patches. He posed with one or several other uniformed men in each photo. In one, the group sat around a table in deep conversation. The name *Frederick Harlan* was written in a margin on the side.

I had never heard of Frederick Harlan and the photos weren't helpful. The next album had papers printed in another language. Frustrated, I closed the album and was about to shut the drawer when my brain niggled again. I grabbed one of the envelopes and pulled out a handful of items—a plastic sleeve containing a scrap of fabric; a photo of two little boys sitting on a bench next to a soldier holding a gun; a flyer of a blond boy staring into the distance with the face of a stern man with black beady eyes and a mustache hovering in the background. More words in another language.

My brain's timer sounded *Red Alert*. I still had to get to breakfast close to the time my run normally finished. I would leave the tracker in the locker, claim I forgot it, and run the extra mile of punishment this afternoon.

I crammed the contents back into the envelope, adding the Wannsee photo, and tucked it into the waistband of my shorts. If I kept my posture straight, my sweatshirt would hide the envelope until I could figure out what to do next.

After breakfast, I reported to the gym, retrieved my tracker, and snuck the envelope into my bag. Fortunately, Hayden and Theo were heading up my group's training exercise this morning.

"We're going to start learning some basic combat techniques," Theo said. "Get in a line at least an arm's length apart."

We spread out, exchanging excited smiles.

"Do we get to punch?" Sakura held up her fists.

"One step at a time," Hayden said. "First thing we're going to talk about is our stance. Who can tell me what a neutral stance is?" He surveyed us, his eyes coming back to Sakura. "What do you think?"

Sakura shrugged. "I'm guessing it's ..." She went flying forward onto the mat. Theo had come up behind and given her a hard shove.

Theo reached out a hand to pull Sakura up. "Neutral stance is what we're in most of the time. When we're going through our lives, not on alert."

"What we're going to teach you today," said Hayden, "is fighting stance. This is where you are prepared and ready to defend yourself or fight back." He gestured to Sakura. "Face me and put your left foot out in front of your right, like you're taking a step. Hold your arms up, palms facing each other."

Looking sheepish, Sakura followed his instructions.

Hayden nodded at Theo who shoved her again. She swayed but remained standing. "Nice job," Hayden said. "Okay, everyone get into fighting stance while we come around and check your positions."

I settled into fighting stance, bouncing up and down on my toes. I hoped for Hayden but got Theo. "What happened this morning?" he asked. "Slept in?"

I groaned. "No, I forgot my tracker."

"You know you'll have to make it up later today. Plus some."

"I know," I forced a heavy sigh.

Theo and Hayden came back to the front and faced each other. "Next is the palm strike," Hayden said. "Starting from fighting stance, you extend one arm directly forward, leading slightly with the heel of your palm." He demonstrated, the heel of his hand touching Theo's cheek.

"Why aren't you using your fist?" Ryan asked.

I half-listened as Theo explained the relative safety and effectiveness of open hand versus fist striking. Now was my only chance to talk to Hayden today since I would be spending IA time running and dinner would be too risky.

I alternated thrusting with my palms and quickly lost patience. Endless repetition was awful—I could never figure out how Emma

Claire could stand practicing ballet pliés over and over.

Finally, Hayden was in front of me. "How's it going?"

"I still need help," I said, striking out with my left hand. My pinky hit the pad and bent back. I yelped.

"Pay attention," Hayden chided. "Your palm should be facing forward. Lead with the heel."

I tried again, this time striking the pad with the heel of my hand.

"Better. Next time push against the ball of your foot and straighten your back leg a little. So, having nerves about your solo tomorrow?"

Why was everyone so focused on the solo? The other Baby Joes were obsessed with the details—where would we be dropped off, how hard would it be to find our way back, what if we got hungry?

The solo was the last thing on my mind. "Have you heard of Wannsee?" I struck out with my right hand, feeling off-balance.

Hayden's brow furrowed. "Don't overdo it. You don't want your weight to get too far forward. Watch me."

He moved next to me. "Follow how I'm moving my body." He began reaching his right palm forward. "Of course, I know about Wannsee. Why?"

I copied his actions. "Because I got into a storage room and found—"

"Nice job everyone," Theo clapped. "We're going to move onto closed fist punches." Before Hayden could step away, I let out a low hiss then directed my eyes toward my gym bag resting along the wall with the others—dark purple with 42 in white lettering.

I wasn't sure if Hayden had seen, but when he got back to Theo, he murmured something and walked away.

Theo chuckled. "Hayden's got to visit the, what do they call it in England, the loo?"

"Enjoy the loo," a Plebe called.

Hayden raised his middle finger, and everyone laughed.

Theo rubbed his hands together. "Until he gets back, I need a volunteer. Who's brave?"

"I'll do it," I exclaimed, doing a kick followed by an awkward shimmy toward Theo. The others burst out laughing, which had the desired effect of drawing their attention away from Hayden.

Theo shook his head. "Okay, Lina, go ahead and stand in front of me." I got into position, glancing toward the wall. My bag was gone.

"Now get ready for a palm strike, but this time make fists," he said.

I bent my elbows and curled my hands into fists. My mouth felt dry, and I wished I had a stick of gum.

"Okay, punch me."

I hesitated.

"Come on," Theo waggled his fingers. "Throw your best punch."

I took a step forward and thrust my fist toward Theo's cheek.

Theo rotated his bent arm outward, diverting my fist, while open palm striking with his other hand. He lightly bumped my chin and grinned. "Gotcha."

The other Joes clapped. We repeated the actions, this time in slow motion so we could follow his movements.

Out of the corner of my eye, I saw Hayden exit the locker room and drop my bag. Nerves flooded my gut. Could he make sense of what I had found?

"Okay, everyone make fists," Theo instructed. "Your thumb needs to be on the outside and below your knuckles."

Hayden's expression was unreadable, but his jaw was tight. He went down the line, inspecting our fists. When he got to me, he turned my fists over and pushed my thumbs away from the knuckles. He stepped away and nodded. "Show me your punch."

I got in fighting stance, focused on tucking my thumbs and punched.

"Not bad. Now this time, I want you to tuck your face into your shoulder a bit to protect it from a counterpunch." He came behind me. "Do it again."

As I punched, Hayden leaned closer and murmured, "We need to talk tonight. Let the others know."

CHAPTER
TWENTY-THREE

BRITT WAS HOVERING at The Chalet's entrance as Gabi, Eric, and I walked in for dinner. "OMG, I need to talk to you," she hissed, pulling me into an alcove. "You are never going to believe what just happened."

"Are you okay?" I asked, startled by her intensity, and the fact that no other Angels were in sight. "Go ahead guys," I told my friends.

Britt glanced around. "I was in the dance studio. Madame Estelle says I need to work on my pirouette. So, I was practicing, you know, turning and turning. When I stopped, Matthew was there. We started talking and he was so funny and smart."

"Girls, you need to get going," a Tore scolded as she walked by. "Talk at the table."

"Sorry." Britt took a few steps then stopped once the Tore was gone. "Anyway, we talked and talked, he's so sweet, and then he kissed me!"

"He kissed you?"

"Shh ..." Britt nudged me. "I've been dying to tell, and I knew you could keep a secret. Matthew said the relationship rules here are relaxed, but we have to be discreet because of who he is."

My head was spinning. I was flattered that Brittany had chosen me to confide in—I had never been included in any dating drama before. "Is it okay that he's on the Council? And older?" I was trying not to sound judgy.

Britt flipped her hair. "Barely three years older. Not a big deal. Someday that boy's going to be something big, like a CEO, or a senator. And I can be right there by his side. We'll make a power couple."

"Britt, come eat," an Angel waved at her.

"Coming." Britt pressed a finger to her lips, waited until I nodded agreement, then flitted toward her friends.

I watched her go, unsure how to feel. As gorgeous and charming as Matthew was, it didn't seem smart to get involved with him. He was on the Council, helping run the academy and starting college in the fall. Or was I just jealous that Brittany could attract a boy like Matthew? They would make a great power couple, and who was I to judge?

My friends were debating sports when I sat down.

"Lina, who is the best quarterback ever?" Charles asked. "I say no doubt it's Tom Brady, but these two," he waved a fork at Gabi and Eric, "they've got all sorts of crazy ideas."

"It's quite simple if you look at it statistically," Eric said. "Peyton Manning has more All-Pro seasons and has been NFL MVP five times. More than Brady."

"But Johnny Unitas completely revolutionized the game," Gabi insisted. "His ability to pass and score touchdowns was head and shoulders above any of his competition. You have to consider the historical context."

They looked expectantly at me as I scooped up a mound of mashed potatoes. "Joe Montana. My dad has an autographed framed photo of him. So, he must be really good, right?"

Charles groaned. "You're an athlete, don't you follow football?"

"I'm not—" I stopped.

"Actions defines identity," Eric said, tipping his head at me.

I considered his words, feeling a sense of pride bloom in my chest—I had spent the morning running and then learning to fight. Maybe I *was* a true athlete now.

Gabi stared at Eric. "Where did you hear that?"

Eric shrugged. "I don't know. It just came to me."

"Huh," Gabi said. "I like it. Say it one more time?"

"Actions defines identity," Eric repeated.

"I've never followed football," I said to Charles. "But I'll start once you're playing."

A loud clap. Hayden was standing on one of the chairs. "The compost bins were not properly secured and got knocked over. I need some Plebes to go clean them up." As his gaze swept the room, we all looked down at our plates.

Not to be left out of a scolding, Becky stood. "Who used those bins last?"

I had joined the IA planting group at the end, and we had thrown weeds into the bins, but we had closed the lids and latched them.

"Gardening gang," Spiky's sarcastic voice rang out.

"Raise your hand if you were in IA planting," Hayden said.

I raised my hand, along with Gabi and the others.

Hayden pointed to our table. "This group. Clean it up before animals get into it."

"Hey, I was baking today," Charles protested. "Us bakers stayed in the kitchen."

"And we're still—" Gabi started to protest, but my hard look stopped her.

Eric's eyes were wide, as he frantically chewed. He hated being yelled at, or even mildly scolded.

"You should have thought about that before you got lazy," Hayden said. To Charles, "Those containers are heavy, so we may need your muscle. Come on, let's move."

"The Council members will be arriving tomorrow for their summer meeting," Becky added. " Behavior and performance need to be perfect."

"Let's go guys." I shoved the rest of my dinner roll in my pocket and picked up my tray.

Outside, Hayden turned and eyed us, his gaze settling on Eric. "What's your name, Plebe?"

"Eric Valentini," Eric gulped.

"Go to the kitchen and get a box of compost bags. The large ones. Ask Dominique how she wants the compost sorted and returned to the containers."

Eric nodded. "Compost bags, Dominique," he repeated, focusing on the ground as he walked away.

"We've got to do something about him," Hayden said.

"He's harmless," I said, unable to imagine rejecting Eric. He had faced so much of it in his life.

"Nobody's harmless." Hayden led us down the path to the parking lot where the recycling and compost bins were normally lined up in a neat row. One of the compost bins was tipped over, its contents spilling across the cement.

He directed us behind the bins, pulled out my envelope and tipped it, letting the contents slide out. "Most of this is in German, which fortunately I am fairly fluent in. I can't believe what's in here."

He pointed to the photo I had first seen—the beautiful building with the circular drive. "This is the Wannsee Villa outside of Munich, Germany."

Gabi inhaled a sharp breath.

Hayden looked at her. "You know about Wannsee?"

Gabi nodded, her fingers moving to her pendant. "The Wannsee Conference was a meeting of Hitler's top Nazi leaders. Where they came up with the plan to annihilate the entire Jewish population of Europe."

I felt like I had been punched. Aunt Lulu had converted to Judaism when she married Uncle Aaron. My cousins were Jewish, and I had once overheard my aunt saying that an entire side of Uncle Aaron's family had been murdered during the Holocaust. "The Final Solution," I breathed. That's why it had sounded so familiar.

Charles touched the photo. "Looks like a fancy hotel. Hard to believe something so evil happened there."

Hayden spread out the rest of the contents. There were four photos of the man from the album, posing with other men in military uniforms.

"Are those guys Nazis?" Charles asked.

Gabi pointed at one of them. "That's Reinhard Heydrich. He created the Nazi SS and organized the Wannsee meeting."

My dinner was threatening to come back up. The man had a ferret face and looked like a math teacher, not a murderer of millions. "And Frederick Harlan?" I managed. "He's an HP'er who ended up being one of Hitler's guys?"

"Frederick Harlan?" Gabi's head whipped toward me. "He's the man in these photos?"

"There's a whole album about him in the drawer where I found this."

Gabi went pale. Hayden picked up a sheet of paper with Harlan's name at the top. "This is his bio. He was born in the US to an American industrialist and German mother. At thirteen, he was sent to boarding school in Germany. His father was well respected there for his business success and Herr Harlan believed in German discipline and academic rigor for his son."

"Did Harlan come to HP?" Charles asked.

Hayden nodded. "Spent all three summers here. When he graduated from gymnasium, he stayed in Germany and enrolled at university. Between his German family and his father's business associates, he was quickly connected with the Nazi Party."

"What was his purpose at HP?" I asked. "Military?"

"Communication and media." Hayden pointed to the poster of the blond boy with the man I now knew was Adolf Hitler in the background. How had I not recognized those beady eyes and black brush mustache? "Youth Serves the Führer," Hayden translated. "All ten-year-olds into the Hitler Youth."

I shuddered, thinking of Emma Claire and how she still loved to chase butterflies and have tea parties with her dolls.

"Hitler was a brilliant manipulator," Gabi said. "He appealed to people's emotions and their love for their children."

There was the sound of footsteps. Hayden jumped up to intercept Eric who was hurrying toward us carrying a cardboard box. "I couldn't find Dominique," he panted. "But the man in the kitchen said you don't need to sort anything. Just throw it all in and lock it up." He handed Hayden the box and tried to squeeze past him.

"Nice work," Hayden stepped to block Eric. "Now return to the dining hall and let Becky know the situation is handled. We will have the compost re-bagged and locked up in five minutes."

Eric looked past Hayden to me. "Okay, but Lina, um, can I talk to you?"

I jumped up. "How about after we're done? We can—" Eric's expression stopped me.

I walked over to him. "What's up?"

"I know you've been really worried," he whispered. "So, I went by the computer lab to check if Emma Claire had answered."

I stared at him. None of us had thought we'd get a response so quickly, if ever.

He pressed a square of paper into my hand. "It sounds like she's doing well."

My heart melted at his worried expression and trembling hands. Eric hated breaking rules but had done so twice for me. And I had done nothing but lie to him.

"Thank you." I tried to show him through my eyes how much his help meant.

"Get going," Hayden said. "You can meet us for dessert."

Eric's slow footsteps retreated. Hayden watched him, lips pressed together.

"Don't worry," Gabi told me. "I've got a plan for Soul Brother."

I turned, hopeful. "You do?"

Gabi tapped a finger against her chin like a mini-Sherlock Holmes. "I need a list of all the brainwash sayings. Hayden can you—"

Hayden ignored her and grabbed the paper out of my hand. "What is this?"

CHAPTER
TWENTY-FOUR

GABI AND I EXCHANGED A LOOK as Hayden unfolded the paper and frowned. "Dear Sis, I am feeling much better, thanks. Let's go to our favorite sweet shop when you get home. Love, Cookie."

He raised an eyebrow at me.

"Is that from Nick?" Charles exclaimed. "The email worked?"

Hayden's look of puzzlement morphed into anger and disbelief. It was the look Ricky would give Lucy right before he bellowed, "Lucy, you've got some 'splaining to do!"

Gabi and I fell over ourselves 'splaining the email we had sent.

When we were done, Hayden looked stunned. "Sweet shop," he murmured, rereading the email. His eyes filled with tears. "Maybe he could be alive. I don't know how but ..."

He shook his head hard twice, crumpled the paper, and shoved it in his pocket. "I'll think on this later. We need to focus on Harlan now." He righted the compost bin while I pulled out a bio bag and shook it open.

"So, what did this guy Harlan do?" Charles began picking up scraps of food and tossing them into the bag.

"Hitler was brilliant in using propaganda to sway the German people," Hayden said. "He didn't care if what he said was true."

Charles and I flashed each other confused looks.

"Propaganda? You know, like advertising. It's powerful images and messages to convince people of a certain view. No facts needed."

Gabi tossed in an apple core. "Hitler said in *Mein Kampf* that all propaganda must have its levels adjusted to the most limited intelligence."

"Keep the message simple," Hayden said. "Repeat it over and over and appeal to people's emotions, not their brains." He gestured to the poster. "This has a written message but the imagery stirs powerful emotions like pride, belonging, security."

"When he gave speeches," Gabi said, "the crowds went crazy. He would spend hours practicing his body language, intonation, and words."

Hayden tied the top of the bag. "And Harlan helped him. His bio says he was trained at HP in persuasive communication by the best. Tutors who had helped elect senators and presidents."

I picked up a half-eaten pear, crushing the fruit in my fingers. I didn't know whether I wanted to scream or cry, but I felt intense anger toward Harlan's tutors who had taught him the skills to convince the Germans to hate and murder.

Glancing at me, Hayden added, "HP trainees ended up on the Allies' side of the war as well. No doubt they played a key role in defeating Hitler. Look at this." He picked up a cloth patch and held it out. It was black with the word *Edelweisspiraten* embroidered across the bottom. In the center was a white flower dotted with yellow buds. "This is the edelweiss flower."

"Like in *The Sound of Music*?" Emma Claire loved that movie and knew all the songs.

"Exactly. The Edelweisspiraten, or Edelweiss Pirates, was a group of young people who defied Hitler. The flower was their symbol."

"Maybe an HP grad helped form that pirate group," Charles said. He pulled out his inhaler. "So, we know that an HP'er became a Nazi leader ..." He put the inhaler close to his mouth, pressed the button, and took a breath. We all waited while he held it for a moment then exhaled.

"And we know that HP develops trainees' purposes. But that doesn't determine if they're going to end up using them for good."

The Apollo 13 drawer celebrated the astronaut Jack Swigert. HP had produced plenty of heroes too. I tossed the pear in the bin and wiped my hands on my shorts. "There were lots of drawers in that room. They must want to include the good and the bad so the museum will have accuracy. I guess there's nothing wrong with that."

Hayden gave Gabi a searching look and she nodded. "There's more to this story." She picked up the plastic sleeve with the fabric star inside. "In 1941, on Heydrich's recommendation, the Nazis started making Jews wear yellow stars. It was one of the steps in making them seem different and inhuman." A tear spilled over her eyelid and ran down her cheek. "One step in the process that ended up with six million deaths."

"Frederick Harlan was a key player," Hayden added. "HP trained him and sent him into the world to commit genocide."

I didn't want to think any more of families being sent to concentration camps. "So, what is your point? Do you think HP is responsible for what their trainees go on to do or not?" I knelt and began sweeping the contents back into the envelope. "Why are we even talking about this anyway? What does it matter if they created a Nazi a zillion years ago? We need to know what's going on right now. And thinking about yellow stars and murders is not ..." I pressed the back of my hand to my mouth.

"You're right," Gabi said. "Of course, HP couldn't have known what Harlan would go on to become. And if we dug around, we would find grads who have done terrible things and grads who have done great ones. That isn't HP's fault." She hesitated. "But it is relevant now."

Hayden nodded. "The quote going above the new library's entrance—*The method to transform a nation and the world is through the spirit and will of its children*—is by Frederick Harlan. So, even if HP was naive when they trained Harlan, they are making the deliberate choice to celebrate him now."

There was the sound of footsteps and scuffling.

"That hurts me," a voice squeaked.

Crystal, Becky, and Eric appeared, Becky gripping Eric's arm.

"Well, what do we have here?" Crystal said. "What are you up to?"

"We're cleaning up the compost," Gabi said. "Just like we were told to do."

"Let him go," I said, starting toward Becky. Charles grabbed the back of my shirt, gripping it tightly.

Becky roughly released Eric and he stumbled.

"Who instructed you to be out here?" Crystal demanded.

"Hayden did," I said. "He ..." I looked behind me. Hayden had disappeared, along with the envelope.

"He made us miss dinner," Charles said. "Didn't even stay to help."

"You've been out here too long," Becky said. "You're either the biggest morons ever, or you're up to something." She eyed Eric. "Something that involves the computer lab, perhaps?"

Eric cringed.

"A trainee saw you sneak into the lab and print out something," Crystal said. "Tell us right now what you were doing."

Eric's lower lip trembled, but he remained silent.

"Let me handle this," Becky said. "Just give me five minutes."

"It was me," I blurted. "I begged Eric to send an email to my sister, just to make sure she was okay." I started rambling about Emma Claire's injury and possible brain damage.

"Enough," Crystal snapped. She glared at Eric. "Young man, is this true?"

He nodded, wringing his hands together.

"We are going to the lab right now and you will show me those emails." Her cold eyes met mine. "If you are lying, there will be severe consequences. Either way, there will be disciplinary action taken for breaking the rules. The Council comes tomorrow, and I won't tolerate acting up."

Becky grabbed Eric's arm and began pulling him up the path.

I tried to follow, but Charles held tight. "Let them go," he hissed. "We got off easy."

"But Eric ..." I felt helpless and terrified for him.

"He'll show them the emails and it will be okay," Gabi said. "There is nothing suspicious in them."

I didn't trust Becky. I waited until Charles released me and darted up the path. I made it about fifty feet before Hayden stepped out from the trees. "You need to get back to your room and prep for your solo," he said. "I will make sure that Eric is safe."

"You promise?"

"Yes, I promise. I'm going after them right now." I watched him jog up the path, waiting until he had entered the back door of The Chalet.

CHAPTER
TWENTY-FIVE

"THIS IS LAME," SAKURA SAID as our van bumped along the road.
"We should be doing at least two nights."

The others voiced their agreement, but I didn't join in. I stared out
the window, still stunned by the awful information we had uncovered.
HP had trained a Nazi leader and was putting a quote by this monster
above the library.

"You'll get your chance next summer," Theo said from the front
passenger seat. The Equites were currently out on a four-day solo. The
Senatores would return to HP in January to spend four days braving
the Rockies' snow and subzero temperatures.

This solo was a waste of time. It was keeping me from helping my
friends dig up more information—unbearably frustrating because
there was so much to figure out. Who had chosen Harlan's quote?
Who else in leadership or the Council knew about it? What were
HP's current connections with Nazis, or other hate groups?

I tried to remain calm. Hayden had sworn he would keep Eric safe,
and the solo was not even twenty-four hours. How much could be

done in that time? I shifted my attention to the items in my pack—a packet of food, a full water bottle, a sleeve of water purification tablets, a compass, a map, and a windbreaker. I wouldn't need the compass and map as I had an innate sense of direction, but it might be good to try them out for practice.

The van stopped and Theo consulted his clipboard. "Lina, this is you." He got out and opened the back door, gesturing with a flourish. I stepped out and he clapped me on the shoulder. "You may not see me, but I'm nearby. Remember the basics and you'll be fine."

I nodded. I couldn't imagine needing help, but I appreciated how supportive he was. Thank goodness I hadn't been placed in Becky's group. She would have dumped me at the top of a mountain where the air was so thin that trees couldn't grow.

The van pulled away and I stood still, taking deep breaths of the piney air. Since I was stuck out here, I might as well enjoy it. The sky was deep blue, with tufts of cottony clouds. A thicket of pines came right up to the road. My mental map told me that HP was approximately four miles away. We were required to stay at our sites until sunrise. Then, if it took me forty-five minutes to hike each mile, I could be back at HP by lunchtime.

The first thing we had been instructed to do was find a water source. The river was a few hundred yards downhill. My water bottle would be enough until the morning when I could fill up and use the purification tablets. Food was not a problem as the packet was enough for an overnight. Hayden had assured me that it was tightly sealed and would not attract bears.

The next priority was shelter. The mountains grew cool at night and I would need a way to stay warm. I stepped into the trees. The ground was thick with dead branches and pine needles. Birds called to each other above and tiny animals skittered in the undergrowth. I spotted a group of dead pines tipped over to one side. Their roots had been pulled out of the ground and were gnarled and exposed, like a giant claw. The area underneath was the perfect size for a cozy shelter.

I gathered dead branches and laid them across the roots in a lattice shape, leaving a small opening next to the trunk. When the claw was covered, I used my windbreaker to scoop up dead pine needles and grass and spread them over the branches, filling in the gaps. I stepped back to admire the messy lump—not pretty but perfect.

The sound of crunching pine needles came from the direction of the road. Theo back to check on me? A mountain lion? I pulled my pocketknife from my boot and flipped out the blade.

The crunching grew louder. A tall boy stepped into view and froze, eyeing me and the knife. "I'm not going to hurt you," he said quickly.

His accent was foreign. Sunlight filtered through the trees, highlighting pale pink skin and blond curls. A pasty Scot?

"Nick?" I said.

The boy tipped his head and walked toward me. "Catalina Jamison, a pleasure to meet you."

I folded up the knife and returned it to my boot. Shaking Nick's hand felt surreal, like we were actors in a play and the director was about to yell *cut*.

"I obviously got your email," he said.

"How did you? What did you ...?" I could barely form words.

He smiled. "I knew you were a Plebe, as we hadn't met last summer. Since you were tied into Hayden, I assumed you were a Baby Joe, meaning you would be on your solo tonight. Your tracker proved me right." He gestured toward my wrist. "Handy things they are. You'd think HP would block their data better but they're just too damn arrogant."

I stared dumbly at him.

He rubbed his hands together. "So, Hayden got Paxton? I thought the ciggie was a nice touch."

"Hayden thinks you are dead."

Nick's smile faded. He held out his arms, which had fleshy red scars running up them. "I did damn near die." He turned his head to show me a scar covering the left side of his neck, his ear twisted like a melted candle. "The explosion and smoke almost did me in, but I managed to crawl to a stairwell. That's where the medics found me."

I waited, a thousand questions hovering between us.

"Listen, we don't have much time. I can't risk being seen." Nick ran a hand through his curls. "Quick story is that a faction in HP wanted me dead. I was getting too close to their secrets. They think they succeeded, and it needs to stay that way."

"But—" I started.

Nick held up a hand. "There is a second faction who shared my suspicions. They whisked me away from the hospital, and then fixed things to look like I had died. I've been in hiding since."

"But Hayden? Couldn't you have told him?"

Nick took in my scowl. "I trust Hayden," he said evenly. "But I needed him to stay safe. I couldn't risk contacting him or increasing his suspicions."

"Then why did you send the dancing pig? That's not playing it safe. And why contact him at all? Why not wait until summer is over?"

Nick steepled his fingers under his chin. "Things are accelerating faster than expected. We need to shut that group down, as soon as possible. And we need proof to do it. Hayden is the only one I trust on the inside."

"Hayden isn't here. I am."

"Yes," Nick nodded solemnly. "A bit of a risk coming here today, isn't it? That should demonstrate how desperate we are."

We studied each other for a long moment.

"What do you need?" I asked.

"We need Hayden to gather proof to justify our team raiding HP. He will be with the Council members this week and can listen in. He should report any intel to General Cole, a Council member on our team. But listen," Nick gave me a hard look. "This is important. Hayden absolutely cannot take any action based on what he learns. It's too dangerous. We will do that once we get the proof."

"Proof about what? What kind of information do you need?"

"Anything related to HP's genetics program, the recruitment process, or their lab testing."

"You need to be more specific."

Nick shook his head.

I crossed my arms over my chest. "If I'm with the enemy, you're already screwed."

"It's not that," he sighed. "The more information I give, the more it puts you and Hayden in danger. And I don't want him trying anything rash. His role is just to gather intel."

"Well, I'm not putting Hayden in danger at all if you won't tell me why."

We eyed each other again. I reminded myself that Nick was an Einstein. He had almost died, which must have toughened him up. But at heart, he was a scientist, not a Joe. He would cave.

"Does this have anything to do with the subliminal brainwashing?" I prompted.

He blinked. "Oh, that. Definitely not. That technology is old—I think they've been using it since the seventies. Rudimentary, but works well for keeping Plebes in line at the beginning."

"The dog chips then?"

His lips twitched. "Dog chips, nicely put. You've figured that out then, have you?"

I pressed my hand to my stomach. "These really are dog chips? We *are* being tracked?"

Nick nodded. "HP has had tabs on all of us since we were born. They bide their time until we reach the age to summon us to the academy."

More crunching sounds. Nick and I spun toward the trees. When the noises grew louder, he said quickly, "Tell Hayden to visit our sweet shop. That will explain a lot." He ran toward the road and ducked behind a large tree.

I stepped into the shade of a tree as two figures appeared.

"She's right around here," Becky said. "She's tracking within ten square feet."

My body tensed. That wrist tracker had helped Nick find me but had also led Becky and Spiky here. They weren't even in my cohort! Becky was supervising her own group of Baby Joes.

"We know you're here," Becky called. "Come out before we get really ticked off."

I glanced toward Nick's hiding spot. The girls couldn't see him from where they stood now.

"Look at this," Spiky exclaimed picking up my pack.

I bent and got my knife.

"I don't know about you, Becks, but I could use an afternoon snack." Spiky dug in my pack.

"Give me her water," Becky said. "I'm parched."

Anger was building deep in my chest. I'd had enough of these two and their bullying. Becky had never apologized for sending me into the swamp. And Spiky was just a miniature Becky. I needed to get rid of them so I could finish up with Nick.

"This is supposed to be a solo," I stepped forward. "Do you need a vocab lesson?"

Becky turned, eyes flashing. Her blond frizz puffed out like cotton candy around her head. "You know what, Jamison? I'm sick of your lousy attitude. You should have been sent home day one, but somehow you managed to sweet-talk Hayden and the others into thinking you were special."

"I've earned my right to be here, just like you. Get over it."

Spiky gestured to my shelter. "That's totally lame. I built a lean-to with a downwind entrance and a fire pit. I even caught a squirrel for dinner."

We weren't supposed to build fires or hunt wildlife, but Spiky just had to show off. "It's not part of this challenge," I said.

"It's not part of this challenge," Spiky mimicked. "You're such a whiner. What would your Geekit boyfriend think right now?"

It was one thing to taunt me, but Eric was off-limits. "What do you want, Barbie doll?" I strode toward her. "Why do I make you feel so threatened? Is it because I know you're a rich bitch fraud?"

Spiky's face flushed.

Becky held up a hand. "Time to pay your dues." She reached behind her and pulled a black baton from her waistband.

Pressing the knife's lever to release the blade, I got into fighting stance. We hadn't learned how to use weapons yet but I would try my best.

Spiky's black-smudged eyes widened and she started digging in her pocket.

Like a snake striking, Becky shot out her foot and kicked the knife out of my hand. In the same motion, she brought the baton around and slammed it into my thigh.

The pain was searing and dropped me to the ground. Becky kicked me in the stomach. "You think you're anything?" she yelled. "You are nothing!"

I curled into a ball, the pain rolling through me in waves. I thought about Nick hiding in the trees and hoped he would stay put.

"Becky," Spiky said, her voice sounding far away.

Becky grabbed my ponytail, jerked my head back, and slapped me.

The slap hardly registered due to the pain in my leg and gut. I tried to get my good leg under me.

"Becky," Spiky said again. "You need to—"

"Shut up, Barbie," Becky's spit sprayed my face. "Unless you want a piece of it, stay back."

"No, I'm serious," Spiky yelled. "Look."

Becky paused, her gaze following Spiky's pointing finger.

I thrust myself up on my good leg and somehow began to run, ignoring the crushing pain in my thigh. I heard the girls yelling behind me and crashing through the trees. I drew into myself and focused only on moving my legs, on pumping my arms, on my lungs inhaling deep breaths to fuel my blood with oxygen.

When I knew I was ahead of them, I allowed my other senses to return. The first thing I noticed was the smell of smoke. A plume of it rose into the sky below us. That must have been what Spiky was pointing at. The arrogant Plebe had been so eager to help Becky that she had broken the first rule of fires and left hers unattended.

If the fire wasn't put out now, it could quickly spread out of control. I ran toward the smoke and came out at the edge of the river. As we had been taught, Spiky had put a circle of rocks around the fire and cleared debris from nearby. But she had built it close to a dead pine and had not considered what could happen if the wind sent sparks flying.

That tree had fire licking up its base and lowest branches. A few trees next to it also had branches that were burning. I stared, horrified. There was nothing we could do without materials or supplies to fight the fire. We were on the banks of a river but had nothing more than water bottles.

Becky burst out of the trees. "Barbie," she screamed. "You idiot, how could you have let this happen!"

"I thought it was out," Spiky said. "I didn't think—"

"Becky, get on your radio and call a Code Red," I yelled. "We have to—"

"Shut up," Becky said, eyes wild, waving her baton. "We can't let them know how this happened."

With a crackle, a cluster of brush caught fire.

"We need to get help," I insisted. "This fire is going to spread. It could burn the entire—"

Becky swung her arm. The baton cracked hard into my head, and everything went dark.

CHAPTER
TWENTY-SIX

I WAS BACK WITH DOCTOR VOLKOV, but this time my whole body was immersed in the tank of freezing water. He pushed a button, and the tank began spinning and churning. I was tumbling, rolling, banging against the hard walls. I needed to take a breath. Through the glass, I saw his hard eyes, his mouth twisted in a sneer. His features narrowed into the evil face of Frederick Harlan.

A bright light and gust of warmth hit my face. I took one gasping breath of air before I was being tumbled again. At least I now realized where I was—in the middle of a raging river.

My shoulder banged against a rock. If the cold didn't kill me, the boulders would. I struggled to maneuver so my feet were facing downstream, and my head was above the surface. My limbs were numb and my chest felt like it was being compressed in a block of ice.

I tried to stroke toward shore, but the water sucked me back to the middle. Up ahead, I spotted a boulder jutting up from the water. Stroking as hard as I could, I moved myself into its path. This decision was either going to kill or save me.

The current swept me hard into the boulder. As my feet hit the rock, I bent my knees and let the force of the water push the rest of my body up and forward. I sprang, angling toward the bank, arms outstretched. When my palms smacked into rocks, I rolled into a somersault. A jolt of pain ran up my spine and I landed on my back in the shallows.

Turning over, I dragged myself onto the bank, spluttering and shivering. After a moment, I recovered enough to assess my situation. Not great—partially frozen, alone in the woods, no water, no food. Yet, a smile played on my lips. I hadn't drowned! I had been in a freakin' river and hadn't panicked—I had kept it together and made it to shore. I couldn't wait to tell Hayden how his swim lessons had paid off. That, and that Nick was alive!

Right now, survival was priority one. I struggled into a kneeling position. I was scraped but didn't see bleeding or crooked bones. I ran my fingers over my skull. There was a painful, swollen area above my left ear.

With the sun going down, the temperature was going to drop. I unlaced my boots and pulled them and my socks off. Peeling off my clothes, I wrung them out and hung them on tree branches. Until drier, they would only suck warmth from my body.

I unstrapped my tracker and held it in my palm. If I kept it, Becky could locate me again. For all I knew, those girls were racing toward me right now. But if I got rid of it, nobody else could find me either. I couldn't be rescued.

I drew my arm back and threw the tracker into the water, watching with a little worry and a lot of pride as it got swept away. I didn't need help. I could make my way back to HP on my own.

Except ... the fire! I sniffed. A faint smell of smoke. I reluctantly pulled on my wet boots and clothes and walked up the hill until I found the perfect aspen tree—slim and branchless with dark bulging knots. I shimmied up, ignoring the rough bark scraping off more skin, until I could see up the river. It was getting dark, but I could make out the plume of black smoke.

The safest thing to do was follow the river downstream. It would take me farther away from HP but also the fire. Once the blaze was controlled, I could cut back up the slope. If I kept moving, hopefully, my clothes would dry and my body would stay warm enough.

I picked my way along the river's edge, the bright moon helping me to navigate. I kept going, even when fatigue hit, and I wanted to settle into a pile of leaves and take a nap. I continued to imagine my Ranger by my side, urging me along.

When the sun finally crested over the mountaintops, I collapsed onto a large flat rock. Thankfully, the sky was hazy but no signs of active fire. A flood of pain rolled through my entire body, starting at my bruised skull and ending at my blistered feet. Incredibly thirsty, I gazed longingly at the river. If I drank the water, I would feel better but would risk getting a horrible infection.

Special Forces are tough. You don't need water. I pushed myself to my feet and started up the hill.

I was running through pizza toppings in my head—yes to mushrooms and pepperoni, no to olives and peppers—when my body instinctively dropped to the ground. Peering through the grass, I saw a pickup truck parked next to a shed. Crawling closer, I spotted two men—one holding a walkie-talkie and the other peering inside a metal box.

"She wants to know how long," the first man said.

The second shrugged. "Maybe an hour. Whole thing crashed when the power went back on. Gotta see if we have the parts to fix it."

The first man relayed the message. He held the walkie-talkie away from his ear as angry squawks came out. "I'll let him know, ma'am," he said when the squawks stopped. "We'll get it fixed as soon as possible."

He clipped the walkie-talkie to his belt. "Don't know why they need an electric fence anyway. One of those brats gets out, where they gonna go?"

"One of those brats gets out, that's a fat lawsuit."

"Rich kids. Let's go back and check on those parts."

I could ask these men for a ride back to HP. But I needed to avoid Becky or Spiky until I knew where things stood. Plus, getting help would violate the rules of the solo and I was determined to finish properly. Once they drove off, I kept walking. After ten minutes, I came to the electric fence on HP's backside. It was ten feet tall with a spindly rope of barbed wire across the top. The men had said the fence wasn't working, but just in case, I stood sideways, put my weight on the leg farthest from the fence, reached out a fingertip and touched the wire. Nothing.

I found an area where the wire was stretched and I could climb over without touching it. Walking through the trees, I encountered another fence. This one was sturdier with a heftier coil of barbed wire rimming the top.

I walked along it, unsure about attempting this one. After a hundred feet, the fence cornered and turned toward the lake. That sparked my curiosity. Why was this fence here if it wasn't a second layer to protect all of HP? I peered through it and saw a stone, one-story building. Its brown color blended in with the trees, and if I hadn't been next to it, I might have missed it completely. It definitely wasn't on the handbook's map.

I vowed to return during one of my runs and check it out, but I needed to keep moving. As I approached the road, I heard the crunch of gravel. Once again, I dropped to the ground. More crunching as a vehicle drove past then stopped. The engine turned off. Doors opened and slammed shut.

"Stand over there," Crystal's sharp voice commanded.

"I need a chance to explain," a girl's voice, tearful and scared.

My body gave an involuntary jerk. Becky.

"Oh, you'll explain. You'll explain to Edmund Blakewell and the Council how you let one of your Plebes start a fire. How your stupidity killed our power and derailed their opening session."

"I didn't know she was doing that," Becky's voice was pleading. "As soon as I found out—"

The sound of a slap. "Get on your hands and knees, Untermensch. You left your post to invade the territory of another Senatore, abandoning your group and your duties."

"I was just checking on my friend," Becky whined. "And when that awful Plebe attacked me, I had to defend myself."

"Are you going to put up with this?" Crystal demanded.

"I've heard enough," a low male voice said. "Nobody ever did, or ever will, escape the consequences of his choices." A pause then a thwacking noise.

Becky screamed.

I lifted my chin, peering through the grass. Becky was on her hands and knees. Her shirt was off, and a rivulet of blood ran along the edge of her sports bra.

Crystal stood between Becky and the lake, her cream-colored suit and high heels out of place in nature. She resembled a hawk, ready to rip her prey to pieces.

A brown-haired man wearing khaki pants and a purple polo stood with his back to me, holding a cord in his right hand.

"I'm, I'm sorry," Becky gulped. "I did it to protect HP. I only—"
The man raised his arm and brought the cord down.

Becky screamed again. Blood flowed off her back, dripping onto the earth.

"Your actions were not about protecting Haverford Pines or serving our ultimate goal." The man's voice was calm with an edge. It sounded familiar, but I couldn't quite place it. "You let your anger overrule your intellect and that is unacceptable and dangerous. You put our mission in jeopardy."

Another snap and a wail.

I fought the urge to jump to my feet, to do something. Even Becky, who I hated, didn't deserve this abuse. Why wasn't the tough Tore doing something? Becky was trained in combat. How could she let herself be whipped without putting up any resistance?

"This is what you're going to tell the Council." The man's voice grew steely. "You went to check on a Plebe. She wasn't at her campsite and had started a fire, which was against protocol. You were about to call a Code Red but spotted her in the river."

"Yes," Crystal mused. "That girl was out of her territory. Another violation of protocol, although not surprising given her history of recklessness and stupidity."

Seriously? I had been out of my territory because Becky and Spiky were chasing me.

"You knew the girl couldn't swim," the man said. "Yet somehow she was allowed to stay on at HP." A pause while his head swiveled toward Crystal.

"If you recall," Crystal said icily. "I wanted her out from the beginning—and I was overruled."

That's why he sounded familiar—this was the man from

Blakewell's study. The one who had said I would fall into line.

"So, instead of calling the Code Red," he said. "You rushed to help her."

"Are you getting this so far?" Crystal barked.

"Yes," Becky managed. "I was trying to save her life. Because I knew she couldn't swim."

Yeah right, I thought, remembering the baton cracking against my head. Becky hadn't known about my swim lessons so was happy to let me drown for real this time.

"But it was too late. You exited the river and immediately called a Code Red."

Silence while Becky snuffled and the two waited.

"What about Barbie?" she said in a small voice. "She was there too."

The man tapped the cord against his leg. "Barbie will not report anything different."

"When they find the body, HP will take a lot of heat," Crystal said. "As soon as the Council is informed, we need to go to the police. Make it seem like we are being transparent."

The body?

The Pirates of the Caribbean boat ride at Disneyland floats through an underground world of treasures, pirates terrorizing villagers, and jaunty music. Occasionally, a scary voice booms, *'Dead men tell no tales.'* Of course—with me dead, nobody would know that Becky had purposely struck me. Nobody would know that Spiky was responsible for starting a fire and leaving it unattended. Nobody would know anything improper had happened. These three weren't preparing Becky to contradict my story, they were planning a total cover-up.

"Get her cleaned up and to the Council meeting in twenty minutes," the man said. He gave the cord to Crystal—who held it out from her body like a dead animal—and extended his hand to Becky.

Becky took it, letting out a strangled sob as he pulled her up. He kissed her on both cheeks. "I trust that you will continue to serve our mission."

Becky pressed his hand to her lips, crying and nodding. When she turned, I had to bite my lip to avoid gasping. Angry red stripes cut across the flesh on her back and blood soaked the waistband of her shorts.

The man turned and I did gasp then, pressing my face into the grass and hoping I hadn't been heard. How had I not recognized the voice? The man who had just whipped Becky was no man at all. It was Matthew! The Chosen One who would direct the Council and HP's future.

CHAPTER
TWENTY-SEVEN

TWO MUSCULAR MEN in black T-shirts and jeans stood at the gates of HP, barely glancing at me as I limped up the drive. It didn't take any acting to appear hurt and exhausted.

The physical pain in my body was nothing compared to the mental. I couldn't process what I had just seen. My charismatic Ricky Ricardo was a monster. Boys, girls, adults, we all loved Matthew! I had never heard or seen anyone disapprove of him.

Except Gabi. I recalled my friend's snide comments. Gabi could read people better than anyone and she didn't like Matthew. Why had I never paid attention to her view of him? My stomach lurched, recalling the wet thwacking sound the belt had made. Matthew had not seemed to mind inflicting pain, had even enjoyed it.

Matthew and Crystal must be part of the faction that Nick had been talking about—working with Blakewell on an important project. He hadn't had time to tell me more, so I couldn't give Hayden much information before sending him into danger.

A cluster of Senatores at the top of the drive let out loud whoops.

Theo rushed forward, his eyes wide and worried. "What happened to you? You disappeared and your tracker went down." He looked me up and down. "Where's your pack?"

I was relieved at Theo's reaction. He had not yet been fed any story so my plan to act clueless might work. Becky was in front of the Council right now telling her version—which would fit with what I was about to say. I grimaced. "It's a long story. Because of the fire, I moved to a different spot. Misplaced some of my stuff along the way."

Theo looked suspicious. "You misplaced some stuff along the way? Your essential supplies?"

"I might have accidentally fallen in the river."

"You accidentally fell in the river." Theo crossed his arms over his chest. "How exactly did that happen?"

I lifted my hair and showed him the bruise. "I don't remember. It's all fuzzy."

Theo leaned in to examine my head. "That's a nasty lump." He rested a hand on my shoulder. "Go straight to the infirmary. We'll meet up later to talk about this more."

I continued my shuffle into HP. Cheers as Ryan jogged in, grinning and waving his arms. He hand-slapped some Tores and hugged his group leader before coming up alongside me. "Wasn't that awesome? I can't wait for our longer solo next year."

I snorted. Besides his mussed hair and sunburned nose, Ryan appeared clean and well-rested. Could he not see that I looked like I had been mauled by a cheese grater?

"Did you see the fire? That was a crazy twist, but then I built this cool shelter in between a couple of big rocks ..."

I let his words wash over me as we walked past The Chalet. More mystery men stood at the entrance. Plebes, headed in for lunch, paused to congratulate us. As we passed the courtyard, the double doors opened and a group of figures wearing khaki pants and HP polos stepped onto the patio. My chest tightened but I kept moving, forcing a smile at Ryan's story about trying to snag a fish.

Out of the corner of my eye, I saw several members of the group spot me and freeze in collective surprise. After a long moment, one of them separated himself and strode toward us.

"Lina, thank goodness. Are you okay?" Matthew's voice dripped with concern. "We heard that you were missing from your site. We were about to send authorities out to search for you."

I channeled all my years of lying and pasted on my most innocent expression. "I'm fine, except ..." I touched my head and winced. "I must have gone to help put out the fire and fallen in the river."

"Dude," Ryan exclaimed. "That's insane. You fell in the river?"

"The last thing I remember was being at my shelter. Then I was on the riverbank with this huge lump."

I willed tears into my eyes—not hard due to the combination of fear and pain. "I was so scared I wouldn't make it back here. But my training kicked in and I just did it." I gazed earnestly at Matthew, blinking hard. "I am so sorry if I worried anyone."

Matthew was staring intently at me as if trying to suck the truth out of my brain.

I blinked, forcing a tear down my cheek.

"You're lucky you didn't drown," Ryan said.

"I know," I turned teary eyes to him. "But I've been working on my swimming skills, so that must have paid off." I grabbed his arm. "Please don't tell the other Joes. It's embarrassing."

"Are you kidding? It's a great story." Ryan looked jealous that his fish adventure might be upstaged.

Matthew let out a breath. He rested a hand on my shoulder. "I'm thrilled you're okay. Go get yourself checked out. If you hit your head that hard, we want to be sure it's not serious."

While Theo's hand had felt warm and comforting, Matthew's was cold and threatening. I forced a smile. "I'll do that right away." I gave a half-wave to Ryan. "See you at the debrief." Feeling the heavy weight of Matthew's gaze on my back, I forced myself to continue toward the infirmary.

As I rounded the corner, Eric, Gabi, and Charles were waiting. Eric threw his arms around me. "I have had the worst feeling something terrible was happening. Gabi felt so too, but there was nothing we could do."

I rested my head against his shoulder. For Eric to touch, let alone hug me, he must have been terrified. There was so much to share with them—the meetup with Nick, the fire, Matthew's cruelty.

"We can't talk now. They're watching me. They'll be watching all of us." I straightened and spotted Eric's face. He had a bruise on his left cheek. "What happened?"

"I'm okay. Hayden stopped them. And since I didn't know anything about the emails, they let me off easy."

I pressed my hands to my forehead. My head was pounding, and I was so thirsty. "Guys, everything has changed. I need to find Hayden. And we can't stay out here in the open."

"Don't worry," Gabi said. "Everyone's distracted with the power coming back on."

"Wait until you hear what we found," Eric blurted.

"Crazy," Charles added. "What we found is crazy."

"What *we* found?" I grabbed Eric's arm. "Wait, are you back with us? Aren't you ... I'm confused ..." I felt a wave of dizziness. Charles eased me onto a bench and Gabi handed me her water bottle. As I gulped, Charles removed a bundle from his pocket and unwrapped two chocolate chip cookies.

I shoved one in my mouth, barely chewing before swallowing.

"I told you I had plans for Eric," Gabi said. "When the fire started and everyone was running around, I decided to take advantage."

Charles clapped Eric on the shoulder. "Me and Gabi fixed him. Or, more like Gabi fixed him and I kept him from escaping while she did it."

I stared at Gabi who puffed up with pride. I knew she was brilliant but hadn't really expected her to cure Eric's brainwashing, at least not so quickly.

"It was sick," Charles said. "Hayden gave Gabi a list of the HP sayings. She talked them through with Eric, making him explain each one. Like "strength in connections, and actions defines identity.""

"Define," Gabi and Eric chorused.

I looked questioningly at Charles. "Isn't that what—"

"Define not defines," Gabi said. "Actions is plural. Actions *define* identity."

"They made a grammatical mistake with their subliminal messaging," Eric said. "And Gabi *knew* I would never have grammatically incorrect thoughts. So, that begged the question, why was I thinking and saying that expression improperly?"

"It had to have been implanted," Gabi exclaimed. "Once he saw that logic, I had him."

Eric rolled his eyes. "I can't believe I just dropped all my suspicions. That those sayings were embedded in my brain without my awareness."

"Nice work, Gabi." I gulped more water and held out my hand for the second cookie.

"The timing was perfect," Eric said. "Gabi finished," he made air quotes, "fixing me," and boom, the power went out. None of the locks were working, so I could sneak into the computer room and get online."

"Without power?"

He waved a hand. "We have backups."

"Tell me quickly," I said, worried about Matthew. I needed to stay off his radar completely. "If I'm not in the infirmary soon, it could get ugly."

As if on cue, Theo came around the corner. "Lina, what's the hold up?" He scowled. "Why aren't you Plebes in your training activities?"

"Sorry," Gabi said. "We were just worried about Lina."

Theo arched a brow.

"I'm going," I jumped up. "I'll catch you guys later."

Dylan smelled like coffee and was wearing an olive T-shirt, jeans, and silver plugs with black sawtooth edges.

"Just can't stay out of trouble, eh?" he said with an amused smile. "Tell me what happened."

I ran through my story—the accidental fall into the river, hitting my head on a rock and waking up on shore.

"So, you lost consciousness?" Dylan asked, examining my head. I flinched as he probed the lump.

"I guess ..." I said, gnawing at my chapped lower lip. If I made my experience sound too bad, he might keep me here. If I didn't stick with my story, he might tell Matthew. "It's all a blur. I feel fine now except for a headache."

Dylan led me through some silly exercises—puffing out my cheeks, sticking out my tongue, and standing on one foot. He shined a bright light in my eyes and had my eyes follow his fingers.

"Your neurological exam is normal," he said. "I think you just have a concussion."

"So can I go?"

"Hold on. First off, spend the next twenty-four hours resting in your room. No training, no studying. I'm going to give you head injury precautions and I want to see you back if anything gets worse."

I nodded as Dylan rattled off a list of things I was supposed to look for, like worsening headaches and vomiting. My thoughts were on finding Hayden.

I smiled my thanks and slid off the exam table.

"Hold on a second." Dylan reached for the purple jar. "Let's get those scrapes taken care of."

Eric was pacing outside. "Are you okay?"

I held out an ointment-smeared arm. "I smell like rotting rose petals. But otherwise, I'm fine. What about you? Who hit you?"

"Fine? You've got a concussion."

I should have known better than to hide something from him, now that the true Eric had returned. "It's mild. Theo is going to bust you. We'd better get back."

"Theo is moderating a dispute between the Baby Joes and the Jocks over who would win *American Ninja Warrior*. And the Council is back in their meetings." He gestured at the path toward the lake. "Can we walk?"

My stomach heaved, thinking of Becky's blood pooling in the dirt on the other side, but I nodded.

Eric was silent, scuffing his toes and rubbing the pads of his fingers together. Unlike Gabi, I was not good at reading people. I preferred blunt communication. But Eric was sensitive and needed a more delicate touch. "Are you ... are you sad? Worried?"

Eric scuffed harder. "It's complicated. What I'm going to say is unfathomable."

"Is it what you found online? Were you able to get that swimmer's medical records?"

"Sort of. Actually, there are files on all of us, including information about our families, our births." Eric took a breath. "When my mom was seven months pregnant, she tripped down a flight of stairs and landed on her stomach. The paramedics rushed her to the hospital. She had what's called an abruption and they had to do an emergency C-section. Her baby went straight to the NICU, the neonatal intensive care."

I nodded, understanding starting to dawn. "Was this in Boston?"

"Yes. My mom was finishing her PhD, and my dad was teaching at Harvard."

I thought of my dream. "I think I was in the NICU in Boston too."

We reached the lake and walked down the slope to the dock. It seemed like forever ago that Hayden and I had meditated in the center of it. Eric took a few steps then stopped and stared down at the wood planks. "You're right about your mom. She was in Boston and went into early labor. Her baby was also premature and taken to the NICU."

"So, we *were* there together," I said, smiling for the first time since Becky had attacked me. "That's why we have this connection." I pictured two preemies—Eric and me—lying in incubators next to each other. The experience of clinging to life together had somehow formed our strong link.

Eric cleared his throat. "That same day, a third woman was admitted to the maternity ward. She had a condition called pre-eclampsia that can give pregnant women high blood pressure and cause seizures and death. To prevent that, she had to deliver her babies immediately, even though they weren't due for several months."

A third woman?

"That woman had a blood clot that broke loose during the delivery and went to her brain. She died."

A feeling of dread formed in my stomach and oozed its way up my throat. "After she delivered her babies?"

"A boy and a girl."

I stared at him. "What does this have to do with our moms being there? What are you saying?"

Eric's chest hitched.

I wanted to grab his shoulders and shake the information out of him. Instead, I forced my voice to remain calm. "Eric, are you saying those babies were us?"

His pale eyes met mine, tears welling up.

"Eric, are you saying we weren't just next to each other in the NICU? That we're ..."

Eric nodded. "We're twins."

Suddenly, tears were streaming down my face. I pressed my palms to my eyes. This made no sense. Eric and I couldn't be twins. We looked nothing alike—he had light eyes and blond hair, and I had brown hair and brown eyes. Plus, our personalities were opposites. I was an impulsive troublemaker and he was quiet and careful. He'd never been sent home for biting a classmate.

My head spun. If we were twins, then our biological mother had died of a blood clot during our birth ... at the same hospital where our moms had delivered their premature babies. Then how had I ended up with my parents and Eric with his?

A horrible question struck me. I dropped my hands. Eric was

wiping his eyes. "I don't know what happened to the other babies," he said. "Our parents' biological children." He sniffed. "Their fates were not important to HP."

There *had* been a real baby Jamison, a Catalina with Emma Claire's wide blue eyes and sweet smile. A little girl who would have had tons of friends, been the teacher's pet and become a star soccer player. I gagged and forced myself to swallow hard before speaking. "So, what happened—we somehow got put in these babies' places? How could that even be?"

"Someone in the hospital manipulated everything."

"Maybe it was just a mistake? The nurses got us mixed up with the dead woman's babies. The real Catalina and Eric could be out there somewhere."

Eric gave me a sad look. "Possible, but I doubt that's what happened."

"Maybe HP's information is wrong," I said, knowing in my gut that wasn't true. All the times I had felt out of place in my family. The way Emma Claire fit in like a perfect puzzle piece, while I remained an awkward jagged reject off to the side.

More tears came, my heart pounding and head wound throbbing in unison. It was as if all the stress of not fitting in my entire life hit me. Dizzy and nauseous, I fell to my knees.

The planks creaked as Eric knelt next to me. "I don't think those other babies lived," he said firmly, resting a hand on my sweaty back. "Our parents never knew about the deaths. They got to go on and raise us. Think how much suffering that prevented."

My sobs became a harsh laugh. "Not sure my family would agree."

Eric pressed a Kleenex into my hand. "They may not understand you, but they love you. And Emma Claire loves you."

I wiped my eyes and blew my nose.

Footsteps on the dock, and I looked up to see Charles and Gabi walking toward us.

Charles held out a hand. "Let's get up to lunch, Scrapper."

I let him pull me to my feet and grab me into a hug, squeezing me until I groaned. He lifted and carried me to shore. "You need to get some meat on you after all that soloing. Let's go get you a big pizza."

I managed to smile. "How did you know I was craving pizza?"

He belly laughed. "Who wouldn't be craving pizza?"

"I still don't get it," I said. "Why would the hospital have secretly placed us with our families? Didn't we have a dad? Or other relatives? You can't just substitute babies like that."

Gabi spun, her ponytail swatting Eric in the face. "You didn't tell her?"

"I didn't get a chance to finish," he said, rubbing his eyes.

"Finish what?" I said.

Eric flicked his gaze at Gabi. "Our embryos were implanted into the same woman. We grew in her womb together, so technically that makes us twins. But we're not biologically related."

"Implanted?" I stared. "Like as in vitro?"

He nodded. "Our embryos were created in a lab and implanted into our surrogate carrier."

"That's crazy. Why wouldn't we be related? Wouldn't the embryos be from the same parents?"

"There you are," a loud voice exclaimed. Samantha was striding toward us, looking pissed. "Lina, orders are to get to your room ASAP and follow concussion protocol. I got this order fifteen minutes ago and I've been looking for you."

CHAPTER
TWENTY-EIGHT

"NO EXERCISE, NO READING, NO VISITORS," Samantha said as we walked toward Madison. "Brittany will bring your meals."

One of the unfamiliar men stood at the entrance.

"Who are these guys?" I asked.

"Council security. We have a lot of VIPs here." She walked me to my room and waited until I was inside.

I sat on my bed, feeling desperate. Eric's story about us being twins but not real twins made no sense. What had happened in that hospital for us to end up being taken from our original mother—I couldn't think of another way to describe her because I didn't know if we were related biologically or not. Then given to other families? Families who had coincidentally had their babies die that same day?

My head and brain ached. I couldn't think about our births right now. The Council meetings had begun, and I hadn't spoken to Hayden about gathering intel. Being stuck in my room for forty-eight hours was ridiculous. Dylan had said twenty-four, but I was guessing Matthew had lengthened it—an easy way to keep me trapped in case I regained my memory.

I couldn't risk setting off the fire alarm again, especially with all the security. I didn't know where Hayden's room was anyway. I sat on my bed and chewed my thumbnail.

Brittany came in, holding a wrapped sandwich. "You've got me scared," she exclaimed. "I heard that you were knocked out cold and can't remember anything."

"Long story, but yes."

Her eyes widened. "Maybe it's like *Grey's Anatomy*. If you hit your head again, your memory could come back."

I grimaced. "Let's not try that."

Brittany looked disappointed. "Well, Samantha said to make sure you didn't leave. I'm not a babysitter, I told her."

An idea sparked. I gestured toward her bulletin board. "How we doing?"

Brittany examined the list of rules. "Not too bad. Of course, there are some we don't want to break." She wrinkled her nose. "Ew, that one's gross."

"Do we each have to break different rules? Or ... does it count twice if we break the same rule?"

"I think it would be fine if ... what are we talking about? Are you finally going to let me give you a piercing?"

I shook my head and tried to look embarrassed—way too much acting for one day.

"No way," she breathed. "The relationship rule? Do you have the hots for someone?"

I squirmed.

"Who? Did you hook up already? Of course, it's cold and lonely on those solos. I wouldn't blame—"

"It's more of a crush. I don't think he's interested, but maybe?"

"Ah …" she tapped a finger against her lips. "Well, I can help with that too."

"I was thinking, maybe I should ask him to the dance next weekend?"

She beamed. "You definitely should."

"Since I'm stuck in here, I'm afraid someone else will ask him first. Would you be willing to—"

"Ask him for you?" She clapped her hands. "Of course. Who is it? Another Joe? Is it …"

"It's Hayden."

Her eyebrows jumped. "Hayden? I mean, he is adorable but isn't he—"

"He's not gay. Please be discreet. I don't want anyone to know."

"Nobody will hear a thing," Britt made a zipping motion over her lips. "After all, I've kept my relationships secret."

"About that, we need to talk about Matthew." I wasn't sure what I was going to say, but Brittany needed to avoid him completely.

"Oh, the Chosen One's old news." Brittany headed to her mirror. "I caught him hitting on another girl. I met someone else anyway. Bryce is an actor and *so* talented."

As Britt continued, I lay back, exhaustion consuming me. Hopefully, Hayden would get the hint.

I awoke to darkness and Samantha shaking me. She pressed a glass of water and two Tylenol into my hands.

I took the pills and gulped down the water.

"I'll check on you again in the morning," she said.

I thanked her and went into the bathroom. Britt had stuck a pink Post-It note to the mirror. THE ANSWER IS YES!! was scrawled in marker with a slew of hearts. I allowed myself a smile at Britt's enthusiasm. Peeling off my filthy clothes, I showered, careful to avoid the bruise, and changed into clean clothes. I planned to stay awake, but I drifted off, and the next thing I knew, a hand clamping over my mouth jolted me back up.

"It's me," Hayden murmured. He waited until I nodded understanding then removed his hand. He was dressed in black, his hoody pulled up over his head. Behind him, Britt was fast asleep.

Hayden tipped his head toward the door and I followed him. He glanced into the hall, gestured me through, and pulled the door behind us, leaving it slightly ajar. He headed to a door at the end of the hall, opened it, and we entered blackness. The sound of a cord being pulled and faint light shone from a dangling bulb, showing shelves holding rolls of toilet paper and cleaning supplies.

"Did anyone see you?" I whispered. "How did you get into my room?"

"We're fine. Are you okay? What happened? Why the urgency?"

"I saw Nick. He used my tracker to find me."

Hayden sucked in a breath.

"He feels terrible about not letting you know. But it was too dangerous."

Hayden listened intently as I relayed our conversation.

"So, Nick wants me to gather information about genetics and recruitment but not do anything with it?" he said when I finished. "Just pass it along to General Cole?"

"They need proof about what this faction is doing. Once they have that, it sounds like they can justify taking some sort of action against it."

"Okay ... not very specific."

"That's what I said. But then Becky and Spiky showed up." I recounted the fight and tumble into the river.

"Becky," he muttered. "It's high time we dealt with her. I'll take it up with the Council tomorrow."

"That's not a good idea." I hesitated, dreading the next part of the story. As I began to describe Becky's beating, I watched Hayden's expression morph from surprise to anger to devastation.

"Are you sure it was Matthew?" his voice cracked. "You were pretty far away."

"Positive. And I'm sure Matthew was the one in Blakewell's office that first day as well. Hayden, I'm so sorry."

Hayden was trembling. First, finding out Nick was alive, and then remembering the trainings he had done with Matthew, the talks about their future plans and purposes. Wondering if Matthew had helped plot Nick's murder.

"I've been an idiot," he said. "Something evil is happening right under our noses, while I've been playing Special Forces and missing all the signs."

I grasped his arms. "That's what Nick and his group wanted. They needed you to act as if nothing was wrong, to work your way up in HP. You've done that."

"While Nick continues to risk his life?"

"You've both got your roles. And now, he needs your help."

Hayden snorted in frustration. "It's got to be something with that lab. Nick was curious about it last summer, angling to get in there."

"Is it that building hidden behind the lake? I spotted it this morning."

"We have to break in there. See what they are hiding. Find out what those snakes are up to." He was vibrating with emotion. I wanted to help him, yet nothing I could say would make the betrayal by one friend and the attempted murder of another less terrible."

"No. Nick was very clear. You are to gather information only. They have a plan and all they need is concrete evidence. Your role is to provide that. Nothing more. Oh, he did say to tell you to visit your sweet shop?"

"Our sweet shop ..." Hayden slowly nodded. "The pig was smoking a cigarette—that's when I knew it might be him. We used to hide our smokes in a crevice in a boulder by the lake. Our code was asking the other if he fancied a sweet. I haven't been there since ... well, I need to check it out."

"Not now," I tightened my grip. "There's security everywhere."

"Security?" Hayden laughed. "Blakewell's security is lazy and untrained. I'll have no trouble."

"Can I—"

"No way. You get back to your room and finish your concussion rules."

The anger radiating from him worried me. "Promise me you won't do anything crazy. At least until we can talk again."

He huffed a breath. "Okay. But same goes for you. Agreed?"

"Agreed."

CHAPTER
TWENTY-NINE

AFTER FORTY-EIGHT HOURS OF PACING, gazing longingly out the window and worrying about Hayden, I was finally released. At breakfast, my friends were happy to see me, and many Baby Joes came over to check on me. We couldn't dare a real conversation, but after I kept giving Gabi pleading looks, she mentioned she had been busy reading important *journal articles* from Hayden.

Hayden had found info at the sweet shop and given it to Gabi! I knew I would drive myself crazy with curiosity until she shared. As a distraction, I picked up my training schedule. I wasn't allowed to do anything strenuous but I could still attend sessions.

An item after lunch read *Cotillion Lesson*.

"Cotillion is a ballroom dance where couples change partners frequently," Gabi said. "It is based on an eighteenth-century English dance and, in modern times, it is a way for young people to learn how to be prepared to go into high society. There are weekly classes to teach ballroom dancing, table manners, and etiquette."

"Ugh," Eric and I exclaimed.

"Ballroom dance?" I said. "What does that have to do with our purposes?"

It turned out, a Tore Angel informed us, that all the Plebes had Cotillion. "Don't forget that for most of HP's history, it was essential to develop certain skills. Impeccable manners and an ability to socialize properly were necessary to achieve success."

I joined in the collective groan.

"Our annual dance is a wonderful tradition started when we welcomed girls into HP," the Angel continued, "as it was a perfect opportunity for trainees to hone their Cotillion skills. Nowadays, it's more relaxed, but we still expect everyone to look spiffy and practice what they have learned."

Brittany caught my eye from across the room and grinned. She couldn't wait for the dance.

"Ha, I don't have any spiffy clothes." I had refused DJ's attempt to slip a dress and sandals in my bag. "Guess I'm out."

"It's compulsory," the Angel said as if reading my mind. "All of HP attends, even the staff and tutors. For those of you who don't have the proper attire, we have plenty to loan you."

Next to me, Eric was trembling. "I can't dance with anyone. I don't—"

"It's okay," I assured him. "You can dance with me or Gabi. We'll take care of you."

It turned out that was not true. In Cotillion, we had to change partners every few minutes. We also had to wear HP-issued purple dresses—unless you were like Britt who had brought her own—heels and white gloves. We were broken into groups and taught how to properly greet someone, shake hands, and make small talk. It was the same stuff my mom had been trying to get me to do for years and I felt ridiculous practicing it with my fellow Plebes.

The dining hall's tables and chairs had been cleared, leaving an open space for us to practice. Shuffling through the dances, stepping on boys' toes, and trying to make conversation was torturous. Eric looked terrified and corpse-like in his suit, and I could tell he was having trouble speaking at all, let alone managing small talk.

The Tores and Quites loved our discomfort, coming around and correcting positioning, encouraging us to "be witty" and "smile". It was obvious which Plebes had taken ballroom dance, as they were moving easily across the floor. Wearing a purple sports coat with a white handkerchief peeking from the pocket, Matthew took turns dancing with each girl, doling out encouragement before moving on to the next. He and Brittany were spectacular and everyone stopped to watch their gliding and twirling. Brittany's eyes sparkled and her long hair flowed behind her. I resolved to warn her away from Matthew again, just in case.

Right when I thought the torture was ending, a group of Council members entered to watch. In front, Edmund Blakewell was shorter than I had imagined but radiated a dark aura. As his penetrating gaze surveyed us, I felt the tension in the room rise. I gave the itchy collar of my dress a hard tug and half of it ripped off in my hand. Letting out a moan of frustration, I spotted Becky and Spiky watching me. Spiky looked amused while Becky's eyes channeled pure hate.

I knew I should look away. My goal was to avoid conflict and steer clear of the pair. But I couldn't let them think that they'd gotten to me. I flashed a death stare back.

A tap on my shoulder and I turned to see Ryan. We laughed as we stepped on each other's toes more than the floor. "I can't imagine ever being good at this," he confided, swiping at the sweat on his forehead with his rumpled handkerchief.

"Just play their game. We'll get the hang of it eventually, right?"

"Perhaps I can help with that?" a voice said. Ryan turned and flushed, stuttering a yes and giving Matthew a half bow.

"Don't worry buddy, you'll get this." Matthew nudged Ryan's shoulder. "You should have seen me my Plebe summer—not pretty."

Ryan flushed deeper and stumbled away. Matthew took my hand and I was suddenly glad I was wearing the gloves so I didn't have to feel his skin against mine. I forced a smile. "You're such a good dancer. Did you learn that at HP?"

"Among other places," Matthew said, propelling me into the waltz. "How is your head?"

"It still hurts. But much better than before." I focused on my feet.

"And how's your sister doing?" Matthew asked, his voice casual. He guided me into an awkward twirl.

"Much better also, thanks for asking."

"San Diego must be a nice place to recuperate."

Why was Matthew bringing up Emma Claire? I twirled back and he pulled me closer, his dark eyes boring into mine. I couldn't believe that I had found him charming. With his too-white smile and over-styled hair, he was pure sleaze. I sensed Blakewell's heavy gaze on us. He had probably met the news of my death with no more emotion than getting the incorrect drink at a restaurant.

"You're not fooling me, you know." Matthew's expression remained friendly, but his tone was ice cold. "I know what you're doing."

A shiver ran down my spine. He knew. How had he found out? Had he figured out the emails? Had he noticed Hayden spying on the Council members?

"What do you mean?" I asked, trying to keep my voice and expression confused. But it was too late. He had seen the flash of fear in my eyes.

He squeezed my hand, crushing the bones of my fingers together. "You are playing a dangerous game. If you do anything to draw attention to yourself or disturb the Council, it won't just be you who suffers."

I imagined the cord coming down on Emma Claire's tiny back and couldn't prevent a shudder.

"Attention everyone." An Angel in the front was waving cheerily. Matthew dropped my hands, turned, and went to join her. I remained frozen, heart racing, sweat pouring off me. I wanted to yank off a high-heeled shoe and beat him with it. Matthew had threatened not just me but my family. He had mentioned Emma Claire to scare me. And I was scared. But also really, really mad.

"In honor of our Council members being with us, we are changing things up a bit this week." The Angel smiled. "Mr. Blakewell will be presenting the Campiones medallions and we will celebrate as a group."

I peeled off the gloves and rubbed my palms against my dress as Blakewell took the microphone. "I am thrilled to have our Council members here to watch our Plebes work on their dancing skills," he boomed. "I'm sure many of you remember being in their shoes, literally."

Laughs and nods from the Council members.

"We have continued our Council's fine tradition of gathering at the academy for our annual meeting. Even as the world expands and progresses, the heart of our organization is here where our seedlings are planted and grown. The future of HP and our world rests in the work done right here."

Everyone clapped and I forced myself to participate.

"Each week we award the Campiones to the top Plebes in each purpose. At the end of the summer, the Plebes who have received the medallion the most times have the honor of joining the Youth Council. I'm guessing most of you received the award one or multiple times while here at HP."

More laughs and nods.

As he began presenting the Campiones, I examined the Council members, wondering which ones were part of his faction. It was easy to figure out their purposes. The Jocks were still big and buff, the Angels beautiful, and the Geekits nerdy. I recognized at least one famous actor and a cable news anchor. Another man with cropped gray hair and a sturdy jaw looked familiar and I wondered if he was a famous politician.

"I'm happy to report that the Baby Joes all survived their solos, even with the threat of a forest fire," Blakewell said when he got to our group. "It's hard to pick a winner with so many heroic acts, but there were two clear standouts." He gave the Campio yet again to Mini Rock who had helped evacuate a camping family, carrying a child in each arm to safety.

I saw Britt's gaze settle on Mini Rock and thought that they would make a great couple. Anyone was better than Matthew.

"And for her bravery in discovering the fire and sounding the alarm, the Campia award this week goes to Barbie Rossi. This is her second week in a row, so excellent job Barbie."

My body jerked. Spiky had started the fire! And Blakewell knew it!

So did Matthew. I couldn't help it—I let my eyes roam and spotted him standing next to Hayden at the door, speaking intently in his ear. Hayden shrugged and said something back. He didn't look angry or scared, just confused. Matthew must not be threatening his family. Matthew spoke again and they both turned toward me. I grabbed

Ryan by the arm. "Let's practice the foxtrot more later this week," I said. "We can help each other."

"That's great," Ryan said. "Actually, I was wondering if you wanted to go to the dance together?"

"What?" I stared at him. "Oh, Ryan ..." No one had ever asked me to a dance before. This should be a big moment in my life, but I was too distracted by the evil around us. "I already ... I mean ..."

"That's okay. I figured you already had a date, but thought I'd ask."

"I'm really flattered. Let's practice together anyway?" I held out my hand.

As he took it, my gaze flicked to where Hayden and Matthew had been standing but they were gone.

CHAPTER
THIRTY

THE COUNCIL MEMBERS were in the dining hall, so we trainees were eating dinner outside. My friends and I sat on a blanket, our hamburgers and potato salad untouched. My stomach was rumbling but I was too anxious to eat. Gabi's somber expression was stressing me out.

"We wait for Hayden," she had insisted. "Nick is his friend, so this is his information to hear first." The only thing she would say was that Hayden's papers had been informative.

"I wonder if Hayden has overheard anything yet," I said.

"He said he's met Cole before and thought he was a good guy," Charles said. "Cole did some training with the Joes last summer."

"They're coming onto the patio," Eric rubbed his fingers together. The tension was making him miserable.

I touched his arm. My twin. I still couldn't get used to that, but I liked it. No matter what our story ended up being, we had our connection.

Council members, wearing dark pants and cloaks, were gathering in clusters on the patio. Tores circulated with trays of drinks and appetizers.

Hayden came down the stairs, carrying a large wooden tray with cups of ice cream. He stopped at the other groups, offered them cups and chatted.

He saved us for last. "Good evening, Plebes. Ice cream?"

"Is this too suspicious?" I asked as he sat next to me.

"Funny enough, earlier today, Matthew asked me to keep an eye on you, so this is fine." He raised a questioning eyebrow.

I was relieved that Matthew still seemed to trust Hayden. And Hayden was doing an amazing job suppressing his anger. "I don't think he buys my memory loss," I said. I didn't want to add to Hayden's burden by telling him about Matthew threatening me.

We all turned to Gabi who was practically vibrating.

"Okay Gabi, tell us already," Charles said.

Gabi looked at Hayden. "First off, I want to state that your pal Nick is an idiot for leaving this information out in the open. My guess is, he didn't believe it was real."

"Until they tried to kill him," I muttered.

"What did you find?" Hayden asked.

"Lina, remember when you wondered what made HP choose us at birth, to chip us?"

I nodded.

"Well, you had it backward. They didn't choose us, they created us."

We all stared at her for a long moment. Then we all started to speak, and Gabi held up a hand. "Let me get this out. It's a lot. So, in 2006, HP halted its traditional worldwide recruiting and testing and switched to the invitation. The big question is why the switch? And how did they know which trainees to choose?"

I thought of the images Blakewell had shown of past teens testing to get into HP. Very different from the shocking arrival of our invitations.

"One of the scientists who developed in vitro fertilization was an HP grad. In the late 1980s, he and several powerful Council members decided the historic system was outdated. To trial a new process, they turned to fertility clinics and their rich source of genetic materials."

"Fertility clinics?" Hayden said. "You're not saying ..."

"Yes. They created babies that would excel in a particular purpose and," she made air quotes, "go into the world and shine."

"Wait," I said. "Are you saying they located embryos from a person who was really good at something—like swimming or science? And then they chipped and tracked their babies?"

Gabi shook her head. "No, they were much more daring than that. This team was powerful and connected. They wanted both parents to be spectacular. Bio mom and dad might not even have known each other. They weren't necessarily in the same city, or country. HP combined genetic material from a man and a woman with identical or complementary strengths."

I thought about the swimmer—the coach had said both her parents had won Olympic medals. "So, like, let's take this Olympic swimmer's sperm and combine it with this Olympic swimmer's egg to create a baby that will grow up to become a super swimmer?"

"Exactly."

"How could they do that?" Eric protested. "Aren't fertility clinics careful? You can't just walk in, steal materials, and take them to your own lab."

"Believe it or not, there has been poor to no regulation of sperm banks or fertility clinics. Their main goal is making money, and when that's their motivation ..." Gabi shrugged. "Although I agree that it must have been quite an operation to steal eggs and sperm from various clinics, bring them to a separate location, create the embryos, then implant them."

Hayden snorted. "Sorry, but this can't be true. No way was I implanted into my mum. My parents were poor and already had two kids. My younger brother and I were both surprises."

Gabi gave Hayden a sympathetic look. "Actually, your mom was the perfect candidate. Having two kids meant she was fertile. She was not likely to question an unexpected pregnancy. Your embryo could have been implanted during a simple medical procedure."

Hayden started to shake his head then froze. "My mum had her appendix out a bit before she found out she was pregnant with me. It took her a long time to figure it out because she thought her nausea was a side effect from surgery."

"There you go. Some embryos were implanted into couples who were coming for in vitro. Some were manipulated pregnancies in women who were poor and not medically savvy, like your mom and mine, and some were paid surrogates. Fewer questions that way."

Charles gestured toward Eric and me. "Their surrogate had two babies from different parents in her, right?"

"I'm guessing with the surrogates, they sometimes implanted two embryos. With Eric and Lina, things went horribly wrong when the surrogate died, and they had to improvise at the last minute."

We fell silent. The enormity of having biological parents out there—unknowing donors who had been targeted to create us and our talents—was beyond belief.

"And Nick figured this out?" Hayden asked. "All of this was in those papers?"

"More or less," Gabi said. "I also know a lot about in vitro and genetics so I'm extrapolating too."

"Is that what Nick needs proof about?" I asked.

"It can't be that. He already has proof," Gabi said. "It's sitting right here on this blanket."

"This has to be specific to Blakewell and his faction," Hayden agreed. "This embryo thing, this has been going on since when?"

"The late 1980s."

"Right. There must be something new. Something that is going down right here and right now."

"Well, we can guess his faction's plan," I said, picturing Blakewell's jowly, evil face. "To create embryos with specific purposes, invite them here, train them, and fire them into the world to fulfill his goals."

Hayden rubbed a hand over his chin. "If Blakewell has specific goals, it's not sending principled trainees out to better the world."

"The method to transform a nation and the world is through the spirit and will of its children," Gabi recited Harlan's quote.

"They want to create a new world," Charles said. For the first time ever, I heard disgust in his voice. "A world that fits their sick ideas of what is right."

"Every purpose at HP is geared toward engendering power," Eric said. "Athletes, supermodels, politicians, scientists, military leaders. If that power gets channeled in the wrong direction ..."

"The coordination it must be taking to pull this off," Hayden said. "All the people involved." He smacked his palm on the wooden platter, then jerked it back.

"Enough to implant chips after we were born." I felt enraged, just like I did every time I thought about that blue pebble. One of the first things I would do when I got home was get that thing removed, even if I had to cut it out myself.

"How has it stayed a secret?" Hayden examined his hand. A sliver of wood had pierced the center of his palm.

"Excellent question," Gabi said. "This program is massively expensive and risky. HP must have confederates all over the world and pay hefty amounts of cash for their help."

"And think about genetic testing companies," Eric added. "They have to create a fake profile if an HP'er tries to get their DNA mapped."

"It's been more than cash that has kept this secret," Hayden said. "Murder is a tool they aren't afraid to use."

I took Hayden's hand. "Hold still," I said, pressing his fingers down so his palm was flat. I grasped the pointy tip of the splinter and tugged.

"Nick's papers referenced recent testing by HP scientists," Gabi said. "It looks like they are working on a way to take simple genetic material from two people and create an embryo."

"Simple genetic material?" Charles asked.

Hayden grimaced as the splinter came out. He put his hand to his mouth and nodded thanks. I felt a warm glow of satisfaction that I had been able to help him, even with something so small.

"Easy samples," Eric said. "Blood, saliva, even skin cells. No need to steal from fertility labs."

Hayden huffed out a breath. "That expands the pool of parents to basically anyone. And if you have a clear goal in mind ..." He looked toward The Chalet. "I'd better get back in there and see what I can dig up."

CHAPTER
THIRTY-ONE

THE NEXT MORNING, I bolted out of Madison, thrilled to finally be done with the exercise restrictions. It felt good to get my heart pumping and leg muscles working. I did a big loop around the edge of HP, going close enough to see the lab through the fence, but not so close as to draw suspicion.

As I neared the main path, I spotted a group of Council members strolling toward me, led by Blakewell, Matthew, and Crystal. Instinctively, I leaped for the nearest pine tree and climbed up into the branches.

"If you continue along this way and keep to the right, you will end up at the lake," Crystal was saying, her voice unnaturally sweet. If she had seen me, she was doing an excellent job of hiding it. "It's beautiful in the morning. You may catch our swimmers out there doing warm-ups."

"I'd love that," a woman said. The group was getting closer. My tree was spindly, and I was perched across several branches. If anyone looked up, they would spot me.

"I'll take you there," Blakewell offered, his rumbly voice sounding almost jolly.

"That sounds perfect. Will we still have an opportunity to see the gym?"

"Absolutely. We have plenty of time."

"Crystal and I will meet you after your tour," Matthew said warmly.

The group chorused thanks and followed Blakewell down the path.

"What's the status?" Matthew said curtly once they were gone.

"I talked to Jasper at the trucking company. The roads are too narrow for a large truck, so they'll have to use several smaller ones that can shuttle back and forth."

"How long will that take?"

"He said they could still get it done within a day. With overtime."

"Good. And?"

"The earliest is the ..."

The branch supporting my leg made a cracking noise. I bit my lip, hoping they hadn't heard.

Luckily, Matthew was swearing and kicking the ground. "Does he know money is not an issue?"

"I still don't get why this must happen now. We should stick with the original plan and wait until summer session is over."

"You want to tell Edmund that?" Matthew snapped. "He says it needs to be now, so we're doing it now."

"We can try a different company."

"No, too risky. Jasper's done work for HP before and keeps his mouth shut. Tell him to make that day work."

"I know, I know," Crystal's voice grew fainter so I could tell she was moving down the path. I didn't blame her—I would be getting away from an angry Matthew too. "The Council members will be gone, and the trainees will be sleeping late ..." She kept going so I only caught a few more words—"no one ... lab ... distraction."

"Make it happen," Matthew strode after her. "With Jasper. This has to go off perfectly."

My mind whirled. Some guy Jasper was bringing in trucks to remove, what? Papers, computers, lab equipment? It was a rush job, and he was doing it on a day the trainees would be sleeping late. When did we ever get to sleep late? Baby Joes had to run every morning, even Sundays. Except ... the dance was a week away. We were going to be allowed to sleep late the next morning.

Blakewell must be planning to empty out the lab. If the trucks were for another reason, they wouldn't need to be hidden or rushed. Blakewell's request was urgent—which meant he must have found out about Nick's faction and their suspicions. It also meant that, even though he and Matthew had seemed buddy-buddy yesterday, Hayden would be in danger. I had to find him and warn him.

Shifting my weight, I heard a loud crack. The branch supporting me gave way and I plummeted toward the ground. My outstretched arm hit first, and pain shot up my wrist. My shoulder and head crashed next, followed by the rest of my body. I jumped up, shook each leg to be sure it wasn't injured, and took off. Matthew and Crystal were headed back to The Chalet, so I wouldn't bump into them on my way to the gym.

Council members smiled and security men ignored me as I ran by. The back door to the gym was propped open. I tripped over the entry rug, steadied myself, ran down the hall and up the stairs into the gym.

Tores were lugging pieces of equipment around and arranging chairs in the middle of the main mat. I was relieved to spot Hayden dragging mini trampolines over to the climbing wall.

"Hayden," I raced toward him, almost colliding with a Tore unfolding a chair.

He spun around, his expression shifting from surprise to alarm as he took in my flushed face. "What's wrong? What happened?"

"I ... you ... it ..." I was aware of the others stopping what they were doing to listen. I held my wrist out in front of me. "I fell on my wrist," I burst into tears. "I think it might be broken."

Hayden was stunned, his gaze shifting between my wrist and my face. "Let's go get some ice," he finally said, putting a hand on my shoulder and turning me toward the locker rooms.

"I can help her," Theo said. "I'm done here."

I let out a fresh sob, reflecting that of all the times I had fake cried, this was the easiest. In fact, I wasn't sure I was pretending.

"I've got it," Hayden said easily. "I've got an ace in my bag." He stopped at the training office, ducked in, and came back with an ice pack. I followed him into the locker room.

"You are the most accident-prone person I've ever met," he exclaimed.

"They know," I blurted. "Blakewell knows."

Hayden removed his gym bag from a locker and set it on a bench. "What makes you say that?" He unzipped it and rooted around, pulling out an ace bandage.

"Yesterday, at Cotillion, Matthew told me he knew what I was planning and threatened me."

Hayden's eyes flashed. "He threatened you?"

"Me and Emma Claire. Warned me not to do anything stupid."

"Why didn't you tell me?"

"I didn't want to upset you even more."

Hayden blew out a breath. "Stay away from him, Lina. Don't do anything that might catch his attention or upset him. He has a lot of power."

"You don't need to tell me that," I recalled the coldness of Matthew's eyes. "Just now, I overheard him and Crystal saying they were going to clear everything out. Like it was an emergency. I was in a tree, and I heard them."

"You were in a ..." Hayden paused, shook his head like he was trying to clear his thoughts, then gestured to the ice pack. "Put that on your wrist. And tell me what happened."

"My wrist is fine," I said, rotating it around. Hayden listened while I told him what I had overheard.

"Did you find out anything last night?" I asked. "Did you talk to Cole?"

"We briefly chatted, that's all. I hope to get more intel at the black-tie event tonight. Once everyone's liquored up."

"Cole must have told Blakewell about Nick's group. So, that means he knows I met with Nick and that you are supposed to gather proof."

Hayden pressed his lips together. "Hold out your wrist." He began to wrap the ace bandage around it. "I don't think it was Cole. He's part of Nick's team. It doesn't make sense."

"It makes perfect sense. You chatted with him last night and today Matthew and Crystal are rushing to get rid of evidence."

Hayden frowned. "I'm not saying they're not rushing to hide something. But if Cole were in on it, they wouldn't need to panic. They could just ride out the rest of the summer and count on him to scuttle things on his end. He could feed false information to Nick's faction."

"Matthew and Crystal know somebody is onto them" I insisted. "Matthew already suspects me and now they'll come after both of us."

"Maybe," Hayden considered. "But in that case, Matthew wouldn't have asked me to surveil you. And Crystal is the worst liar ever. If that woman is angry with you, you will know it. She's been her usual aloof self with me."

He finished wrapping the bandage and fastened the end with a metal clip. He handed me the ice pack. "Keep up the show. No using your wrist the rest of today."

"So why are they clearing things out?" I could hear Baby Joes coming into the gym. "And what should we do?"

"It doesn't make sense." Hayden put his bag back in the locker. "Even if Cole is team Blakewell, he would report that I was instructed to gather intel only, not go into that lab. And he knows I would obey orders."

"Will you?" I pushed. "Even if they're going to empty out that lab? Even if we will lose any chance to collect evidence?"

Hayden slammed the locker door, "Of course not. They tried to murder Nick and are doing something evil in that lab. All bets are off. I'm going in."

"We're going in."

Hayden shook his head. "It's too dangerous. This is personal and I'm willing to risk getting caught."

"Matthew threatened my sister. This is personal for me too."

"It's foolish for either of us." Hayden rubbed a finger over his scar. "I wish there were a way to alert Nick without going through Cole. Another email would be too risky."

"Agreed." I stared at the round tracker on his wrist. "But I have an idea. Lend me your tracker."

CHAPTER
THIRTY-TWO

I LADLED PUNCH INTO A GLASS and turned to survey the dining room, whose walls had been covered with shiny blue and silver cellophane. Clear plastic bubbles and jellyfish hung from the ceiling and the tables and chairs had been moved to create a dance floor painted like a seashell. The music had just started and already the seashell was packed. In the center, Spiky, in a hot pink strapless dress, waved her arms over her head, hip bumping with the twins and Bolton. They hadn't been kidding about the importance of the traditional Cotillion—everyone was there, including coaches, tutors, and staff. Even Doctor Volkov was glowering in the corner with a glass of brown liquid. The Council members had left, so at least we didn't have to deal with them.

Thankfully, I had been able to wear one of Britt's dresses instead of having to borrow an HP monstrosity. The pale pink dress with blue sequin flowers wasn't too bad once we pinned up the straps so the top didn't gape. She had even coaxed my hair into soft curls. With her lowest heels though, I felt wobbly and unnatural.

My internal clock announced it was eight p.m. Time to put our plan into action. Feeling like I was in a crazy rom-com, I waded into the fray. I stopped behind a shimmying Spiky and tapped her bare shoulder. When she turned, I threw the punch in her face.

I can't say I didn't enjoy Spiky's stunned expression as sticky, purple liquid ran down her forehead, over her spidery lashes and dripped off her chin into the cleavage of her dress.

Spiky took a deep breath, let out a dragon roar, and threw herself at me.

I sidestepped and she fell forward and skidded onto her stomach, revealing all of her legs and hot pink underwear.

Other trainees started shrieking and backing away. "Fight!" a Geekit in an ill-fitting tuxedo and purple bow tie yelled, jumping up and down.

Strong arms grabbed me from behind. I recognized the scent of Bolton's cologne and stomped my heel into the top of his foot. He yelped and let me go.

Spiky leaped up. "Get her!"

Multiple hands lifted me almost off my feet and wrenched my arms back. I kicked behind me and heard grunts of pain.

When Spiky pulled her fist back, I couldn't do more than close my eyes and turn my face to the side. Pain rocketed through my left cheekbone, spreading to my entire head. I struggled, trying to open my eyes. My right one cooperated, but the left one was watery and stuck.

The music had stopped, and the entire room was pressing in around us. Spiky drew back again as Hayden and Becky pushed their way into the circle. "All right, enough! Break it up!" Hayden barked. "What is going on?"

Spiky pointed at me. "Lina threw her drink on me. Look at this." She gestured to the purple stain spreading across her dress. "Totally unprovoked!"

The hands released me, and I tried to pull myself up straight, despite trembling legs and those damn heels. "She punched me," I protested, unhappy with how whiny and weak my voice sounded.

"Did you throw a drink on Barbie?" Hayden's eyes were dark, his expression stern.

"It was a joke," I muttered. "I didn't know she'd be so sensitive."

"A joke," Spiky screamed. "You won't think it's a joke when—"

Becky held up a hand. "Let us take care of this." I could see pink remnants of the welts peeking up from the back of her dress.

"Jamison, this is a serious infraction." Hayden grabbed my arm and wrapped his fingers around my bicep. "You're going to need to come with me."

"Ow," I protested. "You're hurting me."

"You've violated our behavior comportment rules. Your conduct will be reported to the disciplinary committee tomorrow." He put his other hand on my shoulder and turned me.

"You think you're hurting now," Spiky called. "Just wait until tomorrow. You won't even know—"

"Don't make this worse than it already is," Becky said, her tone oozing satisfaction. She knew I was in serious trouble, and this would be my last weekend at HP.

Hayden propelled me through the crowd toward the exit. "Being at the Cotillion is a privilege," he intoned. "Until you meet with the disciplinary committee tomorrow, you will remain in your room."

Stumbling, I tried to keep up with his pace. At the exit, he stopped in front of Blakewell and Crystal who were holding glasses of champagne. Blakewell's expression was flat, his eyes cold. "Unwise choice," he said.

Crystal remained silent but her eyes flashed triumph.

"I am going to escort Lina to her room and ensure she is secure for the night," Hayden said formally. "Is there anything else you would like me to do?"

"Can I at least get an ice pack?" I said sullenly.

Crystal started to shake her head, but Blakewell nodded. He wouldn't want me to have a black eye when my parents came to pick me up.

"Let's go," Hayden gave me a shove toward the kitchen.

Hayden pushed open the swinging door, waiting until it shut to turn to me. "Are you okay? You're going to have quite a shiner."

"She punched me," I exclaimed. "That wasn't part of the plan!"

"Well, it worked. I saw Eric and Charles sneak out without anyone noticing. Idiot security. I assume Gabi got out as well." He gestured for me to sit and began rummaging under the counter.

"It *was* part of the plan then?" I said, gently pressing fingers to the puffy area around my eye. "I thought you told me to stop getting hurt."

"We had to make it realistic." Hayden came up with a Ziploc baggie. "With Barbie, I knew physical violence was likely."

"My head is spinning. It has this weird buzzy feeling." Dylan would not be happy when I showed up with another head injury.

Hayden tossed me the baggie. "Put some ice on that eye and gather yourself while I get the others. We'll circle back to fetch you." He headed for the back door.

A row of refrigerators lined the far wall, and I shuffled over to them. The first held cartons of milk and butter. The second had tubs with lettuce, carrots, and other produce. The third was a freezer with giant bags of frozen berries and cartons of ice cream, but no ice. I debated pressing a pint of Ben & Jerry's Cookie Dough to my eye.

I heard the kitchen door swing open. "You are so bad," a lilting voice said. "We're going to get into trouble."

"They won't even know we're gone," a male voice said. "Everyone's distracted right now."

My gut clenched. I knew both of those voices all too well. I closed the freezer door and slipped into a gap between it and a refrigerator.

Matthew strolled into the center of the room, looking perfect as always in a black tux and purple bow tie. Now that I knew his true nature, he reminded me of a slimy weasel from a Disney movie.

He beckoned and Brittany sauntered closer, giving him a coy smile. After trying on all her dresses multiple times, she had selected a form-hugging, sparkly silver one and diamond pendant earrings. He held out a hand and she placed perfectly manicured fingers in his. Pulling her toward him, he wrapped one arm around her waist and put a finger under her chin. "You are so beautiful."

"You're too sweet," Brittany breathed before their lips met.

I felt nauseous. Brittany had assured me several times that she had moved on from Matthew. I would talk sense into her later, but right now, I needed them to go. It had already been two minutes since Hayden had left and I needed to get outside ASAP.

After a long kiss, Brittany slowly extracted herself from Matthew's embrace. "How about some of that ice cream you promised? I've never tried Cherry Garcia." She started walking toward the freezer.

I tensed. While I was excellent at hiding, Brittany was going to stop right in front of me. In the bright light of the freezer, the blue sequin flowers on my dress would pop. Brittany would scream, Matthew would drag me out, and our whole plan would be ruined.

I debated my options. I could try to run out the back. Except, I was wearing these stupid heels and would probably trip and fall. I could stay and confess that I had given Hayden the slip and was hiding from him. Matthew would then summon Crystal or a security guard to deal with me. Would either option give the others time to try and pull off our plan?

What if Hayden and my friends came back and got caught? I was so frustrated! This was our one chance. The dance was the only time the whole academy was together, including the adults. Plus, the trucks were coming tomorrow.

"Wait a second doll," Matthew tugged at Brittany's arm. "Ice cream isn't really what I was wanting." He pulled her closer and kissed her again.

Doll? What a creep. Apparently, Matthew viewed girls as either punching bags or toys. *Ugh*, I did not want to listen to the slurpy sounds of them kissing. Although, if they got more involved, maybe I could sneak out without them noticing.

Brittany broke their kiss and pressed a fingertip to Matthew's lips. "I think we should get back, don't you? Wouldn't want the Chosen One to be caught breaking the rules."

Matthew smirked. "Those rules are for everyone else. You and I are special." He slid his hands up Brittany's back.

Brittany giggled. "Shouldn't all of us follow the rules?"

Matthew paused. "You're cute, you know that. No, babe, there are rules for the masses and rules for the privileged. Guess which ones we are."

Brittany tipped her head to the side.

"Do you have any idea what they're grooming me for?"

"Something very important obviously. Like CEO or a senator?"

"Think higher. Why stop at senator?" He kissed her neck. " With HP's political and financial clout, I plan to become our nation's youngest president."

"President?" Brittany gasped. "Is that your purpose?"

Matthew chuckled. "It is. Did you know I'm the youngest Council member HP has ever chosen? The people in power see my potential." He grasped the zipper on the back of Brittany's dress and pulled it down. "You have that special something too, Brittany. Don't you want to be my chosen one?"

Brittany squirmed. "I do, of course. I just think we need to take things slow."

"We will," Matthew murmured. "But we've got to see if we're a good fit, right?" He slid the spaghetti straps of her dress down her shoulders. "Your skin is so soft."

Brittany held her dress against her chest. "I'm not comfortable with this."

"Just relax." Matthew ran his hands up the backs of Brittany's thighs, sliding them under her dress.

"That's enough." Brittany tried to take a step backward.

Matthew grabbed her wrist. "We can get out the Cherry Garcia soon, I promise."

"You're hurting me," Brittany protested, trying to tug her arm free. "Let go, Matthew."

Matthew's grip tightened and I imagined the bones in Brittany's slim wrist grinding together. My anger flared but I forced myself to remain still.

"Think carefully about what you're doing," he said, the charm gone from his voice. "You walk away now, you're losing out on a huge opportunity."

Brittany's face flooded with fear and indecision.

"I know what's best. You'll learn that I always know what's best." Still holding Brittany's wrist in one hand, he yanked her dress with the other. It dropped to the floor, leaving Brittany in her lacy pink bra and underwear.

The spot between the machines was hot and my eye throbbed. I sent silent messages for my friends to come. One way or another, things were about to get ugly, and I needed their help.

Brittany's lips trembled. Tears bubbled over her lower eyelids and streaked down her flawless cheeks. I knew what she must be thinking. If she gave in to Matthew, she could fulfill her greatest wishes. Being paired with the Chosen One would open wide the elite world of acting and modeling. On Matthew's arm, she would be successful, famous, maybe even the First Lady.

But clearly, she was also afraid. Matthew's true nature was on display, and would she want a future with that, no matter how much success it brought?

Brittany's tears dried up and she pulled herself together. "Let me go, now," she said, her voice firm.

Matthew's back stiffened and I felt his rage fill the room like a gust of wind. "Wrong answer," he jerked Brittany roughly toward him and wrapped his arm around her waist. She yelped and tried to push against his chest, kicking at his shins with her flimsy heels. He grabbed her other wrist, pinning her arms to her side. Struggling frantically, Brittany looked over Matthew's shoulder, spotting me as I stepped out from the gap. Her eyes widened and she opened her mouth to cry out.

I held a finger to my lips then pointed to the floor and mouthed the word *drop*.

Brittany's eyes flashed understanding. She went limp, falling to the ground as I braced one foot against the freezer door, channeled Charles' football brilliance, and launched myself at Matthew.

I hit the Chosen One in the center of his back and we crashed to the floor. Matthew's breath huffed out and his head cracked against the linoleum. I planted a knee on his back and pressed one of his bent arms toward his shoulder blade.

"Oh, my goodness," Brittany exclaimed, pacing in a circle and wringing her hands. "Lina, are you okay? How did you ... what were you ... what happened to your eye?"

Matthew appeared to be unconscious, but I wasn't taking any chances. The pain and adrenaline heightened my determination. "Brittany, I need you to focus," I snapped. "We need rope or something to tie him up."

"Tie him up? You can't be serious."

"Listen, I need you to trust me. I don't have time to explain, but I can't have Matthew raising any sort of alarm right now. I need at least an hour. Can you help me?"

Brittany stopped pacing and stood over us, her gaze flicking between me and Matthew. I was waiting for her to freak out and run screaming out of the room. Instead, my roommate's expression hardened. She turned and strode toward a group of cupboards. "I think I know just the thing," she said, flinging open a door and rummaging.

Matthew made a low groaning noise. I held on tight to his arm.

Brittany's heels clacked as she ran back, clutching a large spool of what looked like gray yarn.

"It's twine," she knelt next to me. "I noticed it when I was doing the cookie class. It's for tying up chickens and roasts before you cook them."

The back door burst open, and Hayden, Gabi and Charles ran in, wearing black clothing. They stared at Matthew lying on the floor, with me and an almost naked Brittany on top of him.

"Bloody hell," Hayden exclaimed. "What happened now?"

"We're behind," Gabi said. "We need to get moving."

As if on cue, the power went out and we were plunged into darkness. There were screams and then cheers from the dance floor. The lights flickered back on to more cheers and yelling.

"Countdown begins," Charles said.

Matthew groaned.

"I've got to stay and tie him up," I said. "Otherwise, he'll ruin everything."

"We need you, Lina," Hayden protested. "We can't handle the fence without you."

"I'll stay," Gabi said. "I'll ..." she looked nervously at Matthew.

"Go," Brittany commanded, unwrapping twine from the spool. "I'll take care of him."

"How are you going to—" I stopped when she started wrapping the twine around Matthew's wrists in quick, deft motions.

"Didn't I tell you that I was the junior Galveston rodeo champion?" Brittany pulled the twine tight, causing a louder moan. "Calf roping was my best event."

"I thought you were a pageant queen. Like bathing suits and big hair."

"Oh, I am." Holding Matthew's wrists with one hand, she reached to grab one of his ankles. "But I'm a daddy's girl at heart." She wrapped the twine around the ankle and pulled.

"And Daddy didn't raise no fool. Y'all get going. I have no idea what the heck you're up to, but I'll keep him quiet. I suspect we'll be left alone." She wound the twine around the second ankle. "Something tells me I wasn't the first girl he brought into this kitchen. Nobody's going to disturb the Chosen One while he takes what he wants."

CHAPTER THIRTY-THREE

OUTSIDE, A HALF-MOON provided dim light. I stumbled and grabbed onto Charles as we hurried to the parking lot. By the time we reached the bins, my vision had adjusted enough to see Hayden retrieve a gym bag and rolled-up tarp. I shed my dress and changed into a black shirt, shorts, and tennis shoes. Gabi handed me a mini flashlight.

"Eight minutes," Hayden said, shoving my clothes into the bag and tossing it behind the dumpster. "Let's roll."

We ran toward the lab building, Hayden easily guiding us away from any potential security. Before, the building had appeared dull and unimportant. Now, as we got closer, it emerged, dark and menacing. Exterior lights shot eerie yellow slashes up the walls and the barbed wire loomed overhead.

"Five minutes," Hayden whispered.

Eric had said that cutting the power would force the entire security system to reboot, which took ten minutes. The power had gone out, so Eric had achieved step two of our plan—the first having been me creating a scene to allow my friends to sneak away from the dance. Step three was getting into the building before the security system came back on.

"Someone remind me, how are we getting over that fence," Charles said.

I elbowed him. "Don't even."

Hayden led us to a dense group of trees. The tall pines blocked the light from the moon, casting a section of the fence and the building beyond it into murky darkness. Even if someone were monitoring the security cameras, they probably wouldn't spot us.

Eric was waiting, bobbing up and down on his toes. He was still wearing his dress clothes, having insisted that no way would he strip down outside, even if no one was watching.

"What took you so long?" he asked. "We've only got four minutes."

"Any problems with the reboot?" Hayden asked.

"Piece of cake."

"Brilliant." Hayden handed me the tarp. "Ready?"

"Yep," I said, although my heart was racing. On the mini trampoline, I had practiced boosting myself high onto the climbing wall. I had also been working on my tumbling skills. But there had been no way to truly be ready for this moment.

My friends were shapes in the darkness, the fence a fortress with pointy claws. I unrolled the tarp and walked forward until I was an arm's length from it. Charles stepped behind me and put his hands on my waist. Having him there made me feel calmer and more confident. "Don't worry," he said. "Like I told you, I help my cousins practice all the time."

"Four minutes," Gabi whispered.

"Okay, here we go." Hayden put his mouth next to Charles' ear. "One, two ..."

I had not been able to practice this part with a person but had imagined it on the trampoline. And Charles had talked me through it over and over. As Hayden said "three," I bent my knees and jumped straight up. Charles lifted me and, in a flash, I was above his head—my feet on his shoulders, my knees locked, and his hands wrapped tight around my ankles. Breathing hard, I paused, focusing on keeping my balance and not dropping the tarp.

"Throw and go over, throw and go over," I whispered. Holding the tarp straight ahead, I bent my knees again. Charles let go of my ankles and I sprang forward, draping the tarp over the barbs as I somersaulted over the fence. I came down hard on the other side, managing to stay on my feet.

I spun in triumph, feeling like a gymnast who had nailed the landing. The boys were watching Gabi scramble up the fence. At the top, she swung one leg over the tarp, brought the other leg over, and climbed down to stand next to me. We fist-bumped.

Eric was next and made whimpering noises his whole way up. He paused long enough at the top that I started worrying we would run out of time. I suspected he had never climbed anything taller than a ladder before. With all of us whispering encouragement, Eric slid one leg over the tarp, then the other. By the time he whimpered his way down into our outstretched arms, Hayden was over. He stopped at the bottom and leaned in to speak to Charles. The consensus had been that Charles should avoid the fence given his spider web experience. His job now was to stay outside and look for trouble.

There was a low-humming noise and I grabbed Eric's arm. "Is that an alarm? We should still have two minutes left."

"We're fine," Eric said, sounding less confident than when he had stated that all HP security doors would be unlocked during the reboot period. That had made zero sense to me—why would a top-secret building have such poor security? Wouldn't they have some sort of backup?

"Arrogance," Eric had stated, just as Nick had. "Blakewell is counting on the brainwashing to keep us compliant. That, plus their cameras and alarms, they figure they've got adequate protection."

"Let's go." Hayden strode to a side door. "If the alarm goes off, we head back over the fence." Holding up one hand, he reached for the door with the other and pulled it open.

Nothing. No wails of an alarm.

"Told you," Eric exclaimed.

We entered a hall and switched on our flashlights. That hall led to a larger perpendicular hall that ran the length of the building. Rows of identical doors lined both sides.

"Split up but stay close," I said. Eric and I turned right while Hayden and Gabi turned left. I opened the first door and ran my light over a square office with a desk, two chairs, a filing cabinet, and a bookshelf. A poster of the periodic table on one wall and framed diplomas on the other. The bookshelf held rows of magazines and textbooks.

I moved to the next room, which was similar, except with a framed poster of aspen trees on one wall and photos of kids pinned to a bulletin board. When the third room was the same, I poked my head into the hallway. "Eric," I called.

He appeared, holding an object that looked like a glass slinky. "The double helix," he exclaimed, grinning like a kid with a new toy.

"Are you finding anything important?"

He shook his head. "These rooms are too small to perform research. We need to locate the lab space."

"Go find Gabi and Hayden. I'll catch up." I jogged down the rest of the hall, opening the remaining doors and confirming they were all offices.

I joined the others in the dimly lit lobby.

"No luck." Hayden gave a frustrated tug at the strap of the miniature camera hung around his neck.

"What if it's something on their computers?" Gabi said. "You wouldn't need lab space for that."

"You also wouldn't need a building like this with physical security," Eric said. "Your focus would be on cyber threats."

"Maybe they didn't want to risk cyber threats," Gabi said. "Self-contained is the safest way to go."

"If we're looking at genetic manipulation and experiments, there has to be physical research going on here," Eric said.

"And something that needs to be removed in trucks," I added. "What about a basement? Hayden, did you see an elevator or stairs?"

Hayden shook his head. "Just offices, a kitchen, and a custodial closet."

"What about the roof?" Gabi asked. "Could they have a lab up there?"

"I already scouted the roof," Hayden said. "Nothing." He ran a hand over his face. "At the very least, Lina and I can go through the cabinets. Eric and Gabi, you get on the computers. There has to be something."

"Wait a second," Gabi held up a hand. "Just be quiet." She closed her eyes.

I flashed the boys a questioning look. They shrugged.

Gabi knelt and pressed her hands to the floor. "Do you hear that? That humming noise?"

We tilted our heads, like dogs trying to hear a whistle.

"I don't hear anything," I said. Actually, I heard gurgles from my stomach as I hadn't eaten since lunch.

"There's a basement. A machine is humming down there."

Hayden snapped his fingers. "The custodial closet. One of the walls looked a little off. Come on."

The windowless closet was clean, with a white-tiled floor and walls. A bucket and mop stood in the corner and metal shelves along the walls held neatly stacked cleaning supplies. Hayden moved to the far wall. He placed his finger on a straight crack running through the rows of tiles. "A door? Maybe an elevator?"

Eric pointed to a keypad on the wall behind the shelves. "We need the code."

"Of course we do," Hayden pounded the tile in frustration.

Eric typed in four numbers. The keypad beeped and flashed a red light. "Okay, here we go," he murmured. He typed in four other numbers. Another beep and red flash.

"How are you going to guess their code?" Hayden exclaimed. "It's probably some random scientist's birthday."

Eric ignored him, typing in more sets of numbers. Gabi stood next to him, offering suggestions.

"Let's see if we can find something to pry this open," Hayden said, just as the keypad flashed a green light. There was a clunk and the tile walls slid aside revealing an elevator car.

Hayden whooped and clapped a grinning Eric on the shoulder. "1783?" he guessed, as we piled into the elevator. "The year HP was founded," he added for my sake.

"I tried that one first," Eric said. "Then 1786, the year the first cohort graduated."

"And Haverford's birthday," Gabi chimed in. "And the ratification of—"

"What was it?" I said.

"1940, the year HP relocated to Colorado." Eric flashed me a smug look. "What did I tell you—arrogance. They must have set that years ago and never changed it."

The elevator doors opened onto a long corridor. A giant framed photo hung directly in front of us—black and white overlapping circles, resembling daisy petals.

More framed photos lined the rest of the corridor. The next was of a weirdly shaped orange blob, the next a tiny alien.

"Embryonic development," Gabi said. "Starting at conception."

"Then this has to be the place where they create the embryos," I said.

Hayden held up the camera. "And we're going to get proof."

Gabi stopped in front of a photo of a tiny, pale fetus sucking its thumb. "Maybe, but why here, in the middle of nowhere? Isn't it more likely they have labs set up closer to big cities? Easier to transfer and less expensive?"

"We're about to find out," I headed down the corridor toward a set of double doors.

A plaque above the doors read *He alone, who owns the youth, gains the future.*

Gabi groaned.

"Another Harlan?"

"No, the OG Nazi. Hitler's rallying speech to his party in 1935. Man was crazy, but he was a genius."

Hayden took a photo.

A paper taped to the door read *Proper Sanitation Requirements*

Must Be Followed Past This Point. Packets of antibacterial wipes, surgical masks, and gloves were stacked on a cart.

"Do you think there are toxic chemicals in there?" Eric asked. "Or some sort of virulent bacteria?" He washed his hands every hour, wore a mask when he traveled, and only ate meat that bordered on burnt.

"No," Gabi reassured him. "I think this is to keep us from contaminating the lab space."

Ignoring the protective equipment, Hayden pushed through the double doors. I followed him and ran right into his back, "What the ..." he exclaimed.

CHAPTER
THIRTY-FOUR

WE STOOD IN A VAST, DARK ROOM. Warm air wafted against my cheeks, a contrast to the cool hall. Lights strung across the ceiling and along the walls gave off a dim glow.

Rows of what looked like giant fish tanks ran the length of the room. They were filled with a thick yellowish liquid. No fish that I could see. Hayden snapped a photo then pressed his hand against the tank. "It's warm."

Gabi and I felt the glass, which was a pleasant temperature. I got the sense that the liquid inside was moving.

Eric entered, wearing a mask, safety glasses, and gloves.

Gabi cupped her hands around her eyes and peered into the murkiness. "Look at that."

I copied her and Eric pressed his goggled eyes next to mine. Something resembling a jellyfish was floating in the middle of the tank.

The jellyfish bobbed toward us. Eric let out a shriek and jumped behind my back. It retreated and I realized it was only shifting with the movement of the liquid.

"Is that some sort of jellyfish?" Hayden echoed my thoughts. "I'm afraid the camera isn't going to pick it up." He took several shots anyway.

"It's a giant bacteria," Eric moaned. "It's a Teenage Mutant Ninja Turtle bacteria."

"It doesn't have tentacles," Gabi said. "So, it's not a jellyfish. And it's not round, spiral, or rod." She twisted around to frown at Eric. "It's not a mutant bacteria. Get over here and look again."

Eric came back out. "It looks like a giant dacrocyte."

"A what?" Hayden and I said.

"A teardrop-shaped cell," Gabi explained.

"Looks like it has a tether," Hayden said.

Gabi stood on her tiptoes. "We need to get higher."

"I'll boost you." Hayden knelt and formed his hands into a step.

Gabi shrank away. "Cheerleading coach thought I'd be a good flyer since I'm tiny. Only time I tried, I fractured my tailbone."

Hayden shifted toward me. I placed a foot in his hands and let him boost me up. I leaned into the glass, cupping my hands. A blob was floating across from me. At the top, its shape tapered into what looked like a thick rope that stretched up toward the top of the tank. As the liquid shifted, the blob bobbed gently up and down, its shape stretching and contracting. "It's springy. Kind of like a water balloon with a string."

"Can you see where the string goes?" Eric asked.

"Not really. Just a hole." I stretched my fingers up to the top of the tank and felt where the glass met a steel cover. "I can get up there. I just need a bigger boost."

Hayden knelt and I hopped down. He cupped his hands again, I stepped and he boosted me, harder and higher. I gripped the edge of the tank cover and swung my legs up.

It was even darker up here, but I could make out a metal mesh that covered the tank, except for a round opening in the middle. I crawled over and pulled out my flashlight.

"What do you see?" Gabi asked.

I shone the light on a thick tube that came out of the opening. Where it left the tank, it was a canvas-like material, then became plastic tubing, like a giant, flexible straw. The tube crossed the metal cover and connected to a machine that sat on a platform against the wall.

I relayed a description to my friends.

"What does the material feel like?" Gabi asked. "Is it biological, synthetic?"

Biological? I flashed to Eric's fears. Could this be some creature or contagious bacteria? Before I could scare myself, I reached out my hand. The material was warm and spongy, like how I imagined an elephant's skin would feel.

"It's pulsing," I exclaimed.

A gasp from Gabi, then excited talking between her and Eric.

"Lina," Eric said. "Look at the clear tube. Can you see what's inside?"

I aimed my flashlight. "More tubes. One is kind of pink and another is greenish." I flashed my light down the length of the tanks. They were identical, with tubes running from the covers into machines. Collectively the machines made the humming noise Gabi had heard from the first floor.

The doors from the hallway banged open. I flattened myself onto my stomach as Matthew strode into the room, followed by Crystal and security men. "Well, well, look what we have here," he drawled. His white shirt was wrinkled and dirty. A rectangular bandage ran across his forehead and his normally perfect hair was messy. I sent up a silent prayer that Brittany was okay.

"Looks like we found our dissenters." Matthew nodded at Eric. "I didn't think you had the guts, Geekit. Apparently, we need to tighten up our cybersecurity."

Eric folded into himself, rubbing his gloved fingers together.

Matthew took a step toward him. "Where is your friend?" He pointed to his forehead. "She did this to me, you know."

Eric cringed and whimpered, "I don't know."

"Hold on," Crystal said. She pointed at Hayden. "Jamison was with him. He was taking her back to her room."

Matthew swiveled. "Where is she, Hayden?"

"I left her in her room," Hayden said.

"Come on my friend. You're on the wrong side of this all, you know."

"I left her in her room," Hayden repeated. "Friend."

A long pause. "So, it's going to be like that." Matthew nodded at one of the men who stepped forward and punched Hayden in the stomach. Gabi screamed as Hayden dropped to his knees. I imagined leaping on top of Matthew, this time crushing his body into the ground and slamming his head over and over into the concrete until he couldn't get up.

Matthew yanked the camera from around Hayden's neck. He dropped it on the floor and stomped on it. "Want to try again?"

Hayden remained silent, breathing heavily. I knew he was hurting. I also knew that he wouldn't talk. With his training, he could be beaten to a pulp and not give information to this weasel.

"Go check her cabin," Matthew ordered two men who nodded and headed toward the corridor. He ran his gaze over the tanks and the space above them. I held my breath as his eyes passed over my spot.

He gestured to more men. "Take them to Doctor Volkov. He knows what to do."

The men stepped forward, grabbed my friends and pulled them away. I knew Eric was terrified and wished I could comfort him. I wondered if Hayden would put up a fight, but he stood and cooperated. No doubt he could break free and escape, but where would he go? And who could help him? He would wait until they were outside to put up resistance.

"The rest of you scour this building," Matthew commanded. "I want that girl found and brought to me immediately."

The remaining men separated and began shining their flashlights in the crevices between the tanks.

"What's the plan?" Crystal asked. "Accidental deaths?"

Matthew steepled his fingers under his chin. "No. A memory wipe is better. Multiple deaths could damage our reputation. We still need parents to be excited to send their kids here."

I tried to corral my anger so I could focus. A memory wipe? Matthew was sending my friends to Volkov to be altered like lab rats. I had to stop it.

A clanging noise caught my attention. One of the men was starting to climb the ladder on my tank. I glanced around for a place to hide. The tanks were in a row, each with a machine behind them. There were gaps between the machines, but I would be easily found there.

I stared at the hole in the top of the tank. There was only one option. It might kill me, but what other choice did I have? Saving my friends was up to me and I would die trying.

Drawing my arm back, I threw my flashlight as hard as I could toward the opposite row of tanks. It hit a grate with a bang and bounced, making a series of clanging noises. When everyone had turned in that direction, I crawled to the hole, took a deep breath and pushed myself headfirst into the liquid.

Bracing for skin digesting chemicals, I was relieved to feel like I was entering a bath of warm soup. The liquid was thick enough to keep me from sinking, so I curled into a ball.

After a long moment, when there was no shouting or hands reaching to pull me out, I knew I hadn't been spotted. I felt the thump of the man's footsteps above me, the pauses to shine his flashlight between the tanks. I hoped he wouldn't think to look inside the tanks.

I opened my eyes, surprised to find the liquid was soothing and it felt like being in a thick fog. In front of me floated the blob and just beyond the glass were the shapes of Matthew and Crystal, their voices low rumbles.

My lungs twinged. It had been one minute. There were four tanks after mine, then the security guy needed to climb back down the ladder before I could come up for a breath.

Matthew was gesturing and yelling. Crystal stepped back and held up her hands. I tried not to fixate on images of my friends in Volkov's lab having their memories wiped. It sounded like something from the *Star Trek* episodes my dad liked to watch. Would they forget me and everything we had discovered this summer? Would it change their personalities forever?

My lungs were starting to ache. I ignored them. The thumps were coming back my way. I felt confident I could hold out until the man left.

There was movement next to me. The blob was rippling and bulging. It almost looked like—my heart thumped hard. I had a sweeping sense of déjà vu, of being in another liquid, floating and suspended.

I stretched out my hand, touching my palm to the blob's spongy side. Something inside shifted. A smaller bulge formed and pressed against my palm. A bolt of understanding as I got what Eric and Gabi had likely figured out a few minutes ago. Pressed against my palm was a tiny hand.

CHAPTER
THIRTY-FIVE

I SURFACED SILENTLY, forcing myself to take a slow breath. Everything made sense. Years of stealing genetic material to form embryos. The Hitler quote: *He alone, who owns the youth, gains the future.* HP wouldn't need to continue their in vitro program because they had a new, terrible solution. They were growing their own babies.

The clack of heels below. "She's not in her room," Becky said.

"She's not here either, sir," a man said. "We've searched this entire space."

"Recheck the upstairs and scour the perimeter," Matthew ordered. I heard him striding toward the door and the clattering of heels as Becky and Crystal followed.

I needed to escape this building and get help. With enough trainees on my side, we could stop Volkov and prevent the trucks from taking away the fetuses. Even with the brainwashing, the other Plebes were not fools. I could get Ryan, Sakura, and most of the Baby Joes to believe me. At a minimum, we would create enough chaos to spoil Blakewell's plans.

But how was I going to get out of here?

I pulled myself out of the tank and waited in the semidarkness, listening to the machines' hum. The tubes were pulsing, in what I now knew mimicked a mother's heartbeat, pumping nutrients through a fake umbilical cord to a developing baby.

Forcing myself to wait two minutes—time for Matthew's gang to get out of the building—I stood and walked to the edge, feeling the thick liquid sliding off of me. I climbed carefully back to the ground. The elevator was not an option as Matthew would have someone stationed at the top. I ran to the opposite end of the room. My chemistry teacher had described labs that had mini elevators that transported materials between floors. If this lab had one, maybe I could squeeze myself into it and ride it up.

Every cabinet door in the room was flung open. No mini elevator. I grabbed two X-Acto blades from the counter, sliding them into the elastic of my sports bra, next to my spine. Last time I had tried to use a knife, I had ended up unconscious in a river. Still, I would try again to save my friends.

Next to the lab, I shoved open double doors into a trash room. Red bins on the left wall had *Biohazard* printed on them. Black dumpsters with wheels were on the right. Directly in front of me was an elevator. I ran to it and pressed the button next to the door. It didn't light up. There was a keypad and I tried 1940. No luck. 1783. No. 1786. No. I tried other combinations like 1234, 2468, and 1776, but the keypad just blinked red.

I pounded on the doors. My friends could be in Volkov's lab right now. The next time I saw them, if I ever saw them, would their gazes look through me as if we had never met?

I grabbed a black bin overflowing with trash and rolled it into the center of the room. Muscles straining, I pushed it forward, letting go at the last second and sending it crashing into the elevator. The bin shuddered, and trash flew out of the container. The doors didn't budge.

I wanted to scream. My only choice was to brave the main elevator and hope for slacker security. Turning, I stared at a space where the black dumpster had been. The piled-up trash had been blocking a large round hole in the wall. With a rush of hope, I ran over. The hole went into the wall at an angle, stretching up and out of sight. A trash chute, just like in the apartment building on *Friends*!

I stuck my head inside. It smelled like rotten food, but the metal walls were clean and dry. Boosting myself up, I planted my hands and feet against the metal, wedging myself into the space. Moving my hands and elbows first, keeping them pressed against the wall, I then shifted my feet up. Within moments, my muscles were aching and I was sweating. A little sweat would help my skin stick to the metal, but too much would have the opposite effect, leading to a fall onto hard cement.

After what seemed like an hour of moving inch by inch, I reached a panel in the wall. Bracing myself with my other three limbs, I pushed the panel with my foot. It wouldn't budge. Trembling, I drew back the leg and kicked hard.

There was a pinging noise, and the panel swung open, revealing darkness beyond it. I thrust my body through the opening and tumbled to the floor. I was in one of the hallways. I waited for the sounds of footsteps or voices yelling. Silence. I needed to get out of the building and back over the fence.

Was Charles still there? Had he tried to help? I crawled into the closest office, opened its window, and climbed out. Fortunately, I was close to where we had entered. The tarp was still there, draped over the barbed wire. I scrambled over the fence and dove into the brush. Within moments, I heard noises and a flashlight beam played over the grass.

"We can't keep searching this whole area," a man's voice grumbled.

"We're not going to find her until morning," another man said. "I told Drexler we needed to bring the dogs."

"Nowhere to go anyhow with that electric fence." A yawn. "Let's head back."

I waited until the voices faded. If Matthew's men were ready to give up for the night, I had a chance. If I could get to the lab, I could ... I could ... okay, I didn't know what I could do. But I would figure it out or rally the Baby Joes.

I began moving toward The Cube, scanning for Charles. I kicked something hard. Charles' flashlight. He wouldn't have left this willingly. It was a cloudless night, so I aimed the flashlight at the sky and clicked the button: three fast, three slow, three fast. It was worth a try, just in case Nick or another ally was out there watching. Slipping the flashlight into my pocket, I kept going.

The courtyard in front of The Cube was illuminated. Blakewell, Matthew, and Crystal stood in the center, their heads bowed together. A group of security men surrounded Charles, who was bent over and breathing hard. There was no sign of my other friends. I crept through the trees toward the back entrance. If I could get in that way, I could locate Volkov's lab and free them.

A bright light shone on my face.

"Gotcha," Becky crowed. "I knew you'd come to rescue your boyfriend."

Before I could react, I was pulled off my feet by a man standing in the shadows. Kicking and struggling, I was dragged into the courtyard.

The trio turned and Blakewell's face lit up in a Jack-O-Lantern grin. "Excellent work." He nodded approvingly at Becky. "You were right, young lady."

The man set me in front of them. Matthew touched a hand to his bandaged forehead. "Your time at HP seems to be coming to an end." He looked me up and down, ran a finger along my arm then touched it to his lips.

He gave a disbelieving laugh. "She was in one of the tanks. Can you believe it?"

"Smart girl." Blakewell regarded me like I was a disobedient show dog. "Too bad you will never get to show us your potential."

I pulled myself up as tall as I could. "You won't succeed. Even if you get rid of all of us."

Charles' head struggled up. His face was bloody, one of his eyes swollen shut and his breathing fast and wheezy.

Blakewell pursed his fat lips in amusement. "But we have, and we will succeed. Well into the second trimester and all the parameters are excellent. We've had some kinks we needed to work out, but the fetuses are developing nicely."

"Fetuses?" Charles rasped.

"They're growing lab babies," I practically spit. "No mothers needed."

"Hallelujah," Crystal raised her clipboard in the air. "You have no idea what a hassle it has been using human carriers. Collecting the specimens, arranging the swaps, tracking the urchins. A nightmare."

"This almost seems simple in comparison," Matthew said. He winked at Becky. "Simple solutions are often the best."

"They'll figure you out," Charles croaked.

The group shared a condescending smile. "People are idiots," Blakewell said. "So many couples out there desperate to adopt a healthy baby." He looked pointedly at Charles. "Especially a healthy white baby. Nobody is going to question anything. They haven't so far."

"Not true. Nick figured it out," I said. "He knew you were using genetic engineering to create embryos. So, you tried to kill him."

The security men's faces were neutral. How could they hear this and do nothing?

Matthew chuckled. "You mean we *did* kill him, or didn't sweet Hayden tell you the truth? Maybe he thought you were too sensitive."

Blakewell scowled. "Nicholas Shaw should have been strong-armed to join the team. He had an exceptional scientific mind."

"He didn't agree with our principles, and we couldn't take the risk," Matthew said. "Sometimes you have to sacrifice one to benefit the many."

Matthew and Blakewell didn't know Nick was alive! That meant there was still a tiny chance. I needed to buy more time.

"HP has a long history of doing just that, doesn't it?" I said. "Getting rid of trainees or grads who don't blindly follow the rules, who come too close to the truth. Where is that mentioned in your handbook?"

Blakewell smirked. "There's a lot that isn't in the handbook."

"So, you're planning to grow your own HP army? Let me guess, they'll all be perfect soldiers, just like you?"

Blakewell ran his eyes over my body and made a face. "Well, certainly, few to none will look like you." His eyes flicked again to Charles. "Or him. Although we'll always have a need for our negro athletes." He clapped his hands together. "Anyway, take LeBron here to the memory wipe with the others. I'm sure nobody will notice a drop in his IQ."

I tried to get to Charles, but one man grabbed me while another wrapped ropes around my wrists and ankles and shoved a cloth in my mouth. It tasted like gasoline and sweat. I gagged, trying not to puke.

Charles was thrashing and struggling. One of the men smashed him in the head with a baton and he collapsed. They dragged him into the building.

I tried to scream but gagged more. When I managed to stop retching, Blakewell and the gang were watching me, like cats waiting to devour a mouse.

Blakewell turned to Becky. "You found her so she's all yours."

Becky's eyes lit up and she clapped her hands together like a child getting a Christmas present. "Really?"

"Just be sure you finish the job this time," Matthew said.

Crystal held up a hand. "I thought you said deaths of trainees would be too hard to explain."

"It would," Blakewell said. "The deaths of five trainees would be hard to explain. Not so the death of one troubled girl."

Becky gestured to the security. "Bring her to me."

I was lifted, carried, and set in front of Becky—her sacrificial offering.

Blakewell flicked his hand to the men. "Go. Be back here at six a.m. sharp to load the trucks."

The men nodded and headed toward HP's exit. I watched them go, feeling helpless. Where had they found men who would abandon a teenage girl to be murdered? And return the next day to load up a truck with tanks of fetuses? More brainwashing? A lot of money? Both?

As Becky walked slowly around me, I thought about how my Ranger would behave if he were captured by the enemy. No weakness. No fear. I stared straight ahead.

Becky pinched my arms, ran a finger up my neck, flipped my hair. "How would you like to go? I'll give you a choice. Fire. Hanging." She planted herself directly in front of me, staring into my eyes. "Drowning?"

I met Becky's gaze with defiance.

She yanked the cloth out of my mouth. "Well?"

I stuck out my chin. "Sine missione."

Becky blinked in confusion, then let out a laugh. She turned to Matthew. "Did you hear that? This shrimp wants a fight to the death."

"Are you afraid?" I challenged. With a measly few weeks of training so far, I had little hope. Besides having two more years of experience, Becky was at least six inches taller and forty pounds heavier. But a fight would give me a chance, and take time.

Becky whooped. "Are you kidding? I'll even let you choose the weapon. If I were you, I would stay away from a knife this time."

I thought of the blades tucked in my bra. I might do some damage with those, if I could get them out.

"Enough," Blakewell said, glancing at his watch. "The dance is ending and we need this done." He gestured toward the maple tree. "String her up there. We'll call it a suicide."

Becky's face fell, but she nodded obediently. Grabbing under my arms, she half dragged, half carried me toward the tree.

"Why are you listening to them?" I hissed. "They don't care about you. You're not important."

"False," Becky said. "Next summer, I'll join Matthew on the Council. Our inner circle will grow in power and direct HP's future."

"You think someone who whips you is going to let you in his inner circle?"

Becky's nostrils flared.

"Yeah, I know about that. And he'll be stringing you up next."

"Shut up." She shoved me against the tree. "Matthew and I will shepherd the next generation of trainees to greatness."

I struggled to free my wrists, which were not well bound. If I could get a hand free, I could reach a blade. A well-aimed slice would stop Becky, at least temporarily. "Maybe that's why he was kissing another girl earlier—because you're his choice to shepherd the next generation?"

Becky backhanded me. My head slammed into the tree. When my vision cleared, Crystal was handing her a rope. Becky quickly tied one end into a noose and looped it around my neck. Crystal dragged a decorative stump over and set it next to Becky. "Leave it tipped over here. Make it look like she climbed up then kicked it away."

Behind my back, I was twisting my wrists back and forth, ignoring the pain from the rope cutting into my flesh.

Becky handed the end of the rope to Crystal. She climbed up the tree to a sturdy branch above my head.

Blood was trickling down my arms, but I kept twisting and pulling. The blood made everything slippery and, with a hard tug, I managed to slide a hand out. The rope loosened and both hands were free.

Crystal was holding the rope in one hand and examining her nails on the other. I considered an elbow strike, but my feet were still tied together. I wouldn't be able to free them before Becky made it back down.

"Give me the rope," Becky said. Crystal threw Becky the end of the rope, then walked back toward Matthew and Blakewell.

"Climb up on the stump," Becky commanded.

When I ignored her, she began pulling on the rope. As it tightened around my neck, I stood on my tiptoes, then was forced to climb onto the stump to relieve the pressure.

Blakewell, Matthew, and Crystal were watching as if they were spectators at a football game, and their team was winning.

Becky tied the rope around the branch, then climbed back down. She flashed me a look of triumph. "Here we go, Kitty Cat. Any last words? Want me to tell your boyfriend that you cried out for him?" She put a hand to her mouth in mock surprise. "Oh wait, that won't work. He won't even remember who you are."

My body flooded with anger as Becky kicked the stump out from underneath me. Hard, thick rope cut into my neck. I choked and grabbed at it with both hands, trying to pull myself up, to give myself a chance to breathe. I was able to hold myself up for a moment, then the weight from my body was too much. Kicking and spinning, my vision blurred as the rope cut off the blood supply to my brain.

CHAPTER
THIRTY-SIX

AS BLACKNESS CONSUMED ME, I heard noises and yelling. Suddenly, the pressure was gone and I was being lifted. The rope was loosened and pulled over my head. My vision cleared and I was looking into Nick's concerned eyes. He was holding me on his hip like a toddler. I wrapped my arms around the pasty Scot and took hitching breaths. "It worked. You're here."

"It worked," he agreed. "Using the tracker was brilliant." He set me down, keeping his arm around my shoulders to hold me steady. "We were outside, ready for action tomorrow. Then we saw the SOS and knew we'd better get in stat."

Soldiers had filled the courtyard. Becky was unmoving on the grass nearby, a soldier's foot planted on her back. Across the courtyard, Blakewell was trying to charm the stone-faced woman gripping his arm. "It was just a training exercise, nobody would be harmed."

Crystal sat on the cement, a broken heel next to her. "You don't know who you're messing with," she screamed as two soldiers yanked her up.

"Hayden," I grasped Nick's arm. "The lab. They're being memory-wiped."

Nick's eyes widened. "General Cole," he gestured to a man with cropped gray hair. The man strode over, his expression darkening as he took in my bloody wrists and black eye. "Unbelievable."

His piercing green eyes and strong jaw were familiar. He was the Council member who I had thought looked familiar at Cotillion practice. "My friends are in there," I gestured toward The Cube. "They're being memory-wiped."

The general called over a soldier. "Take Collins and Keyes and go check it out."

I looked around. "Nick, where is Matthew? He was here too."

Nick turned in a circle. "We need to find Matthew Drexler now. He's extremely dangerous."

Cole beckoned over more soldiers.

"I'll come with you," Nick said to them. "I know the places he might hide." He gripped my arms and looked into my face. "I'll be right back."

I watched them run toward The Chalet. On unsteady feet, I spun and stumbled toward The Cube. General Cole took my arm and, instead of stopping me, helped me up the stairs and inside.

Sounds of running footsteps and shouts. At the end of the hall, a bank of windows looked into what resembled a hospital nursery. Instead of bundled newborns in bassinets, my friends lay motionless in hospital beds. Wires ran out of black helmets on their heads.

"No!" I shoved the door and tumbled into the room. It was cold and smelled like rubbing alcohol. Two soldiers had a man in black pants and a dress shirt pinned against the far wall—Doctor Volkov, his dark eyes cold, his lips curled into a sneer.

I ran to the closest bed. Hayden looked like a little boy with his pale face, dark eyelashes, and fringes of damp hair poking out from underneath the helmet. The scar on his chin was puffy and red, like someone had slapped him. The black wires traveled into a machine that hummed and beeped. Next to it was a screen with a moving, jagged line, and a bunch of numbers. I recognized that screen from TV shows. My dad had explained that it measured a patient's heart function. Clear liquid dripped from an IV bag into plastic tubing that ran under a thick white bandage on Hayden's arm. I imagined it sending poison into his body, through his veins and into his brain to eat away at his memories.

I tried to pull off the helmet. The plastic lifted partway off, revealing rubber suction cups that were attached to his head. I glanced around the room, looking for scissors or a knife, anything sharp. Suddenly, remembering, I reached under my T-shirt. The X-Acto blades were still there, held snugly between my shoulder blades. I slid one out, yanked off the cap, and began slicing through the helmet's wires.

A crash as Doctor Volkov was thrown against the wall. "I'm not going to ask you again," the soldier yelled. "How do we turn these machines off?"

"Enough," General Cole commanded from the doorway. "Let him go."

Finished with the wires, I turned my attention to slicing through the IV tubing. The memory erasing poison would now flow onto the floor instead of into Hayden's veins.

I raced to the next bed. Eric was ghostly pale, like I imagined a dead body would look. It was the first time I had been this close to my twin and felt no tug, no connection between us.

"Stop that, girl," Volkov snarled.

I shot a hateful look toward the doctor, who was jabbing a finger at me. "Stop cutting the tubing. It is dangerous."

I ignored him. "Make him fix this," I yelled at the general. "Make him tell us how to stop this. We can't let them—"

"He will bleed out," Volkov yelled. He tried to step forward, but the soldiers blocked his path. With a grunt of frustration, he gestured toward Hayden. "You must stop the bleeding."

A stream of blood was flowing from the cut IV line in Hayden's arm, forming a red puddle on the floor. The general nodded to a soldier who yanked on gloves, rushed over and picked up the tubing. He tied it into a knot and then began unwrapping the bandage around Hayden's arm.

The general turned his attention to me. "Stop cutting."

His voice was stern and authoritative, but I ignored him, finishing the helmet wires and reaching for the tubing.

A soldier came over and put a hand on my shoulder. "Listen to the general," she said, her voice kind but firm.

I hesitated. Would cutting the tubing make any difference? Or was it too late? Hayden was still unconscious and there was still Gabi and Charles. I grabbed for the tubing. I had to try. What did I have to lose?

The soldier gripped my wrist and squeezed until I was forced to open my hand and let the knife clatter to the floor.

"We need to help them," I begged. The woman's expression was sympathetic as she picked up the knife and deposited it in a red container.

The other soldiers were watching the general for further orders. He and Volkov faced each other across the room. "Come over here," the general ordered.

I felt a twinge of hope. Cole had the upper hand. He and Nick had brought a team of soldiers into HP. The general could force Volkov to fix my friends. Surely with all of HP's incredible technology, there was a way to reverse the memory wipe.

Volkov walked slowly forward, smoothing down his white shirt and purple tie. I remembered that he had been dressed for the dance. It seemed like the Cotillion had been ages ago, even though it was just now ending. My fellow trainees had danced the night away and were headed back to the cabins, having no idea what was going on.

The general and doctor regarded each other for a long moment. Then both their faces relaxed into wide smiles.

"It's been too long, Tommy," Volkov said, holding out his arms.

"You too L'vionachick," Cole said, grabbing the doctor into a big hug.

My blood froze. *Tommy? L'vionachick?*

I stared back and forth between the two of them, mentally kicking myself. I had been so stupid. How had I not realized it before? That's why Cole had looked familiar when I saw him at Cotillion practice.

Photos of the general had been projected on the theater screen, an example of the enduring connections made between trainees. *Ivan and Tom met at HP when they signed up to plant a vegetable garden ... Ivan received his MD/PhD from Johns Hopkins and teaches neurobiology at Stanford. Tom obtained a PhD in history from Yale and is currently a leader in the US military.*

I sank onto Eric's mattress, taking his cold hand. Cole was in on it. On the whole thing. He and Volkov had been working together all these years, had likely masterminded the latest genetic engineering. A US general would be a powerful ally in distributing the newborn HP minions throughout the country and the world.

"Is everything under control?" Cole asked.

"Mostly. How about for you?"

"Messy, but yes. You have quite an operation here." Cole gestured to the row of beds. "Put the memory wipe to use often, do you?"

"Not so often," Volkov smirked. "Certainly not as often as the US military."

Cole chuckled. "True. It's been a boon to our intelligence service." He peered at Hayden's IV bag. "What did you give them?"

"Propofol. Quick and easy. I needed them silent."

I twined my fingers through Eric's. My brother, not genetically, but that didn't matter. Our connection was strong, as it was with Gabi, Charles, and Hayden. None of our genetics matched, but with my friends, I belonged. I hadn't wanted to come to HP, but it had given me a gift I never thought I would have—not an ultimate purpose that would shape my life, but a family.

A fire kindled in my gut, sending pulses of heat into my chest. Volkov and Cole were taking that away. What right did they have to manipulate people's lives like puppets? What right did they have to destroy my friends?

Volkov walked to Hayden's bed, swiftly removed the needle from his arm, and pressed a piece of gauze onto the wound. He nodded to a soldier who put a piece of white tape over the gauze.

I hung my head next to Eric's, shoulders shaking. Making snuffling noises, I shifted sideways, moving my knees underneath my body. There was nothing I could do about the master plan. HP would grow their lab of fetuses, birth them, and raise them as their own little army. But there was something I could do to avenge my friends.

When Volkov came to Eric's bed, I was ready. In one swift motion, I leaped to my feet, grabbed his thick black hair with one hand, and pressed the second X-Acto blade against his neck.

Volkov let out a squeak of surprise.

"Don't move," I yelled at Cole and his soldiers. I pressed the tip of the blade against what I knew, thanks to all my textbook reading, was Volkov's jugular vein.

Cole held up his hands. "Whoa, calm down. Everything is going to be okay."

"Everything is not," I yelled, my rage continuing to swell. "He needs to undo what he's done. He has to fix my friends." I knew my face was deep red, spit dripping from my lower lip.

Cole flicked his eyes toward the soldiers.

"If they move, I cut." I let out a sob of half anger, half despair. "I'm a Joe, so you know I'll do it."

Volkov took a shaky breath. "I will fix things," his voice cracked. "Nothing bad has happened, I promise you."

I yanked his head further back. "I don't believe you."

"It's not what you think," Cole said. "Give us a chance to explain."

I knew they were manipulating me, trying to buy time until they could disarm me. With one cut, I would get revenge for my friends. Did Volkov deserve anything different after all the evil things he had done? Trying to murder Nick, manipulating genetics, creating babies who would follow the ideals of Adolf Hitler?

Can you really kill someone? I had never considered myself a potential murderer.

Yet in my core, I knew that I could kill, would kill if someone I loved were threatened. If murder would protect Emma Claire from harm, I could do it without hesitation. And wouldn't making it into Special Forces have meant I was willing to kill to defend my country against enemies?

What was Volkov if not the worst kind of enemy—to myself, my family and my country?

"You've got ten seconds," I snapped. The blade nicked Volkov's skin, and a trickle of blood ran down his neck.

"Do something," Volkov whined to Cole.

Cole pressed his palms together. "Young lady, I am not your enemy. I have been working with Nick and following our plan. We spotted the tracker signal and came in tonight to demobilize Blakewell and protect your group."

"This is protection?" I nodded toward my friends. "All of a sudden, Matthew knew to get rid of the evidence. He orders trucks to take everything away. Why? Because you knew I had met with Nick, and we were onto you. Once we're taken care of, you'll cover everything up."

Cole brought his steepled fingers up to his chin, as if in prayer. "Your friends are going to be fine. I know this looks bad, but it was necessary for their safety."

A beeping noise came from Hayden's monitor. On the screen, the jagged line had gone flat. The numbers all read zero.

I located the exact spot on Volkov's neck to plunge the blade in. A quick motion and there would be massive bleeding—he would die. Which was what he deserved.

Blood was soaking the collar of Volkov's shirt, oozing onto his lilac tie. A tie patterned with white flowers.

I froze. "What is that?" I demanded.

"What?" Volkov's voice was barely audible above the machine's beeping.

The flowers had triangular white petals with yellow buds in the center. "Those things on your tie. What are those?"

"They're edelweiss," he sputtered. "It's a flower."

My mind whirled. If those flowers meant what I thought, it could change everything. "Why are you wearing it?"

"I wanted to ..." Volkov gulped, seeming to realize that his answer would determine his fate. "Make a statement. About what is happening at HP." Another gulp. "I didn't figure those idiots would be smart enough to make the connection."

Hayden had shown us the patch with the white flower. *The Edelweisspiraten, or Edelweiss Pirates, was a group of young people who defied Hitler. The flower was their symbol.* "Edelweisspiraten?" I asked.

"Yes." Volkov let out a sob. "Yes, Edelweisspiraten."

I let go of his hair and lowered my arm to my side.

He darted to the far side of the room, clutching his neck.

The soldiers started to advance but Cole shook his head. He gazed at me. "How did you know about the Edelweisspiraten?"

"We know a lot more than you think."

"We sure do," a faint voice said.

My whole body jerked in surprise. Hayden was awake and trying to push himself up. His eyelids drooped and his face was pale, but he was alive.

I dropped the blade, jumped off the bed, and ran to him. "I thought your heart had stopped." I buried my face in his shoulder. "There was a flat line."

"Get me a bandage," I heard Volkov command. "Idiot girl."

"Hey, can you help me sit?" Hayden asked. "I'm pretty knackered."

I wiped my eyes with the edge of the blanket. Putting my arms under Hayden's shoulders, I helped him into a sitting position.

Cole's strong hand clapped Hayden's shoulder. "Mr. Murray, good to see you awake. I have to admit I had a moment of panic when you flatlined."

Hayden cleared his throat. "Thank you for coming, sir."

"You did the right thing sending the SOS signal. It was clearly time to intervene."

"SOS signal?" Hayden looked confused then turned to me.

I nodded and he squeezed my arm. "You saved me this time."

"Are we allowed to wake up yet?" a voice squeaked.

I spun to see Eric peeking out from his covers.

I raced to his bed and hugged him, feeling a swell of relief at the renewed sense of connection. Over Eric's shoulder, Gabi and Charles were also stirring.

"I gave them only a short-term sedative," Volkov said. "Wears off in ten minutes." He touched his hand to his bandaged neck and scowled. "I could have explained that if only—"

"Breaking the rules as always, aren't you HM? Didn't we say to stand down and just gather intel?" Nick stood in the doorway, a huge grin on his face. He strode to Hayden's bed and enveloped him in a bear hug. "I'm so sorry, mate. I wish I could have told you sooner."

"We couldn't stand down," I said. "Matthew has trucks coming in to move everything out tomorrow. Our proof would have disappeared. That's why I did the tracker message."

"You did that?" Nick said. "Brilliant move."

"What tracker message?" Gabi asked me.

"I knew Nick could see our trackers since that was how he found me on my solo," I said. "I didn't have a new one yet, so I borrowed Hayden's tracker, went to the meadow and ran in crazy loops to spell out SOS SUN. I hoped that would be enough to bring help here and catch them loading up the evidence."

"We could also see that you got into that lab building," Nick said. "Did you find anything?"

Charles yelped and slapped a hand over his mouth. He and I stared at each other. "Don't let anyone go down to the basement," I said. "There's something you need to know."

EPILOGUE

PACKING TOOK AN HOUR. Less than five minutes of that was my duffel and the rest was helping Brittany. Now that we had our phones back, she had to take tons of photos of herself and the room. Then, we took each item from the bulletin board and slid it into a plastic sleeve, folded each item of clothing, and placed them in her trunk. Arranging the makeup and brushes in their special holders was too much so I insisted on stripping the bed instead.

"Should we be roomies again next year?" Brittany asked, tightening the lid on a tube of mascara.

I stopped folding a pillowcase. "Really?" It hadn't crossed my mind that Brittany would want me again, especially after the incident with Matthew. "I assumed the Angels would stick together."

"It's okay. Never mind. I just thought that ..." she turned to face me. "Being with Angels all the time can get boring. It's nice to have some ..."

"Variety?" I supplied. "Danger?"

Brittany pursed her lips. "Variety, yes. Danger, not so much."

Her makeup skills were so good that I could barely make out the bruise that still covered the left side of her face. The punch Matthew had delivered when the security detail untied him had knocked her to the floor. No bones were broken, but the blow had caused a deep bluish-black bruise on her cheekbone that, over the past two weeks, had spread towards her ear and morphed into a pea-green color.

Matthew was still missing—somehow, he had escaped before HP was locked down. Cole had reassured us that he would be found and handled. "Matthew Drexler is a bad apple and a coward. True, he charmed enough of us to earn a position on the Council. And he seemed to be doing a fine job with the summer academy." He had grimaced. "But behind the scenes, he was getting cozy with Blakewell and other Council members enacting this genetic experiment. Now that their operation is shut down, he'll scurry away like a rat. The last thing he'll care about is coming after you or Brittany."

I hoped Cole was right. Brittany wouldn't realize it until she unpacked at home but I had folded Cairo up in one of her pillowcases, my best way to provide her with a sort of protection—and a reminder of me too.

I smiled. "Let's do it!" Truth was, Brittany had helped make my life at HP interesting and fun. When else would I get to help pick bikinis and give advice on relationship drama?

"It's too bad I won't see you at the Youth Council meetings. You totally should have been the Joe's Campia. That Barbie girl is so ..." she screwed up her face.

If only Brittany knew the truth! Yes, I should be the Campia and on the Youth Council. But few knew about the events during the solo or the night of the dance, so I had only received the medallion that first week. Spiky had gotten it a total of four weeks and ended up winning.

A voice called my name. I looked out the window to see Hayden waving. "Next summer, then," I said, giving Brittany a hug.

"Don't forget, my handle is @brittany_roselee." She pulled me into another selfie before I picked up my duffel and went outside.

"You ready?" Hayden asked, taking my duffel and handing me the #42 gym bag.

Hayden also had fading bruises—on his stomach where the security had kicked him and in the crook of his elbow from the IV. "I still don't see why Volkov had to knock you out," I said. "He could have just hidden you away until Cole arrived. Or you could have faked being unconscious."

Hayden sighed. "It had to be real. We didn't know if Blakewell or Matthew would come into the lab and check on everything." His tone was patient, despite having repeated this multiple times since that night. "If they had realized we were pretending, it could have turned deadly." He hefted the duffel higher. "There was no way I could have brought my heart rate down with all the stress." He gestured toward the front of The Chalet. "And how do you think our germaphobe would have done?"

Eric stood at The Chalet's roundabout, twisting his hands and watching the cars pulling into the parking lot. "All right, you have a point. But Gabi could have done it."

"Done what?"

I spun around. "How do you always do that?"

"How are two Joes so oblivious? And what could I have done?"

"Kept your heart rate down and pretended to be getting memory-wiped if Matthew appeared."

"Um, probably, but …" she tipped her head toward the grassy area in the middle of the drive. Charles and his football buddies were hooting and line dancing. "Not all of us have the same skill set, right?" Charles spotted us, dropped out of the group and came loping toward us.

"I don't know why I'm waiting for my parents," Eric said anxiously as we reached him. "They are always late." He looked at Gabi who didn't have a bag. "How are you getting home?"

"Same way I came. The bus with the rest of the group going to the Denver airport."

"I'll be on it with you," Charles said holding up his palm for Gabi to high-five. "When are your parents coming, Lina?"

"Oh, they're here," I pointed toward the girl with flowing blonde hair racing across the grass. A Mercedes SUV was entering the round-about, a sun-glassed DJ videoing out the open window.

Emma Claire threw herself into my arms. I stumbled as her pink cast smacked me in the face. "I danced really well in Aspen. But then I broke my arm and they put screws in it. Daddy let me have ice cream every night, even though Mommy said it was too much sugar, especially since I wasn't dancing. And ..." she took a deep breath.

"Whoa, hold on," I laughed. "You've got plenty of time to tell me all about it. I'm coming home, remember?"

Emma Claire noticed my friends. She smiled and held out her good hand. "I'm Emma Claire, nice to meet you."

"Sounds like she's already done Cotillion," Eric murmured.

"Nah, she's just naturally good with people." Gabi took Emma Claire's hand and gave her a warm smile. "Aren't you?"

"I guess," Emma Claire said, beaming.

"Catalina," my mom strode toward us in heels and a yellow floral sundress. "We need to get going. There's terrible traffic."

I felt a twinge of panic. What if my parents took me back to California and it was like HP hadn't happened? Could I stand going back to being the lonely, talentless girl?

As if sensing my fears, Eric and Gabi each grabbed a hand.

DJ stopped and inspected my friends. I knew she was thinking that none of them looked like a Kennedy or future superstar. "Well, did you figure out your purpose?" she asked, her voice a mix of hope and skepticism.

My friends' hands still in mine, I felt a surge of confidence I had never experienced around my mom. "Actually, yes. And I also met—"

"She certainly did," a deep voice interrupted. General Cole stood behind us, wearing his Air Force uniform. "You should be proud of your daughter. She shows excellent promise. I look forward to working with her next summer."

DJ pushed her sunglasses up on her head and blinked. "She does? You are?" Her eyes scanned the uniform's numerous medals and patches. "And who ...?"

"General Thomas Cole, United States Air Force. Proud HP grad and interim director of recruitment and training."

"So, you're the one who ... chose her ...?"

Cole hesitated. My friends and I glanced at each other and then burst out laughing. "It's a long story," I said. "I'll explain later."

Although I wouldn't. Time and planning were needed to figure out what information would be shared—not just with HP'ers but with parents and the public. In the last two weeks, Cole and Volkov had been intent on stabilization. Cole had taken over running the academy. Volkov had arranged for neonatology specialists to care for the fetuses through the rest of their development. Who would adopt and raise them was still being figured out.

The sudden absence of Matthew, Crystal, and several Einstein tutors had been explained away as an urgent crisis. The trainees hadn't seemed to notice or care, likely because they were still somewhat brainwashed.

We still didn't know why Blakewell had decided he urgently needed to move the fetuses. Had he been paranoid, or did he have actual information about Nick's group's plans? So far, he wasn't talking, but that would change. His future was something Cole and Volkov discussed in their frequent online meetings with trusted Council members.

Later, they would decide whether to reveal any HP secrets, including our biological origins, the chippings, and the genetic manipulation. And I was okay with that for now. I didn't know when I would be ready to think about my genetic parents, my surrogate, and the way I had ended up being created and brought into this world. I trusted the two men to make wise decisions. Plus, Hayden was taking Matthew's position on the Council, which made me feel even better.

The Mercedes pulled up and my dad waved. "Hey, honey! Let's get going so we don't miss our flight."

"Be right there. I need to say goodbye."

DJ looked like she might object but nodded and even smiled at my friends before ushering Emma Claire back to the car.

"See you next summer, dream team," Cole said. "Excellent work, all of you." He saluted then strode away to greet more parents.

Eric squeezed my hand. "FaceTime."

"Every Sunday," I agreed. Eric and I still hadn't been able to completely figure out our connection. We had been in utero together for nine months, but how did we know so much about each other's lives since then?

"Maybe more experiments were going on that we don't know about yet," Nick had said. "Time will tell." Nick had made a beeline for Scotland as soon as he could—his family hadn't known he was still alive. He and Hayden had plans to meet up at Paxton's Pub as soon as Hayden returned to England.

"You will try to visit," Eric said to me.

"I told you," I tipped my head toward the Mercedes, "once my parents find out your parents are profs at Dartmouth, I'll be on the next flight. Anything to tempt me toward the Ivy League."

"FaceTime for all of us," Charles exclaimed, wrapping his arms around Gabi and me and lifting us into the air. He knew better than to try and include Eric in any sort of hug. "But not during Sunday Night Football." He set us down and kissed the top of my head. "Gotta get back to my boys. Love you, Scrapper." Slapping Hayden on the back, he ran back toward his team.

"Lina, give me your hand," Gabi said. She unclasped her necklace and placed it in my palm. The gold chain and pearly pink crown felt warm and comforting.

"You can't give me this," I protested. "It's from your quinceañera."

"You can return it next summer. In the meantime, it will remind you of your HP family."

Tears welled in my eyes. "As usual, you know exactly what I need." Now, every time I worried that HP had been a dream, I could hold the pendant and know the truth.

"Let me help you." Hayden hooked the necklace with his finger. I held up my hair while he drew it around my neck. "Don't let your physical fitness slide," he said, fastening the clasp. "You're going to train hard next summer. If you come in soft, you'll be miserable the first few weeks."

I turned to face him, tears sliding down my cheeks. "You'll still be here, right?"

Hayden pulled a tissue from his pocket. "Of course. I'm the new and improved Matthew, aren't I?"

"Well, you're no Ricky Ricardo," I sniffed, wiping my eyes. "But you're a pretty decent substitute."

Hayden shook his head. "You know who Ricky Ricardo is, but not Charles Dickens. Unbelievable."

I threw my arms around him. "Thank you for thinking I could do it. You were the first one."

Hayden snorted. "When I met you, you were sprawled on that web, trying to save a boy four times your size with a flimsy jumper. It was all you, luv."

My dad beeped the horn.

Hayden squeezed me and turned me toward the Mercedes.

"323 days," Eric called as we pulled away. "See you back here in 323 days."

323 days. I wrapped my fingers around Gabi's pendant. *In 323 days, I'll be back home.*

LEARN MORE ABOUT CAIRO, THE HERO DOG OF SEAL TEAM 6 BY SCANNING THE QR CODE BELOW!

You can join in celebrating Cairo and all our "hero" pets and animals by sharing a picture on our website or social media using the hashtag **#whosyourCairo**

RACHELBYRNEAUTHOR.COM

ACKNOWLEDGMENTS

THIS NOVEL HAS BEEN A LONG TIME COMING, with a lot of support and encouragement along the way. My kids, Danielle and Nathan, have been my cheerleaders, providers of source material, readers, and plot adjusters. Predestined is much better because of them! My niece, Julianne, was an early reader and provided suggestions and answers to my multiple questions along the way. My niece, Cadence, was an eager first reader and has helped with marketing ideas and spreading the word. My nephew, Jacob, was enthusiastic about reading the novel and passing it on to his friends. Thanks to my mom who is my biggest fan and has kept asking "When are you going to get this published?!?" It's finally here, Mom!

For additional help with editing, I owe so much gratitude to Traci Jones for wrangling my original draft and Jennifer Rees for her wise advice on both big-picture and smaller edits. Their help was invaluable!

Many friends have supported me through this process, giving me much-needed confidence and gentle nudging. Cris Roskelly was an early reader and so positive and encouraging. My husband, Greg, tolerated the angst of an insecure writer and supported the time and energy I poured into the novel. Other friends who cheered me along the way (and finally get to read it) are Randi Waldman, Sarah Shikes, Kara Cannon, Tanya Fernandez, Stefanie Jacobs, and David Hicks. A special loving thank you to Kay Collins who never got to read *Predestined* but was a constant cheerleader for me and my kids in all our endeavors.

A final thanks to the team at My Word Publishing who has supported *Predestined* over its final hurdles. Thanks to Shelly Wilhelm for her enthusiasm, encouragement, and help with editing and guidance on cover design, Amanda Miller for being positive, keeping me on track, and guiding me through the entire process, Victoria Wolf for her amazing book design, Cheryl Isaac for final editing and Melissa McQueen for my fantastic website.

ABOUT THE
AUTHOR

RACHEL BYRNE, a Colorado native, is inspired by her state's majestic landscapes. With a BA in psychology from Dartmouth College and a Master of Science from the University of Colorado, Rachel has forged a career in psychiatry and addiction medicine.  Her role as an educator has fueled her passion for teaching and understanding human behavior.

Driven by a lifelong fascination with the complexities of human nature and a love for American history, Rachel enjoys a career that explores the depths of the human psyche. As a devoted mother and dog lover, she treasures family moments and indulges in hobbies like reading, writing, tennis, and travel. Rachel's commitment to literature stems from her childhood as a shy bookworm, aiming to create engaging stories that resonate with readers and leave a lasting impact.

Made in the USA
Middletown, DE
04 January 2025

68268244R00191